THE ISOLATOR

realization of absolute solitude

Sect.003
The Trancer

3

REKI KAWAHARA
ILLUSTRATION BY SHIMEJI
CHARACTER DESIGN BY BEE-PEE

THE ISOLATOR
realization of absolute solitude 《◎》 CONTENTS

THE ISOLATOR
realization of absolute solitude

Sect. 003 The Trancer

"I'M LOOKING FOR ABSOLUTE SOLITUDE... THAT'S WHY MY CODE NAME IS ISOLATOR."

REKI KAWAHARA
ILLUSTRATIONS BY SHIMEJI
CHARACTER DESIGN BY BEE-PEE

YEN ON
NEW YORK

Yen On
1290 Avenue of the Americas
New York, NY 10104

Visit us at yenpress.com
facebook.com/yenpress
twitter.com/yenpress
yenpress.tumblr.com
instagram.com/yenpress

First Yen On Edition: November 2016

Yen On is an imprint of Yen Press, LLC.
The Yen On name and logo are trademarks
of Yen Press, LLC.

The publisher is not responsible for websites (or their content) that are
not owned by the publisher.

Library of Congress Cataloging-in-Publication Data

Names: Kawahara, Reki, author. | Shimeji, illustrator. | ZephyrRz, translator.
Title: The Isolator, realization of absolute solitude. Sect.003, The trancer /
    Reki Kawahara ; illustrations by Shimeji ; character design by Bee-Pee ;
    translation by ZephyrRz.
Other titles: Zettai naru kodokumono. English | Realization of absolute solitude.
    Sect.003, The trancer | Sect.003 The trancer | Trancer
Description: First Yen On edition. | New York, NY : Yen On, 2016. |
    Series: The isolator ; 3
Identifiers: LCCN 2016034807 | ISBN 9780316552721 (hardback)
Subjects: | CYAC: Science fiction. | BISAC: FICTION / Science Fiction / Adventure.
Classification: LCC PZ7.K1755 Iu 2016 | DDC [Fic]—dc23 LC record available at
    https://lccn.loc.gov/2016034807

10 9 8 7 6 5 4 3 2 1

LSC-C

Printed in the United States of America

For what must have been the hundredth time today, Minoru heard a sigh from the small headset attached to his left ear.

"Ugh...why are we stuck coming to a place like this when it's almost New Year's Eve?"

Before he could respond, the voice spoke up again.

"I still have to do my homework from winter break, and I haven't even bought anything to cook for New Year's yet." Another sigh, then another complaint: "I haven't even done a big end-of-the-year cleaning of my own room yet! So don't you think it's ridiculous for me to have to help someone else clean *their* home?"

As this last complaint came in the form of a question, Minoru Utsugi was finally able to reply. "Erm... I don't know if *cleaning* is the best word for the job we're doing here..."

The girl who was standing by his side, Yumiko Azu, aimed a kick at a piece of the rubble that was scattered at their feet. "We're taking something dirty and making it clean again, right? What else would you call it?"

"Technically, I guess you're not wrong, but still..."

Both of them looked up at once, gazing at the enormous structure that loomed some distance away. Rectangular in shape, it stood about fifty meters tall and thirty-five meters wide. There was not a single window anywhere on the ashen gray surface. At first glance, it seemed to be nothing more than smooth masses of concrete, but just looking at it with the naked eye brought on a feeling of suffocation.

Why? Because it housed the nuclear reactor at the Tokyo Bay Nuclear Power Plant.

And why was Minoru using a headset to communicate with Yumiko when she was right next to him? That would be because they were both wearing protective anti-radiation suits that were enclosed in sheets of tungsten.

The Tokyo Bay Nuclear Power Plant was built on the reclaimed land of the coastal area Uchibo. Utilizing a third-generation boiling-water reactor, the latest model at the time, and located right next to the coastline, it was hoped that the plant could be used as an alternative to thermal power stations. However, eight years ago in the summer of 2011, the magnitude 7.8 "Uraga water supply earthquake" caused a serious incident to occur there.

Flooding due to the land subsidence and tsunamis caused the nuclear reactor to lose power, and with the emergency reactor core cooling system not functioning, a meltdown occurred. Fortunately, the concrete structure did not sustain major damage, but the interior and the surrounding grounds were polluted by the radioactive material, and now in 2019 the nuclear decommissioning process was still barely making progress.

Atomic fuel debris had most likely melted through the bottom of the containment vessel and fallen below, but more details about the situation would be needed before the deadlock could be broken. Therefore, the previous week, the Nuclear and Industrial Safety Agency and the Eastern Electric Power Company had deployed a new weapon: a completely autonomous probe robot able to operate without any human control through the use of both wired and wireless communication.

Manufactured on an astronomical budget, the robot was able to arrive at the underside of the damaged containment vessel. However, the signal was somehow lost at that point, so the robot was unable to return. The only way to recover it would be to build a second robot; however, fearful that a similar incident would occur, the committee refused to approve the budget. And so the organization Minoru belonged to received an unusual, desperate, and highly confidential proposal from the Ministry of Health, Labor, and Welfare.

Of course, Minoru didn't know the exact wording that had been used, but he could guess at the contents. Most likely, some bureaucrat or politician was trying to use the Ministry of Health, Labor, and Welfare Industrial Safety and Health Department Specialized Forces Division as a pawn in a power struggle and had promised in some fancy restaurant near Akasaka that "my department's SFD can definitely get the robot back for just one little favor!"

Then, someone way up at the top of the ministry gave orders to Chief Himi, the head of the department; their commander, Professor Riri, reluctantly agreed; and now, on Saturday, December 28, 2019, here were

Minoru and Yumiko paying a visit to the Tokyo Bay Nuclear Power Plant.

"...Really, though, I thought I had prepared myself for wearing this thing, but it's even worse than I thought!"

Yumiko tugged at the gray material of the protective suit as she resumed her grumbling. "It's so stiff and crinkly, it's sweltering hot, the mask is way too tight, it stinks of rubber, and it's just not cute at all!"

Under his mask, Minoru couldn't help but smile—in all her complaints, she had somehow left out the immense weight of the suits. Unlike regular anti-radiation clothing, which can block out only a lower level of radioactivity, these suits weighed about 150 pounds. The two were still able to move in them, since the Third Eye parasites raised their strength to several times that of an average human, but they could certainly still feel the extra weight... Compared to that, the suit's stiffness or smell seemed like trivial concerns.

Forgetting to complain about the biggest issue, despite finding fault with almost everything else, seemed to indicate that Yumiko, too, was feeling the gravity of their current mission. Eight years after the earthquake, the nuclear accident had become an ordinary fact of life, but it was still one of the most difficult ordeals this country had ever gone through. It could even rank on the same level as the bizarre calamity that had rained down from outer space, the Third Eye.

"Hey, what are you smiling about?"

Caught off guard by the question that suddenly rang out in his earpiece, Minoru hastily shook his head. "...I'm not smiling."

"Oh? Well, that's fine, then... Still, they're awfully late, aren't they? We were told to wait here and they'd send a car to pick us up, but it's been at least five minutes already!"

"That's true..."

Once again, Minoru surveyed his surroundings through the lead glass of his goggles.

The two of them stood at the front entrance of the anti-seismic building that served as the control room of the repair work. As it stood some distance away from the structure that housed the nuclear reactor, the radioactivity levels in the air were fairly low; the wrist communicator installed on the left side of the suit (which, despite the name, was essentially just a waterproof smartphone affixed to a wristband) displayed the microsievert levels every five minutes and at the moment read "no effect on health at present level." The protective suit would absorb the majority of the radiation anyway, but still, it was difficult to feel at ease in such a place.

"Um…I know I said this earlier, Yumiko, but it's okay if you just want to wait here," Minoru said as he lowered his left hand, knowing full well what her response would be.

"Yeah, right! What would be the point of my coming in the first place, then?"

"But I'm going to have to go into the building by myself in the end…"

"Yeah, but we have no idea what it's like in there! If anything happens to you, who do you think is going to have to save you?"

She was right: The weight of both suits plus Minoru's body weight added up to almost 204 kilograms, which only someone with a Third Eye like Yumiko's could carry. Still, hearing her words, Minoru couldn't help but feel like a princess whose knight was coming to her rescue. He cleared his throat uncomfortably.

"Hey… Come on, I was just stating the facts." Yumiko nudged Minoru as she spoke, the tungsten lining on her elbow digging into his right arm.

It had been more than three weeks since Minoru had met Yumiko, but he still had no idea how to respond to her at times like these. Luckily, just as he was searching for the right words to say, the sound of an engine came roaring from the direction of the parking lot.

"Oh, good, the car is finally…here…" Minoru trailed off as the car came into view. Instead of the Ministry of Health, Labor, and Welfare minivan that had brought them here from Tokyo, an enormous olive-green off-roader pulled up in front of them.

"What is this…? The Self-Defense Forces?" Just as Yumiko muttered these words, the driver-side window rolled down to reveal a man whose clothing confirmed her speculation.

He was wearing a suit and mask like the two of them, but he also wore a helmet, and most of his equipment was in a camouflage pattern, which in this country could only mean a member of the Japan Self-Defense Forces.

The driver gave a crisp salute with his right hand, then used the same hand to motion her toward the back of the truck. Minoru and Yumiko exchanged glances before reluctantly complying, heading around the large HMV and opening the double doors on the back, then hoisting themselves inside.

The interior of the HMV had benches lining either side, almost like a train car. As soon as the pair sat down, the diesel engine noisily roared into action, and they were on the move. Perhaps because they had been used by so many working vehicles in the past, the roads were full of cracks and holes, each one sending a jolt through the seats in the HMV as its tires rolled over the gaps.

There was not a single bush or tree to be seen among the dreary mortar grounds of the power plant, and since it was nearly New Year's, there were no workers around, either. Minoru had seen images of the contaminated water tanks lined up along the right side of the road, on TV and online, but in person their size was truly overwhelming. In this surreal landscape under the ashen winter sky, the HMV traveled slowly onward.

Suddenly, a quiet electronic buzz sounded in Minoru's headset. Looking at his wrist communicator, he saw a message requesting a new connection, so both he and Yumiko pressed the Yes button. Immediately, a voice just as noisy as the engine came blasting through the earpiece.

"Sorry to keep you kids waiting! It took ages to get this thing on!"

The speaker seemed to be the person in the passenger seat, not the driver. Since they were wearing camouflage from head to toe, it was impossible to see anyone's face, but judging by the speaker's physique and (more importantly) that voice, they were probably—no, definitely—a woman. Of course, there were plenty of female members of the Self-Defense Forces, but this one's manner of speech seemed rather unbefitting of a soldier.

As Minoru sat dumbfounded, Yumiko responded in a rather sharp voice, "We arrived right on schedule, so you should have had plenty of time to prepare… But more importantly, who are you people?"

"Ah-ha-ha, yikes! You're scarin' me!"

Pop.

That was the sound of Yumiko's anger meter going up a level. Minoru hurriedly cut into the pair's conversation. "Erm… We're from the Ministry of Health, Labor, and Welfare Industrial Safety and Health

Department, Specialized Forces Division, code names Isolator and Accelerator. Would you mind telling us your affiliation?"

"Ooh, you're just as stuffy as the rumors said!"

Minoru was beginning to get the sense that she was deliberately trying to annoy them, but he couldn't think of any reason why a Self-Defense Forces member would want to do that. As he tilted his head in puzzlement underneath his protective suit, Yumiko half rose from the seat next to him. A short, sharp gasp came in through the headset, followed by an increasingly hard voice.

"Don't tell me... Are you people...*red*...?"

"Huh...?"

Stunned, Minoru stared back and forth between Yumiko and the Self-Defense Forces member in the passenger's seat.

The slang term *red* could refer to only one thing. When the spheres had come down from outer space and affixed themselves to people as "Third Eyes," some of those life-forms were red, and they instilled in their human hosts an overwhelming urge to attack other humans. These violent individuals were known as "Ruby Eyes."

Minoru and Yumiko, on the other hand, were known as "Jet Eyes," who were infected by black spheres and destined to do battle with the Ruby Eyes. Normally, the easiest way for them to detect a Ruby Eye was with their sense of smell. The violent, carnivorous Ruby Eyes had a distinctively strong and savage scent; it was strongest when they used their powers but would certainly be detectable if they were in the very same vehicle.

Quickly, Minoru inhaled deeply through his nose, but all he could smell was the acrid stench of fresh rubber from his protective mask. Was the mask's charcoal filter absorbing even the Ruby Eye scent, or was Yumiko just jumping to false conclusions?

All at once, a childish giggle broke through the tension in the air. "You're a sharp one, aren't you, little Miss Accelerator?"

Immediately, Yumiko started to unzip the front of her protective suit with her left hand and reached inside with her right. But before she could take anything out—Minoru was expecting a high-power Taser or an automatic pistol—another voice broke in.

"We are members of the Japan Self-Defense Force Ground Staff Office Operational Support Intelligence Department Special Task Squad." This speaker must be the driver who was grasping the large steering wheel. Without turning his head, he continued in a low, husky voice, "My name is Nishikida, and this is Kakinari. We may not have code names, but we are allies of the SFD."

Yumiko's right hand stopped moving immediately, but she didn't let go of whatever it was holding inside her suit as she responded tersely, "Allies…? What do you mean exactly?"

"Heh, isn't it obvious? This, of course!" Replying in an easy drawl, the passenger whose name was apparently Kakinari bent around her seat to face them and unzipped her suit as Yumiko had; however, instead of drawing something out, she pulled the front wide open with both hands.

Underneath her suit she wore only a close-fitting olive-green tank top, revealing her considerable bust. Yumiko was speechless, and Minoru hastily moved to avert his eyes; however, when he noticed something shining out from her cleavage, his eyes widened.

Right beneath the silver dog tag that hung from her neck, embedded in her slightly tanned skin, was a jet-black sphere. Bearing a strong resemblance to a living eye, it was unmistakably a black Third Eye, just like Yumiko and Minoru each had.

"…Are you both…Jet Eyes…?"

"Yup, you betcha!"

With that casual confirmation, Kakinari languidly withdrew back to her seat.

Slowly, Yumiko brought her empty right hand out of her suit and zipped it back up. As if he had been waiting for her to do so, Nishikida spoke up again. "You can call us the STS, since you two are from the SFD. We'll be your escorts today, so I hope our short time together will be a pleasant one."

"Th…thank you, it's a pleasure to meet you."

As he gave this reflexive response, Minoru was mentally repeating the organization name the man had given a short time ago. *Japan Self-Defense Force, Ground Staff Office, Operational Support, Intelligence Department, Special Task Squad.* An even longer name than the organization Minoru was affiliated with, the Ministry of Health, Labor, and Welfare Industrial Safety and Health Department, Specialized Forces Division. Did a longer name mean a more prestigious organization? Not necessarily, but the news that a group of Jet Eyes like the SFD existed within the Self-Defense Forces was still a significant shock to Minoru. Quietly, he leaned over toward his partner.

"Um, Yu— I mean, Accelerator. Did you know about this? A group of Jet Eyes in the Self-Defense Forces..."

After a moment's pause, a bemused voice responded through the headset. "You know, Isolator, there's not much point in whispering when we're communicating via radio."

She was absolutely right, of course. Kakinari let out a little snort through the headset, and Yumiko huffed irritably, pressing a few buttons on her wrist communicator.

There was another little buzz in Minoru's ear, this one indicating that the previous communication channel had been temporarily disconnected. After a moment, Yumiko's voice came through, more serious than before.

"I've heard rumors about it, yes. People said that there was another team in the government like ours, anyway... But I didn't know it was in the Self-Defense Forces."

"...Then...do you think the Special Task Squad is made up of only Self-Defense Forces personnel who were infected by black Third Eyes...?"

"I wonder about that. There may be over 250,000 people in the Self-Defense Forces, but that's still much less than even the population of Shinjuku alone. Considering that we scraped up only eight SFD members from the Tokyo metropolitan area, I doubt there would be enough Third Eye hosts in the Self-Defense Forces to put together a functional team. I wouldn't be surprised if most of their members were recruited from outside the organization, just like us."

"I see..."

If most of the STS's members had been recruited like Minoru, it would certainly explain Kakinari's laid-back personality. Nonetheless, he found it reassuring to think they'd have battle-trained professionals from the Self-Defense Forces fighting alongside.

As he reached this conclusion, Minoru abruptly realized the meaning of a phrase Nishikida had used some time before. Hurriedly restoring the communication channel, he impulsively posed a question.

"Um, excuse me, Mr. Nishikida... You said you would be our 'escorts' today, right? Does that mean Ruby Eyes might try to interfere with our mission?"

"We haven't received any concrete information to indicate that. This is simply part of our duties here," Nishikida responded, his tone much stiffer than Kakinari's. "The Tokyo Bay Nuclear Power Plant is an obvious target for the Ruby Eyes who want to wage war on humanity, so it is closely guarded by the STS. If they were to destroy the containment building before the nuclear-decommissioning process is complete, all of Tokyo could be contaminated with radioactive materials, and we would effectively lose our capital city... We cannot allow any such attempts."

Nishikida's words held such firm resolve that Minoru felt himself automatically thinking, *No, never!* in response.

The two Ruby Eyes he had fought, Biter and Igniter, had both been driven by personal motives, using the powers given to them by their Third Eyes to kill for pleasure. If they had turned their abilities on the nuclear power plant, they could have thrown Tokyo—no, all of Japan—into chaos, but their own everyday lives would be ruined as well. Surely they wouldn't go that far... But before he could voice his thoughts, Yumiko cut in with another huff.

"Those are fine words, Mr. Nishikida, but I can see right through them to your real objective."

"And what would that be, Miss Accelerator?"

"I'm sure that part of your *duties* today includes spying on us, right?"

"...!"

This thought hadn't occurred to Minoru, and he listened for Nishikida's response with bated breath. Instead, though, Kakinari chose this moment to break her silence.

"Ah-ha-ha, you're something else, Accelerator! Must be tough on your boyfriend, huh? You better not cheat on her, Isolator!"

"Wh..." Yumiko's voice cracked with rage, and Minoru attempted to stammer out an answer instead.

"I...I wouldn't! I mean, wait— I'm not her boyfriend!"

At that moment, Nishikida slowed the vehicle to a halt.

"Here we are, you two."

Yumiko looked for a moment as if she was struggling to decide whether to say anything more, but in the end she stood up in silence, opened the back doors, and hopped out of the truck, Minoru following shortly behind her. When he closed the doors and looked up, a smooth gray tower loomed before his eyes.

Tokyo Bay Nuclear Power Plant, No. 1. Built in 2001 with the latest technology of the time, it had now been sitting in disuse for several decades, simply waiting to be decommissioned.

At the base of the enormous gravestone-like structure was an air lock with double doors, though of course they were no longer in use. Two large radiation shields loomed on either side of the door, giving the impression that the place was the ancient ruins of some bygone era.

Getting out of the car and walking up to stand next to Minoru, Nishikida pointed at the air lock.

"Go in through those doors and you'll find the entrance to the containment vessel about eighteen meters down the hall. This is as far as Kakinari and I can accompany you..."

"Ah, that's all right, thank you. We received a map of the building and such."

Minoru pulled up the map on the fifteen-centimeter LCD screen of his wrist communicator. Bending down to look at it, Nishikida tapped near the entrance.

"Once you get inside, the radioactivity levels in this immediate area will be around three millisieverts per hour. In front of the doors to the containment vessel, it'll rise to ten, and inside the vessel, it could be anywhere from several thousand to ten thousand millisieverts. At those levels, even Third Eye hosts like us wouldn't be able to survive if exposed unprotected... Are you sure this is all right with you?"

Whatever orders he might have been under, the concern in Nishikida's voice was undoubtedly genuine. Minoru looked up at him through his mask and nodded.

"Yes. I'll be fine."

"This kid's not talkin' about his suit, is he? Do you have some kinda Jet Eye power that'll protect you from all that radioactive junk, Isolator?" Kakinari once again muscled into the conversation, but her question was intercepted by Yumiko.

"That is highly confidential SFD information!"

"Aww, gimme a break!"

"Kakinari, please refrain from engaging in idle chatter before an important mission," Nishikida reprimanded his colleague, then turned back to Minoru's wrist communicator, scrolling across the map with a rough gloved finger. Zooming in on the round containment vessel, he tapped part of the interior.

"This is where we lost contact with the probe robot, Muser. Your job is to open the double doors, enter the room, and locate and retrieve Muser. Of course, there are no lights inside the containment vessel, the heat and humidity levels are considerably high, and the room will be completely clouded with steam. It won't be an easy mission..."

"Yes, I know... I've already been lectured extensively about it. But it's all right... I think I can do it."

Giving another nod to the tall Self-Defense Forces personnel, Minoru looked at the clock in the top right of the LCD screen. Ten fifty-five a.m. The mission was set to start at eleven, so there were only five minutes... No, there were *still* five minutes left. Though the response he'd given Nishikida had been brimming with confidence, it wasn't as if Minoru wasn't nervous. He was eager to get in and out as quickly as possible and get the mission over with.

As he stared intently at the painfully slow progression of the clock, Yumiko, standing next to him, clapped him on the back. Once again disconnecting their communication channel from the STS members, she brought her mask in close to his.

"...Utsugi. We've already seen in countless SFD experiments that your protective shell can completely block out radiation like alpha, beta, gamma, and X-rays. But on the other hand, that also means that if you drop that shell for even a second, you'll be exposed to lethal levels of radiation. You know that, right? If anything goes wrong... No, if anything even *seems* like it might go wrong, turn back immediately. That's an order."

"Right...understood."

As he responded, Minoru glanced at Yumiko's face, which he could just barely make out through the thick lead glass of his mask. Her beautiful features, normally set into a cold and distant expression, were currently so full of concern that Minoru unwittingly held his breath.

It had been only three weeks since he'd first met Yumiko Azu, a Jet Eye and member of the Special Defense Forces with the code name Accelerator.

But in that short time, they had paired up to defeat two terrifying enemies, the Ruby Eyes Biter and Igniter. And Yumiko had been the one to come up with Minoru's code name, Isolator. Minoru could still barely wrap his mind around the idea that he was a member of a secret organization that protected humanity, but he knew one thing: The reason he had been able to carry out his duties so far was because his partner, Yumiko, had been there, urging him on.

But this time, he would have to take on this difficult mission without Yumiko there to back him up. Even with the 150-pound protective suit, she wouldn't be able to withstand the radiation inside the containment vessel, which far exceeded the sievert levels that a normal human being could survive for even a short period of time. Professor Riri had mentioned the possibility that a Third Eye might be able to restore DNA damaged by radiation, but that hypothesis was still being investigated and could hardly justify jumping into a nuclear reactor containment vessel.

But it's all right—I can do it by myself. Professor Riri and Chief Himi both told me I could decline if I wanted to, but I said I would do it.

As Minoru took deep breaths and said this to himself repeatedly, Yumiko lightly slapped him on the back again, then sighed loudly and made a remark that caught him by surprise. "Honestly, Utsugi. If you had been able to pull it off in that last experiment, I would've been able to come, too."

"Wh…what?! It wasn't my fault that experiment failed…"

"Hmph! Are you saying it was mine?!" As she responded in a disgruntled voice, Yumiko nevertheless pressed her goggles up against Minoru's mask.

"I-I think it was half your fault, at least!"

As he pushed back against her, he recalled the events that she was referring to: Christmas Eve, just four days earlier.

2

"Hey, don't touch me in weird places!"

Minoru was perplexed by Yumiko's sharp words, unsure of how he was supposed to judge which places were weird and how to avoid touching them.

After all, the entire front of his body, from head to toe and even to his fingertips, was currently pressed up against Yumiko. More specifically, she was standing upright with her arms spread wide, and he stood directly behind her in the same position, with virtually no space in between them. It was therefore completely unreasonable to ask him to somehow not touch her, but nonetheless, Minoru automatically leaned his hips away from her. Immediately, another voice chimed in from nearby.

"Don't move apart, Mikkun! Your desire to put distance between yourself and Yukko is going to cause this experiment to fail!"

"A-all right…"

Minoru nodded, and the tip of his nose brushed against Yumiko's hair, so that he caught a slight whiff of the sweet smell of her shampoo. Instinctively, he bent his head away this time.

"You're doing it again!"

The Professor—Riri Isa, an elementary school girl who also happened to be the commander of the SFD—shook her head with a sigh, her pigtails swaying back and forth. "Hrmph…the ability to do the same thing over and over with very little show of improvement is one of our species' special gifts. According to my research, a young man your age should be thrilled to press his body up against a girl of the same generation as his…"

"Don't say creepy things like that, Professor!" Yumiko exclaimed before Minoru could get a word in.

The Professor's retort was immediate.

"It's not creepy! That's how normal high school girls and boys are. And you're to blame, too, Yukko! Mikkun wouldn't want to get away from you if you weren't being so crabby! You're his senior in this organization, so you should be leading by example!"

"……I don't think I like your tone…," Yumiko grumbled, but she leaned into Minoru anyway as if out of spite. "See, Utsugi? I'm not rejecting you one bit. So make sure this next attempt works, got it?"

Sure you're not, Minoru thought to himself, nodding nonetheless.

"All right…here goes."

"Okay! This is attempt number twenty. Recording now… Whenever you're ready!" The Professor pressed a button on the video camera and stepped aside.

Minoru took a deep breath, closed his eyes, and focused.

Accept her.

This person is not an intruder who needs to be rejected. This is a friend who has fought alongside me, who I can trust with my life. And I've done this once before. It was only a week ago that I managed to bring her into my protective shell to keep her safe from the shock wave of a hydrogen explosion. I just have to remember what I did that time...

Minoru pressed himself tighter against Yumiko's body, and with his eyes still closed, he brought out his protective shell.

His sense of sound, temperature, and finally touch all vanished.

Cautiously, he cracked open one eye. The sight before him was bathed in pale-blue light: Yumiko in front of him, moving farther away in a straight line. Flailing her arms wildly, the Accelerator crashed into the polyurethane-padded wall of the small room and stuck there.

Two minutes later...

In the center of the large room on the fifth floor of a musty old apartment building in Toyama Park, Shinjuku, Tokyo, which served as the secret base of the SFD, Yumiko sat on the couch and glared at Minoru out of the corner of her eye.

"So, basically, the fact that you were able to accept me in the battle against Igniter was a total fluke, right? If you hadn't happened to get lucky, then I'd either be dead or at least covered in burns and compound fractures. Delightful."

"Erm... Well...I wonder..." Minoru placed a cup of black tea down on the glass table in front of Yumiko and gave a small shrug.

Glancing at the experiment space in the room's west corner, he noted sheepishly that the faint outline of a sprawled-out human body could still be seen in the padding on the wall. Privately, he felt it was a little unfair to think it was entirely his fault, but considering that Yumiko had now been launched into the wall and stuck there twenty times in a row, he couldn't exactly say so.

Instead he silently handed the Professor her drink of choice, a café au lait that was mostly just milk, which she blew on a few times as she spoke.

"No, no, it's not necessarily all Mikkun's fault, Yukko. If you are mentally rejecting him, it's entirely possible that..."

"No, it's not!"

In a flash, Yumiko took a big gulp of her milk- and sugar-filled tea, then shook her head furiously. "When it happened that time, I didn't even know Utsugi was nearby until I was pulled into his shell! Doesn't that mean my will has nothing to do with whether it works or not? If anyone's rejecting somebody, it must be Utsugi!"

"No, that's... I'm not rejecting you or anything..." Minoru made a reserved attempt to object as he sat down across from Yumiko, dropping a lemon slice into his own cup of black tea.

"I'm very well aware that I'll be much more useful in the next fight against a Ruby Eye if I learn to control my ability at will. And I know I have to put my duties above my emotions. So I think in the end, the fact that Yumiko didn't notice me might have been a big reason it worked that time..."

Through the steam rising from his tea, Minoru saw Yumiko throw another glare in his direction.

"Now wait just a minute. Is it just me, or did that phrasing sound a lot like 'I personally don't want to, but if it's for the sake of the mission, I'll just have to bear it'?"

"I-I didn't say that at all! Aren't you just looking for reasons to reject me now?!"

"And while we're at it, don't you think you should stop acting so stiff and formal around me? It's so obvious that you *want* there to be distance between us!"

"I can't help it if you're going to be so scary all the time!"

The pair's back-and-forth argument was interrupted by a loud sigh from the Professor.

"Ugh...listen, you two. From where I'm standing... Ugh, how do I say this...? Could you just start dating already, please?"

Like clockwork, they both sprang back, widening their eyes and protesting in unison:

"N-no thank you!"

"No thanks! Who would want to...... Wait."

Midsentence, Yumiko stopped and turned slowly and deliberately toward Minoru, a dangerous glint in her eyes.

"Just a moment. Hold it right there, Utsugi."

"...Y-yes?"

"Did you just say 'No thank you'? You did, didn't you? You said 'No thank you' without a moment's hesitation, did you not?"

"...But, w-well, you said it, too, didn't you?"

"Of course I did! Oh, forget it already. I've had quite enough of being paired up with you! It's obvious what happened that time was just a fluke, end of story!"

With that, Yumiko threw back the rest of her tea in one gulp, slammed the cup back onto the saucer, stood up brusquely, and stomped toward the elevator.

However, she stopped partway across the room and looked over her shoulder with a toss of her long hair.

"You'd better be making a nice Christmas dinner tonight to make up for your rudeness today! I expect a cheesy seafood gratin and a nice meaty beef stew, got it?"

Then, with a dramatic flourish, she used her accelerating abilities to propel herself to the elevator in a single step, jabbed the down button, and disappeared into the elevator.

Minoru, incredulous, watched her leave and then sank back onto the sofa, muttering into his lemon tea:

"...It's impossible... I can barely pair up with her as a team, never mind as a *couple*..."

"Ugh...well, I guess that's it for today, then." The Professor shook her head. "I'm still not giving up, though. The combination of your protective shell and her acceleration powers has incredible potential, after all. If you could master it, you'd have an attack that would be almost impossible to counter or defend against."

"Ah... Well, that may be true, but..."

One week ago, in the battle against the Ruby Eye who could manipulate oxygen molecules freely, Igniter, Minoru had somehow absorbed Yumiko into his protective shell in order to defend her from the hydrogen explosions she had rushed into. Still inside the shell, Yumiko had used her accelerator powers to slam them into Igniter, knocking him out in a single blow. If they could use this same tactic at will, they would essentially have nothing to fear from any future Ruby Eye attacks. Between Minoru's protective shell, which was harder than any known substance on Earth, and Yumiko's ultrahigh speed, they would practically be invincible.

Therefore, one week after the battle with Igniter, Professor Riri Isa had ordered a series of tests in an attempt to re-create that situation. However, Minoru had failed to envelop Yumiko in his protective shell every time he produced it, instead sending her flying into the polyurethane wall, which still showed the vague outline of her repeated impact.

But I tried my best...

Minoru was wrapped up in his thoughts when the Professor's voice reached him again. "By the way..."

"Y-yes?"

"Have you given any thought to what we talked about before?"

Minoru knew right away what she was talking about, but he still looked down, unable to give an immediate reply. Feeling her eyes on him as she intently awaited his response, he answered haltingly, searching for the right words.

"...Yes...I understand that it would be best if I proceed as you suggested, Professor. But to be honest...I'm not sure if I can do it. Moving away...transferring to a new school..."

"Nonetheless, Mikkun..." Still holding her café au lait, the Professor spoke in a voice that was at once quite serious and adorable. "Your request in exchange for joining the SFD was for Chief Himi to use his abilities to 'erase any memories of you from existence,' wasn't it? If that day comes, won't you have to move and change schools, anyway? Maybe you can think of this as practice for all that."

"...That's true, but..."

The Professor's reasons for suggesting that Minoru move to SFD Headquarters were twofold: so that he would be more immediately available to fight against the Ruby Eyes and to prevent them from targeting his stepsister, Norie Yoshimizu. Ruby Eyes and Jet Eyes like Minoru and the others could detect the use of one another's abilities from a fair distance away, so if Minoru were ever to activate his protective shell at home, there was a strong possibility that a Ruby Eye would figure out where he lived and attack Norie.

No, there was more than a possibility—the first Ruby Eye Minoru had fought, the Biter, had already used just such a tactic. He'd saved Norie that time, but he couldn't afford to let that happen again.

But...

At the school he currently attended, Yoshiki High School in Saitama,

Minoru had gone to great pains to ensure that his presence was barely noticed by the other students. To Minoru, who feared above all else the creation of more painful memories, the very thought of going into a new and unknown environment was unbearable. Just picturing himself transferring into a new school and standing in front of a class of strangers made him break into a cold sweat.

Minoru sank into silence and faintly heard the Professor heave another sigh.

"Well...having you transfer schools is mostly just a matter of convenience, so that there won't be any holes in your academic records. You don't necessarily have to go every day, but you can't exactly skip all the time, either. Take that into consideration and get back to me soon, okay? Well, anyway... I'd like to have some chocolate cake tonight, Mikkun."

"...Yes, ma'am."

Giving her a meek nod, Minoru roused himself, rose from the couch, and headed toward the kitchen, which stood across from the experiment space.

3

"...Well, it is too bad that the experiment didn't work, but even if it had, in the end I'd still be going in alone today."

Awakening from his brief reverie, Minoru voiced this thought aloud, and Yumiko responded without removing her face mask from his.

"...Why?"

"I mean, if something happened inside and my protective shell vanished, both of us would go down at once. It's better to minimize our losses, right?"

"I don't like the way you said that one bit."

With one more irritated huff, Yumiko pulled away.

At last, the clock display ticked up to 10:00 a.m. Restoring their connection to the STS channel, Yumiko spoke now in a much more composed, businesslike voice. "Well then, let's begin the operation. Isolator, please proceed to the air lock of nuclear reactor containment vessel number one."

"R…roger that."

Taking a deep breath, Minoru stepped forward with his right foot.

He walked slowly and deliberately, mindful of the radiation screens that stood to his left and right. Along the way, he checked the screen of his wrist communicator, but the radiation levels in the air hadn't risen much just yet. In a little over a minute, he halted, having reached the first checkpoint.

"I've arrived in front of the air lock."

"Radioactivity level report?"

"Um…currently 9.3 microsieverts per hour."

"Roger. Now please begin the locking mechanism release procedure."

"Roger," Minoru responded, glancing over his shoulder. Yumiko and the two Self-Defense Forces personnel stood motionless next to the parked vehicle, watching him from about twenty-one meters away. Kakinari waved at him vigorously, and he quickly turned back before the urge to wave overcame him.

Up close, he could see that the wall of the containment vessel was cracked and stained, the damage unchanged from the incident eight long years ago. The paint on the steel doors of the air lock was peeling away in places, too, with brown specks of rust blooming here and there along its surface.

Above the door handle, a red light indicated that the lock was currently closed.

On the other side of this door was a death trap, full of lethal levels of radioactivity. In fact, since they had measured the radioactivity levels in SFD Headquarters to be about 0.03 microsieverts per hour, the radioactivity levels out here were already three hundred times that of the Tokyo metropolitan area.

Naturally, his adoptive stepsister and guardian, Norie, didn't know anything about today's mission. As a matter of fact, any time he had SFD business, he simply told her he was going to "a prep school in Tokyo." Since he did occasionally study with Yumiko and the Professor at SFD Headquarters in their free time, it wasn't a total lie, but that didn't change the fact that he was deceiving his beloved stepsister.

However, in reality he had already committed the ultimate betrayal of Norie by joining the SFD in exchange for the promise of eventually being erased from the memories of everyone around him.

It wasn't as though Minoru wanted to be separated from Norie. She was the only person with whom he could create new memories every day without fear. He would have liked to continue living with her... but doing so would mean tying the thirty-year-old to the role of being Minoru's guardian indefinitely.

No, things would be better for her this way. In order to allow Norie to forget about her adopted brother and live for her own happiness, Minoru would continue to fulfill his duties with the SFD to the best of his abilities—even if it meant fighting more Ruby Eyes...or retrieving a probe robot from a nuclear power plant.

"...Releasing the lock now," Minoru said into the headset, and he stepped up to the double doors to grip the locking mechanism with both hands. Just as he'd been instructed in a lecture earlier, he turned it to the left with all his might. It was difficult to budge at first—no doubt it hadn't been opened very often, especially in recent years—but it was nothing his Third Eye–given strength couldn't handle. After three full turns, there was the sound of the bolt creaking loose, and the indicator light turned bright green.

"Release complete."

"Roger that," Yumiko responded, her voice a bit tenser than before. "Commence opening the air lock."

"Understood..." Minoru shifted both hands back to the handle and again grasped it tightly.

Though they hadn't mentioned it to the Self-Defense Forces members, there was one more thing he had to do before opening these doors. Breathing in quietly through his mask, he filled his lungs with air and activated the small black sphere-shaped parasite that lived in his chest—his "Third Eye."

Minoru's body floated up slightly inside his protective suit, and all outside sound was cut off at once. His view of his surroundings through the lead glass of his mask was tinted blue. Even the pressure of the mask's elastic band and the weight of the tungsten-lined suit disappeared.

This was Minoru's power as a Jet Eye: the ability to create a colorless, transparent, and utterly indestructible protective shell that projected about three centimeters around his entire body. In other words, Minoru was currently encased in an insulated inner shell that fit to the contours of his body (and the small earpiece in his left ear), which in turn was protected by the tungsten suit.

As his colleagues had confirmed in experiments at SFD Headquarters, the shell could deflect not only physical attacks but also electromagnetic and radio waves. As a result, it had so far been impossible to communicate via radio once Minoru was inside the shell, but they had recently come up with a solution.

Between the headset in his left ear and the left side of his protective mask, there was a white LED light transmitter. The device was automatically activated when the protective shell cut off communications, at which point radio waves from Yumiko's headset and the wrist communicator were now captured by the mask's internal receiver, converted into light-wave communication in order to pass through the protective shell, and changed back into sound waves in Minoru's earpiece. In the test run back at headquarters, it had permitted communication with no problems aside from a bit of time lag; DD, who designed and produced the device, had been extremely proud.

I hope it still works now that we're in the field...

"I will now open the first door. Please be mindful of the radiation levels," Minoru said hesitantly into the headset.

"Roger. Be careful on your end, too."

Yumiko's voice came through loud and clear, if with a little more white noise than before. Breathing a sigh of relief, Minoru checked that his connection with the wrist communicator was working as well, then grabbed hold of the door handle through the shield. Pushing against it hard, he slowly slid the door to the left.

The small microphone in his earpiece picked up the loud grating noise as the first door creaked along the rusted rail. When it had moved about fifteen centimeters open, Minoru let go momentarily to check his wrist communicator. Though the radiation levels had increased to fifteen microsieverts per hour, it was still not high enough to be a serious threat.

A second door awaited behind the first, visually identical to the first except that it had much less visible wear and tear. Since this door was already unlocked, he had only to grab on to the handle once again.

"Opening the second door."

"Go ahead."

After this brief exchange, Minoru pushed with about the same force as before.

Although the rail and wheels weren't rusted, the second door put up much more resistance than the first. It was as though the building itself

SPECIAL DEFENSE FORCE ANTI-RADIATION PROTECTIVE SUIT FOR THE ISOLATOR

Protective shell

Anti-radiation suit

Transceiver
&
Light transmitter

White LED light

Headset
&
Light transmitter

Check Point

Illustration by Tatsuya Kurusu

was refusing to be opened. Nonetheless, Minoru planted his feet firmly and pushed the door with all his weight.

The heavy steel door gave a mighty creak and moved about twenty centimeters. And then...

BREEEEEEE!! A high-pitched warning sound screeched through Minoru's earpiece, and he caught his breath.

A glance at his wrist communicator showed that radiation levels had now reached 2.8 *millisieverts*—180 times higher than before he had opened the door. Of course, this was the level detected by the wrist communicator outside his shell; in theory, not one single beta ray would be reaching Minoru's body. If any of the radiation did get through, a separate counter inside his headset should set off an alarm to let him know. Still, he felt a bead of sweat drip down his forehead.

"Th...the air lock is now open. Radiation levels at 2.8 millisieverts."

"R...roger." Yumiko's voice sounded a bit ill at ease, too.

"Whoa, wait a sec! Two-point-eight?!" This voice was obviously Kakinari. "You're seriously still fine at a level like that?!"

"Y...yes, it's fine."

It is fine, right?! Minoru sent a silent and emphatic plea toward the Third Eye in his chest.

"I'll continue toward the nuclear reactor containment room now."

"...At the first sign of danger, you are to retreat immediately, no matter what. You know that, right?"

"Roger that. I'm going in!"

This is part of my duties, too... A part that only I can do, as a matter of fact. Directing a silent encouragement toward himself this time, Minoru stepped over the rail and into the building.

In the dim light of the nuclear reactor containment building, dust particles danced silently in the rays of winter light shining through the door behind him. Since the reactor itself was kept in a vacuum-sealed vessel, there should be no danger of radioactive material leaking into this part of the building. Nonetheless it was probably best to keep the time that the air lock was open to a minimum.

Changing the wrist communicator's display back to the map and switching on the LED lamp on the forehead of his protective mask, Minoru stepped into the wide passageway. He proceeded with caution, following the red navigation line displayed on his map.

Soon, he was able to see a bulky radiation blocker that had likely been installed after the incident. Since this would also interfere with the radio waves of his communicator, he reached into a pouch on the waist of his protective suit, pulled out a battery-operated repeater, and placed it next to the blocker.

"Repeater number one, installation complete."

"Understood. Signal levels satisfactory."

"Proceeding now."

By the time he had traveled another five meters or so, Minoru's surroundings were almost completely pitch-black. The radiation level on his wrist communicator now measured four millisieverts per hour, the air in the hallway polluted by radioactive elements scattered by the damaged containment vessel. Just standing in this hallway for fifteen minutes would bring your exposure level up to one millisievert, the maximum annual dosage deemed safe by the International Commission on Radiological Protection.

Since particle radiation from emitted alpha particles or photons could be blocked with even a sheet of plastic, they posed no threat to the suited-up Minoru except through internal exposure, but the real problem was electromagnetic radiation like gamma rays and X-rays. At least ten centimeters of lead would be required to block out gamma rays, meaning that the thin layer of tungsten inside Minoru's suit would do little to protect him.

It was strange to think about. Gamma radiation was nothing but electromagnetic waves with a wavelength shorter than that of visible light, yet they could damage a living being's DNA by inhibiting the repairing abilities of cells and, in the worst-case scenario, even lead to death. If the Earth's atmosphere didn't absorb the gamma rays that constantly rain down from outer space, all of humanity would have long since perished.

The survival of human beings is really based on a delicate, dangerous balance, Minoru thought. The shifting of tectonic plates, the eruption of volcanoes, a slight increase in the average temperature—any one of these things could cause that delicate balance to crumble. And Ruby Eyes could be a threat to that balance, too. What set them apart from the other disasters, though, was that they were beings with minds of their own.

He had been deeply alarmed when Nishikida had pointed out this possibility earlier, but thinking back now, he remembered that Igniter had intended to turn all the water in Tokyo into hydrogen and cause a massively destructive explosion. And it was entirely possible that another Ruby Eye could target this nuclear reactor in Tokyo Bay as a show of their power. In order to protect the peaceful lives of the people closest to him—his stepsister, Norie; his friend from the track and field club, Tomomi Minowa—he had to make sure this mission succeeded.

With these thoughts churning in his mind, Minoru continued his slow progress through the dark hallway.

The map on his wrist communicator indicated that the distance from the air lock to the containment vessel was only about eighteen meters, but to Minoru it felt ten times as long. Finally, a plain rectangular door appeared in the wall before him. Finding a label that read CONTAIN-MENT VESSEL AIR LOCK, Minoru took a short breath.

"I've arrived at the containment vessel door. Radiation levels, fifteen millisieverts per hour."

"Roger......a bit farthe......od luck."

Since it was now coming through three different repeaters, Yumiko's response was choppy with noise. Nonetheless, encouraged by the sound of his partner's voice, Minoru gave a loud "Right!" in response as he stepped up to the door.

Compared to the building entrance above, this set of double doors was much smaller. However, the first set of doors had nothing on the pressure of these off-white, steel-armored doors.

Since the incident in 2011, not a single human had been inside these doors. During his briefing, Minoru had seen the images collected by the probe robot before its signal was lost, but seeing up close how the doors had been ravaged by the radiation, he had a keen sense of just how terrifying the situation was inside the containment vessel. Just thinking about the fact that he was about to go inside was enough to make his heart leap into his throat, but he knew he couldn't turn back now.

Through his protective shell and suit, Minoru touched his hand to his left cheek, where the Divider, SFD member Olivier Saitou, had punched him not long ago. Then he clenched his hand into a fist.

"I'm opening the containment vessel!" he shouted, half at himself. Reaching out and gingerly grasping the handle, he unlocked the door and pulled it open. He met with a great deal of resistance at first, but soon the stuck gaskets came loose, and the door creaked open for the first time in eight years.

Inside was a room only about a meter around, with another set of double doors. According to the information Minoru had received, an interlocking mechanism prevented the doors from being opened at the same time, so once he entered the room, the threshold would close back up.

With this, Minoru was now completely cut off from all contact with Yumiko. He would have to make decisions on his own from this point on. The agreement was that if more than twenty minutes passed without any communication from Minoru, Yumiko would assume that something had happened and come rushing in—so he couldn't afford to let a single second go to waste.

Turning around, he shook off his fear of unlocking the next door and gave it a push. Once again, the door slowly came unstuck with a loud noise and began to move. Three centimeters...five centimeters...the opening widened ever so slowly.

Once again, the wrist communicator gave off a shrill alert. Minoru stopped pushing for a moment and looked with dread at the blinking number on the LED screen: 3.2 sieverts per hour. Or in the units of measurement they'd used back at SFD Headquarters, 3.2 million microsieverts.

...It reached that high a level just from opening the door five centimeters?

Minoru planted his right foot in the opening and, after double-checking that his protective shell was activated, pushed the door open with all his might.

The headlamp's white light shone faintly into the gloomy darkness. He had been warned that the inside of the containment vessel would have very high heat and humidity, but there was even more steam than he'd expected. The goggles he was wearing were supposed to be fog-proof, but he still saw some white blooming at the edges of his vision.

"...So this is the inside of a nuclear reactor containment vessel..." In an effort to keep himself calm, Minoru commented out loud, but there was still a bit of an audible tremor in his voice. But he could still move his legs, and there was no numbness in his hands. So far, he didn't feel any headache or stomach pains to indicate that anything was wrong with his body, either. Compared to the fight against Biter on the rooftop of the Saitama Super Arena, he was still pretty calm...at least he hoped so.

Moving on, he carefully scanned around the room with his headlamp. He could more or less make out the grating on the floor but wasn't able to see the wall of the nuclear reactor pressure vessel that should be in the center of the room. A few bolts that had probably come loose in the aftershocks of phreatic explosions were rolling around on the floor, but there didn't seem to be any serious damage.

Looking down between the gaps in the grating beneath his feet, he could see the light from his headlamp reflected in the water far below. Underneath that water, the atomic fuel that had melted through the containment vessel and the pressure vessel was most likely still radiating huge amounts of heat. He had been told that the most difficult part of the nuclear decommissioning process would be retrieving that debris, and indeed, Minoru had no idea how they would go about removing something that no human could get anywhere near.

According to Professor Riri Isa, the Ministry of Health, Labor, and Welfare had indeed expressed the opinion that, if he could retrieve the robot, Minoru might also be able to investigate the debris in the contaminated water below. However, apparently Chief Himi had firmly refused, even going so far as to threaten to remove the memories of this operation from everybody involved if the request was not retracted. Even then, he had bowed his head deeply to Minoru, apologizing for "asking him to do a job like this."

True enough, this mission had nothing to do with eliminating Ruby Eyes, but Minoru's bargain with Chief Himi was only that he would work as a member of the SFD in exchange for the use of the chief's memory-altering abilities once the organization was dissolved. If this was part of his duties as an SFD member, Minoru would simply have to do it.

"...Now then, where are you, Mr. Robot...?" Since he wasn't being recorded in order to protect the secret of his Third Eye, Minoru was free to mumble to himself as he slowly circled clockwise around the diaphragm floor, installed to protect the structure of the reactor from seismic activity.

The diameter of the room was about twenty-four meters, meaning the room's outer circumference was a little over seventy-six meters. Minoru had seventeen minutes left to locate and retrieve the robot.

Fortunately, since the floor was relatively free of debris, it should be fairly easy to locate the large form of the robot. If he couldn't find it, there was a high likelihood that it had fallen through some hole into the water below, so there would be no choice but to give up.

Please be here...

Minoru pleaded silently as he walked, while the number on his wrist communicator continued to rocket upward, soon surpassing ten sieverts per hour. If for some reason Minoru were to drop his protective shell for even a moment, the tungsten suit and even the restorative powers of his Third Eye would almost certainly not be enough to keep him from dying of radiation exposure.

As Minoru continued forward, he imagined that he could see the high-energy radiation flying all around him as small, countless sparks.

Navigating around the pressure vessel, Minoru arrived at the opposite side of the room from the double doors he'd entered through. Then, at last, the white light of his headlamp illuminated a promising shape not far away.

It was a cylindrical object that lay curled on the grating of the floor, about a meter in length. Attached was a long series of metal rings, which he assumed expanded and contracted to move the robot like a snake. This part looked to be about ten centimeters thick and seventy-six centimeters long. On its head was a sensor comprised of several lenses, but it didn't look to be functioning at the moment.

The reason the robot had stopped moving was obvious at a glance. A large gash in the center of its body had damaged three or so of the rings, exposing the mechanisms beneath. The mysterious cause of this damage was nowhere to be seen nearby, but Minoru's job was only to retrieve the robot, not to determine what had happened to it in the first place. Reaching out with both hands, he gathered the little metal snake into his arms.

Suddenly, the indicator on the robot's head blinked green, and at the same instant, a small beep from Minoru's headset indicated a request for a new connection.

"Huh...?"

Without thinking, he automatically looked around the room, but of course, nobody was there.

Then the request must have come from the robot in his arms.

Dubiously, he tapped the button on his wrist communicator to accept the request. The standard Bluetooth icon flashed, confirming that the connection was established, and in the next moment...

"WHAT IS YOUR NAME?"

Muddled with noise though it might have been, there was unquestionably Japanese speech flowing through Minoru's earpiece. He blinked, startled, and looked around once again, but there was still nobody else in the room. Looking down at the metal snake in his arms, he spoke up timidly. "Was that you who said something just now?"

"I AM PROBE ROBOT MARK-22. MY NAME IS MUSER. WHAT IS YOUR NAME?"

On closer inspection, the indicator on the robot's head was blinking erratically in time with the voice in the earpiece. *It really is this little snake that's talking to me.*

Thinking back, Minoru had been told that the robot he was here to retrieve was completely autonomous, able to function without any human control needed. But he hadn't expected it to have such an advanced AI system that he would have to tell it his name.

Minoru wondered for a moment if it was all right to ignore the robot's query and simply carry out his mission. But after three seconds of silence had elapsed, the metal snake—Muser—spoke up again.

"YOU ARE NOT RECOGNIZED AS AN AUTHORIZED USER. FOR SECURITY PURPOSES, CONTROL CIRCUITS WILL NOW SELF-DESTRUCT."

With some difficulty, Minoru tried to translate into words the noisy synthetic voice in his mind. *"Not recognized as an authorized user"..."security purposes"..."self-destruct"?!*

"COMMENCING COUNTDOWN. TEN... NINE... EIGHT... SEVEN..."

"Whoa, w-wait a minute!"

In a panic, Minoru leaned down to address the robot, pressing his goggles against its biggest lens. "I-I'm from the Ministry of Health, Labor, and Welfare Industrial Safety and Health Department, Specialized Forces Division..." After a second's hesitation, he used his real name instead of his code name. "Minoru Utsugi. I came here to retrieve...to rescue you."

"...TO RESCUE ME?"

Interrupting the self-destruct countdown, Muser's indicator blinked rapidly and adjusted the focus on its lens. Despite being a robot, the uncertainty was palpable in its voice as it spoke. "THE RADIOACTIV-ITY LEVEL IN THIS ROOM SURPASSES THE MEDIAN LETHAL DOSAGE FOR A HUMAN. WHY HAVE YOU COME TO RESCUE ME?"

"The median lethal dosage..." That most likely meant the level of radiation that would kill at least half the humans exposed to it. If one thought about it logically, it did seem like there would be no reason for a human to risk death just to rescue a probe robot. Unless, of course, that human was capable of completely protecting himself from radiation. However, Minoru doubted that the robot's AI would understand if he tried to explain about his protective shell.

"Umm, well, that's..." He trailed off for a moment, trying to come up with a satisfactory answer. "Because...you are very important. We couldn't afford to lose you here, so I came to rescue you."

The robot's indicator light flickered for a few moments before it responded in its artificial voice. "...YOU HAVE BEEN RECOGNIZED AS AN AUTHORIZED USER."

Breathing a sigh of relief under his mask, Minoru checked the time. Twelve minutes had already passed since he first entered the contain-ment vessel building; another eight, and Yumiko would come charging in to rescue him.

"All right, we're going outside."

Cradling Muser in his arms as carefully as if it were a wounded ani-mal, Minoru returned to the set of double doors. In the opposite order from before, and with a little more difficulty, as he was using only one hand, he made his way back out. Turning the handle again and locking the outside door, he took a deep breath.

With the headset automatically having reconnected to the repeater, Minoru spoke into it loudly. "This is Isolator. I have successfully recov-ered the robot!"

Yumiko responded without a moment's delay, as if she'd been await-ing the news with bated breath. "Roger that. The repeaters can be left where they are. Please make a speedy exit from the building."

"All right, I'm on my—" Minoru started to respond but was quickly interrupted.

"WHO IS SPEAKING ON THIS CHANNEL? STATE YOUR NAME," the robot in Minoru's arms cut in abruptly. There were a few seconds of silence, and then Yumiko responded in something of a shriek:

"*ME?!* Who are *you?!* Utsu… I mean, Isolator, is there a *girl* in there?!"

"A…a girl?!"

Minoru sputtered, wondering why she had leaped straight to that conclusion, but he supposed that if anything the robot's synthetic voice was somewhat high-pitched.

Muser responded to her question in a cautioning tone.

"YOU ARE NOT RECOGNIZED AS AN AUTHORIZED USER. FOR SECURITY PURPOSES, CONTROL CIRCUITS WILL NOW—"

"Wh-whaa—?! Both of you, please just wait a minute, I'll explain as soon as we get outside!"

Minoru quickened his pace through the hallway. This time, it was Kakinari's bemused voice that cut into the conversation.

"What in the heck is going on in there, kid?"

"I…I don't know, either!!" Minoru wailed. Straight ahead of him, he saw the light of winter shining white through the open air-lock doors.

Thus, the probe robot recovery mission, Minoru's first job for the SFD outside of fighting Ruby Eyes, ended more or less successfully.

The damaged robot Muser was returned to Eastern Electric Power Company, and its recordings from inside the nuclear reactor containment vessel before its signal was lost were uploaded to the Internet. However, there were no images of whatever caused the recording to be interrupted.

What was the cause of the damage "she" had sustained?

And what effect had her first contact with Minoru had on her AI?

It would be a little while longer until Minoru would find out.

Interlude I – End

1

Rain is wonderful.

When you stop to think about it, rain is actually pretty miraculous. Water that previously existed only as humidity in the air turns into liquid when the atmospheric pressure drops below a certain point, gathering together into droplets, and is finally pulled down to earth by gravity. Depending on the atmospheric temperature, it can even cool on the way down, freezing into beads of ice before hitting the ground.

No other substance found in the course of everyday human life alters its phases so drastically. Water is nearly imperceptible in vapor form, drenches the world in liquid form, and in solid form, bares its fangs at humanity.

And so, humans everywhere should devote more of their thoughts to rainy days.

About the mystique of water. About the deep question of why, at that specific temperature of one hundred degrees Celsius, it enters such a chaotic state.

And yet, those people...

Ryuu Mikawa shook his head slightly as he looked at the group of four high school–aged boys, who were making a racket three tables away from him.

Since it was winter vacation now, there wasn't much to be done about the fact that high school students were flooding into family restaurants in the middle of the afternoon, but he wouldn't allow them to ruin this precious, solemn, quiet, rainy New Year's Eve.

Crowded into their booth, the young men were screeching like monkeys as they took huge gulps from different glasses of foul-looking liquid. It seemed that they were making a game of mixing different drinks from the soda machine and tasting the results. It was bad enough to take perfectly colorless water and add gobs of sugary, artificially colored syrup, but to mix those already disgusting beverages together and not even finish drinking them afterward was simply unforgivable.

Swallowing a sigh, Mikawa closed the paperback he'd been reading with a snap.

Should he call the waiter and complain so that they would be given a warning, or should he use his powers to teach them a lesson himself?

Mikawa thought for only a moment before choosing the latter. As a member of the organization known as the Syndicate, he had to be careful about unnecessary bloodshed, but he had gotten permission to use his powers when he went into town today. And more importantly: It was a rainy day.

He lowered his head so he wouldn't be seen by the young men about nine meters away and glared at them, focusing not on any of their faces but on the glass that one of them was holding. The other three were pounding on the table and chanting, "CHUG! CHUG!" as he held up the murky brown liquid with a grin, then brought it to his lips.

The boy tilted the glass; the liquid that could hardly be called a drink anymore poured over the brim and into his mouth. At that moment, Mikawa pursed his lips and blew a tiny puff of air in that direction.

Kshh. Though he should have been too far away for the sound to reach him, Mikawa was sure he heard a small, sharp cracking sound from the young man's mouth.

The high school boy's Adam's apple swelled up suddenly, and his eyes widened, his pupils rolling back. The glass slipped from his hand and smashed into pieces on the table.

"Hey, man, what are you doing?!" one of his friends yelled, the other two bursting into laughter. But all three of them quickly fell silent.

The boy who was now standing moved to clutch his throat and suddenly coughed up a frightening amount of blood. Then he keeled forward onto the table, knocking over a myriad of glasses as he let out a strange, strangled scream. Blood spilled over the table and into the drinks that remained, adding a tinge of red to the mixtures.

Still listening to his victim's screams, Mikawa stood up quietly. He tucked his paperback into his coat pocket, picked up his umbrella and receipt, and began to walk away. Behind him, the restaurant was in an uproar. The screams had reached the ears of the other customers, and a waiter was rushing over with blood draining from his face, but none of them seemed to know what to do.

It was certainly a showy amount of blood, but the young man wouldn't die. The instant the liquid had entered his mouth, Mikawa had simply frozen it into sharp spikes, which cut up the mucous membrane on the inside of the victim's mouth and throat as he swallowed. At most, he would be unable to eat for a while and could possibly lose his voice.

Of course, there was nobody at the cash register, so Mikawa put his silver tray, receipt, and a thousand-yen bill on the counter and left the restaurant.

Opening up the umbrella he was carrying today—one of his favorites from his collection—Mikawa spun it in his hands as he walked down the wet sidewalk. The rain made a pleasant noise as it pattered against the water-resistant material, drowning out the clamor from the restaurant behind him.

The rain was so wonderful.

A blessing from the skies soaking, enveloping, covering everything.

Unfortunately, one of the few people who might have fully understood this sentiment had been hunted down by *them* a few days ago. If only he had accepted the Syndicate's invitation, things might not have ended with his powers and memories being snatched away, then forced to live in disgrace as an ordinary human once more.

Today would be his memorial. Though he might still exist as a living creature, the person who had shared the same will, Igniter, was dead.

Once again, Mikawa lamented the stupidity of humans. Their powers, based on oxygen and water respectively, were not the same by any means, but they carried the same will: to wash this polluted world clean.

And so, diminishing the numbers of the car- and motorcycle-driving humans whom Igniter had so detested was the least Mikawa could do in his fallen comrade's memory.

Lifting his umbrella, he looked up at the dull gray sky. The low-hanging winter storm clouds were beautiful, still dark and heavy with the promise of more rain.

* * *

"Good work today, Utsugi."

Minoru gave a slight bow to Yumiko, who had accompanied him down to the first floor of the SFD building to see him off. "Thanks, Yumiko. You, too."

"Make sure you go straight home today without any loitering around, got it?"

Minoru couldn't resist a wry smile at Yumiko's usual bossiness.

"I don't have the energy for loitering right now anyway, considering that we just got back from a nuclear power plant."

"True enough... All I did was stand outside and wait, and I'm still absurdly tired."

The Accelerator leaned back against the concrete wall by the elevator as she spoke. Judging by her casual jersey and the damp sheen of her hair, she had probably just showered in her room on the fourth floor. Brushing a wet strand away from her cheek, she looked up at the skies, which had been rainy all afternoon.

"Honestly...between meeting those weird escorts and getting mixed up with that weird robot, it's been a very strange day."

Minoru guessed that the "weird escorts" referred to the pair from the Self-Defense Forces and the "weird robot" was Muser. Again, he smiled wryly. "The STS...I mean, Kakinari anyway...was definitely pretty dodgy, but you're the one who came at Muser with all those weird accusations," he remarked, opening his folding umbrella.

"I didn't 'come at' it with anything! It's just an AI, anyway," Yumiko said with a huff, though her expression said differently as she straightened up and stepped away from the wall.

"...At any rate, it certainly is coming down hard..."

"Yeah..."

Minoru nodded, holding out his opened umbrella past the overhang they stood beneath. The sound of water dripping on top of the umbrella mixed in with the incessant sound of the falling rain.

"...Well, I'd better head home. As long as nothing major comes up, I think the next time I come here will be in the new year."

Yumiko nodded briskly. "All right. I'll stock up on ingredients."

"Huh? Uh, I didn't mean I'd be coming to cook..."

"Come on, you don't mind, right? I happen to like your cooking. It's certainly homier than the stuff DD makes." Yumiko gave Minoru such an uncharacteristically bright smile as she spoke that he blushed and had to look away.

"Th...that reminds me, I didn't see DD or Oli-V today..."

"Ah, those two... Oh, actually, on rainy days, they're usually out on patrol. DD probably went along to act as his 'radar.'"

"Huh? Why on rainy days?" Minoru tilted his head, puzzled.

Yumiko's smile faded. "They have a Ruby Eye they can't ignore, just like me with Igniter."

"Can't ignore…?" Minoru repeated, but Yumiko didn't seem to want to elaborate any further.

"I'm sure they'll tell you about it eventually…," she said as she reached out to press the worn elevator button. "See you later."

"…Have a good evening."

With a wave and another light nod, Minoru walked away into the woods that surrounded SFD Headquarters. Rain continued to fall from the twilit sky, dyeing the toes of his sneakers a dark gray.

* * *

With a thunderous roar, a large trailer truck sped past the sidewalk, splashing up a sheet of water that soaked into Mikawa's jeans.

However, he didn't so much as raise an eyebrow, strolling in silence as he gazed over the main road.

Four twenty p.m. With the winter solstice having passed not long ago, not to mention the overcast weather, night was already fast approaching by this time. Most of the cars driving along Route 246 through Aoyama had their headlights on, countless white streaks illuminating the rain-slicked surface of the road.

The rain showed no signs of letting up. In fact, the online weather radar he'd pulled up on his smartphone showed a bright red storm cloud approaching from the west, bringing even more torrential rains. With the global warming of recent years, it wasn't unusual for cumulonimbus clouds to appear even in the winter.

Mikawa had been waiting for this.

The people coming and going on the sidewalk were all shrinking under their umbrellas, their faces contorted as if they were enduring some misery. Mikawa, too, had once despised the cold midwinter rain that soaked into his shoes and froze his toes. But now, this cold was nothing to him. No matter its form, coming into contact with ice gave him a sense of calm. Truthfully, he would have been happy to go without the umbrella, but since standing in the pouring rain, getting soaked to the skin, would inevitably draw attention, he had reluctantly brought it along.

All at once, the pattering sound of the rain lightly bouncing off the top of his umbrella intensified. The cluster of cumulonimbus clouds had arrived overhead. Soon, the sound reached an overwhelming volume. The weight of the umbrella in his right hand nearly doubled, and the throng of headlights was swallowed up in a torrent of water.

It really was miraculous.

Every one of these countless drops of water had been floating as clouds in the sky just seconds ago. If water couldn't go through such remarkable phase transitions, there would be no rain, no rivers, nothing but deserts on this planet.

I'm sure you would've understood how I feel...

Wrapped up in his intoxicated reverie, Mikawa silently called out to his fallen comrade.

Igniter, the Ruby Eye whose near death by drowning triggered the awakening of his oxygen-manipulating abilities. Through a strict training regimen, he had perfected his powers to the point where he could separate water into hydrogen and oxygen molecules. By that same token, he had undoubtedly learned how to do the opposite, taking the hydrogen and oxygen in the air to create water. If he had joined the Syndicate and formed a team with Mikawa, the two of them would have surely been unstoppable.

So today, if nothing else, at least I can incinerate these humans with fire from their internal combustion engines and appease your spirit with their screams. Muttering this in his thoughts, Mikawa took a deep breath as a lump formed in his throat.

As the midwinter downpour reached its peak, the cars on Route 246, heading down the ramp toward Akasaka, looked as though they were coasting on a waterslide. Mikawa focused his attention on the water that was rushing down the asphalt like a river.

He pursed his lips and blew.

Fwhooo...

It was a long, thin, gentle exhale.

KSHHHHH! The sound seemed to resound through the city—the same noise he'd heard from the high school boy's throat at the family restaurant but magnified by a thousand.

The slick black surface of the asphalt had transformed into a pure white.

Immediately, the brake lights of all the cars on the ramp, already going several miles over the speed limit, turned red. Their disc brake calipers pressed into action, trying to slow the rotation of the tires by transforming the kinetic energy into thermal energy.

However, the friction that should have existed between the tires and the surface of the road was all but gone. Because Mikawa had frozen the entire road into ice, from the beginning of the ramp to the bottom of the hill.

Dozens of cars moving over eighty kilometers per hour avalanched down the road, which was now as white and sparkling as a skating rink.

At the bottom was the Akasaka crossing, where the traffic signal had just changed, and a tanker truck had just appeared on the intersecting Sotobori Street.

The first car to reach the bottom, a black minivan, spun wildly into the front wheel of the tanker, its front end denting with a crunch. The tanker's driver panicked and hit the brakes, blocking the entire intersection in the process. Then the next group of cars came crashing down.

There was the screeching sound of metal and a low rumble.

Mikawa cast aside the umbrella in his right hand, half closed his eyes, and flexed his fingers as if settling them onto an invisible keyboard. For each car that crashed, he fiercely played a minor chord.

In the intersection below, the body of the tanker, unable to take the repeated impact of the cars, finally gave way and cracked open in the middle, gasoline spilling in a golden waterfall onto the street. Then the last vehicle to come down the slide, a truck that looked to have about a ten-ton capacity, plunged into the middle, ripe with kinetic energy. Mikawa raised both hands high into the air.

As he slammed his fingers down on the invisible keys, a flash of light swelled up from the intersection, and the entire area was swallowed into a blazing pillar of flame that billowed up to the dark clouds above.

* * *

On the panel above the door of the outbound train on the JR Saikyou line, a news flash began to spell out in white letters.

As he hung onto one of the overhead straps and read the headline uneasily, it took Minoru a few moments to process the news before he let out a small gasp.

On Route 246 in Harbour Ward, a multicar collision had occurred that included a gasoline tanker. The area was still in flames. A high number of casualties.

Could a Ruby Eye have done this?

Minoru considered the thought for only a moment before rejecting it as impossible. The scale of the accident was just too large. Maybe Igniter, the villain they'd fought two weeks ago, would have been able to cause such destruction, but even then he would have needed a large amount of water in the area in order to do so.

Besides, it would take him over an hour to get from his current location, not far from Yonohonmachi Station (the stop near his home), to Harbour Ward. The culprit, if there was one, would be long gone by then, and even the lingering "red" scent of his powers would have vanished.

If I was at SFD Headquarters in the middle of the city, I'd probably make it...

Minoru shook his head again to clear away the thought. He knew that moving to their headquarters would make his job with them easier, but he still couldn't make that decision so easily. What would he tell Norie? *I suppose Chief Himi or Professor Riri could come up with a convincing story, but...*

As Minoru was lost in these thoughts, the train arrived at Yonohonmachi Station, and the doors in front of him slid open. Pushing against the cold breeze as he walked toward the ticket gate and home, Minoru pulled up his scarf and quickened his pace.

＊ ＊ ＊

Do not get drunk on murder.

This was the first doctrine of the Syndicate.

The deep crimson Ruby Eye parasites instill their hosts with an overwhelming urge to kill. It's impossible to resist it. When experiments were conducted that prevented Ruby Eyes from killing for an extended period of time, the hosts slowly lost their minds and were soon completely taken over by the crazed parasite. Thus, members of the Syndicate could periodically request permission to use their abilities and murder people.

When allowed to kill, the parasite responds by flooding the host's mind with an intoxicating feeling of power. According to a member of the Syndicate who had been a regular drug user as an ordinary human, the sensation felt after killing far surpassed the high he'd experienced from heroin.

In other words, it was just like training a monkey to do tricks. If the Ruby Eye killed according to the alien's wishes, the parasite would reward its host with a trip.

However, the Syndicate taught its members that they must not let that intoxication overwhelm them. Just like any powerful drug, if a Ruby Eye user were to kill haphazardly in order to chase that high, they would gradually start to lose their sanity. Down that path lay only the humiliation of being hunted by the "black." The only way to avoid losing one's powers or life was to resist the intoxicating trip that came with committing murder and withdraw immediately.

Once, Mikawa asked a question about this to the woman who taught them—their leader, who was known as Liquidizer.

"If we're going to resist the Ruby Eyes' will that much, why not just surrender to the Jet Eyes and ask them to take out our Third Eyes and turn us back into regular humans?"

Liquidizer had replied with a smile.

"The Ruby Eyes who are strong enough to be accepted into the Syndicate invariably have emotional trauma of an equal strength, you know. In other words, they hate the Syndicate and the human world alike. The murderous urges inside me may be induced by the parasite, but my desire to see this world destroyed has been with me for much longer. You are the same way, are you not?"

"Yes" was the only response he could muster. Still, a bit peeved, he pushed a little further.

"But still, that being the case, don't you think the Syndicate is aiming a bit low? Our entire purpose seems to be just to help one another run away from the 'black' who keep hunting us."

At this, Liquidizer simply chuckled and flicked Mikawa's forehead lightly.

"Now, when have I ever said that? The Syndicate is not some benefit society that aims to survive by sneaking around. Our ultimate goal is one simple thing.

"The extermination of humanity."

"......Heh."

Walking along the back alleys from Akasaka toward Aoyama Cemetery, Mikawa laughed to himself a little as he remembered.

That comment had really captured his attention.

The extermination of humanity? If all the Ruby Eyes in the Syndicate were to combine their powers and attack Shinjuku Station during rush hour, they could probably take out a thousand people at best. She was full of hot air. Besides, if they attempted such a major act of terrorism, the Japanese government would surely abandon their current concern for discretion, make an official announcement about the existence of Ruby Eyes, and finally devote the entire police and defense force to hunting them down. He doubted the Syndicate had anywhere near enough power to stand a chance against that.

Mikawa was just one lowly member of the Syndicate, so he had no idea what the organization's leadership—which apparently included several people above Liquidizer—might be thinking. But he didn't really care if it was just to kill people off slowly over the course of several decades. As long as he could go out into town once a month on a rainy day and reduce the population by however many people, he would be content.

At least for now.

In that regard, he may have gone a bit overboard today. When he got back to the hideout, it was possible he'd receive a scolding from Liquidizer. However, he imagined she'd give him a pass if he explained that it had been a memorial for their dearly departed Igniter.

Mikawa suppressed another smile. The rain had abated slightly but nonetheless continued to fall as he crossed Gaien Higashidori, the main strip in the Roppongi district, and entered Aoyama Cemetery.

The expansive cemetery appeared to be empty of people. Rainwater splashed around him as Mikawa made his way west through the lines of tombstones. Once he crossed through here and got onto the subway at Omotesandou Station, there should be no chance of any "black" pursuers capturing him.

As he was thinking this to himself, he drew near the part of the graveyard set aside for graves of foreigners, in the middle of the cemetery. At that moment, the hair on the nape of his neck suddenly stood on end.

"......Tch!"

Just as he tossed his umbrella away and leaped aside, a puddle on a nearby stretch of road suddenly burst upward with a snap.

Was this an attack from the black ones? No, surely not. Someone was sniping at him with a gun, probably from the rooftop of the building on the west side of the cemetery. They must have been using a suppressor, since he hadn't noticed the shot being fired.

Even as his mind raced, Mikawa kept on the move, jumping aside once again to narrowly dodge a second bullet that broke through the raindrops where he'd been just moments ago and left a deep hole in a gravestone to the east. Live ammunition. And these were no warning shots, either.

Usually, the black group's objective was to neutralize a Ruby Eye, remove their Third Eye, and erase their memories, turning them back into an ordinary human. But this time, they were aiming to kill. Still, Mikawa guessed that the gunshots were meant to keep him in place while a nearby Third Eye user prepared to attack with their abilities.

Mikawa ducked behind a large gravestone into what he hoped was a blind spot for the sniper on the west side of the graveyard and gathered his thoughts. How these people had tracked him down was of secondary importance right now. Right now, he had to figure out whether to get away or fight back.

But this decision took him less than a second.

It's raining today, Jet Eyes.

With a thin smirk on his lips, Mikawa stood up. If he could hold this position, the sniper wouldn't be much of a threat for a while. During that time, he would deal with the attacker he suspected was nearby.

Leaning his back against the gravestone and looking around, Mikawa dodged the attack by sheer luck.

Just less than a meter to his left, a long metal blade cut deep into the gravestone, then slashed through, aiming at Mikawa. Had he rolled forward even half a second later, it would probably have been more than the hem of his jacket that got cut clean through.

Mikawa rolled once on the wet flagstones and landed in a kneeling

position, watching the blade silently sink into the center of the gravestone. In the next moment, a tall figure came into view from behind the
stone. Mikawa recognized his face at once.

"...Oh, it's just you?" he drawled, flashing a smile.

"Of course, who else?" the black user answered lightly, but there was
no trace of a smile on his face. He was wearing a glossy gray bodysuit and a stern expression, and he was holding in his right hand a
Western-style long sword, which he whipped briskly through the air a
few times, his left hand behind his back. The raindrops his blade made
contact with were all sliced neatly into two halves.

Mikawa stood up unhurriedly, the strong chemical scent of the black
ability reaching his nose. "You don't know when to give up, do you,
Divider? I thought I showed you last time that your power is no match
for mine."

"Sorry, but I'm not in the mood for a pissing contest today, Trancer,"
the Jet Eye responded, whipping out his left hand to reveal an automatic
pistol, its jet-black muzzle leveled directly at Mikawa's forehead.

The handgun: the pinnacle of humankind's development of deadly,
portable weapons. Even to a Third Eye user—for all their enhanced
speed, stamina, and unusual abilities—it posed more than enough of
a threat.

In fact, to be honest, a single pistol packed more punch than almost
any Third Eye user's abilities. Well aware of this, the black forces often
used Tasers or knives to bring in "victims" of the "red" parasites so they
could be treated.

However, this compassion did not extend to Ruby Eyes who were
found out as members of the Syndicate. Last time Mikawa had fought
against Divider, some sneaky black agent had crept up on him from
behind and zapped him with a Taser, nearly capturing him. He'd made
a narrow escape thanks to the help of Liquidizer, but as a result, the
"blacks" now knew he was a Syndicate member.

So this time, Divider had come to kill him, no questions asked.

Mikawa reflected on all this in the short moments before Divider
unhesitatingly squeezed the trigger. But of course, he had nowhere to
run. The muzzle of the gun was only six meters away. Even if he used
his Third Eye–induced speed, the bullet would be in his chest almost as
soon as he saw it fired.

But it's raining today, you know.

Mikawa stood fast and took in a lungful of the cold, wet air.

Divider's finger pulled the trigger three times in rapid succession.

Aiming at the gun's muzzle, Mikawa pursed his lips and blew.

In the darkness of the rain, three yellow flashes blinked in succession. With a dry bursting sound, three nine-millimeter bullets were fired, and the first round made contact with a raindrop.

Kshhh. Instead of being scattered into smaller droplets by the rotating bullet, the raindrop froze around it.

Kshh! Kshh! Kshh! Kshh!

As they flew through the six meters of air between the gun's muzzle and Mikawa, each of the bullets made contact with dozens of raindrops, which all froze onto the bullets, dragging them down with the added weight.

The first and second bullets flew off course and passed by Mikawa harmlessly; the third hit him in the left shoulder, but by then the snowball-sized lump of ice around it had created enough air resistance to slow it down to a speed that wasn't nearly high enough to pierce the tough skin of a Third Eye user. Still, its impact was akin to taking a hit from a blunt weapon, but even as Mikawa's body was shaken by it, he continued to let out sharp breaths of air.

Kshh! Kshh! Now the sound of freezing ice came from the pistol in Divider's hands. The water that had permeated the gun's mechanisms turned solid, stopping the firing hammer before it could strike a fourth time.

Quickly, Divider tossed away the gun before the ice could freeze it to his left hand. By the time it hit the flagstones, there was nothing but a hunk of ice.

"...Phew, that was close. Even bad cops in Hollywood movies don't just start shooting without warning, you know," Mikawa remarked with another smile. "See, this is why I hate firearms."

His gun rendered useless, Divider licked his lips and spat off to one side, but his expression was as determined as ever. He grasped his heavy-looking sword with both hands, holding it out at the ready. The last time they had fought, he'd been using a Japanese sword that may or may not have been the real thing, but this time his weapon was so absurd that it looked like it had been pulled straight out of a fantasy movie.

"So hey, where do you buy a sword like that, anyway? Or did you make it yourself?" Mikawa asked, genuinely rather curious.

But Divider just shook his head flatly, his curly hair bobbing. "No way, I'm not tellin' you that so you can go off and attack their shop or somethin'. I mean, not that you're making it out of here alive today anyway, but y'know."

"Aw, c'mon, I wouldn't attack them. I just wanted to buy one for myself."

He shrugged and sighed deeply. Then, focusing on Divider's feet, he exhaled lightly.

Kshhh! Kshhh! The sharp noise resounded through the graveyard as pure white ice formed quickly around both of the black agent's legs. However, instead of freezing him in place, as it should have, the ice cracked and fell away as soon as Divider took a step forward.

"Hah!" With a strident battle cry, Divider leaped toward him at a dizzying speed, attacking with sword aloft. Glittering in the light of the distant streetlamps, the blade came straight down toward Mikawa's neck.

Continuing to blow out cold air, Mikawa was only narrowly able to dodge by freezing over the flagstones underneath Divider's feet. His boots, connected to his bodysuit, slipped slightly on the fresh ice, altering the trajectory of his blade so that it only just cut through the right side of Mikawa's jacket. Mikawa quickly put some distance between them as the sword continued straight down, cutting nearly a meter into the flagstones of the cemetery path like a knife through butter.

The sharpness of his cuts was as absurd as ever. Underneath his jacket, Mikawa was wearing a Syndicate-distributed knife-proof aramid fiber undershirt, but against Divider's sword, it would do about as much good as a thin sheet of paper. But more importantly...

"...So that fancy new suit of yours isn't just cosplay, huh?"

"Yeah, we came up with it after you froze up all my clothes last time. This suit's totally waterproof, so you can huff and puff at it all you like."

"I see... You're actually getting smarter." Mikawa had to admit, the black group was a step ahead of the Syndicate when it came to developing this kind of equipment. They did have the government on their side, after all.

Narrowing his eyes, he glanced up at the sky. The rain clouds were still dark and heavy; it didn't seem like he'd have to worry about the worst-case scenario of the rain letting up anytime soon. However, he still couldn't let this battle go on for too long. The sniper was probably well on his way to a better vantage point by now and had quite possibly called for backup, too.

That invisible black agent was much more concerning to him right now than even the sword-wielding maniac in front of him. Like most attack-based Third Eye abilities, Mikawa's powers required the target to be within his sight line, so cheap tricks like invisibility rendered his talents practically useless. If that black agent had used a knife or a gun instead of a Taser last time, Mikawa would probably be dead.

As much as he wanted to keep playing with the swordsman, it was probably time to wrap things up. With that decided, Mikawa's smile left his face. Perhaps sensing his resolve to kill, Divider narrowed his eyes as well.

Mikawa breathed in deeply through his nose and mouth.

Divider charged at a terrifying speed, white sparks flying as his sword glided along the wet pavement.

In the instant when the blade hung in the air, glinting in the twilight as it shifted downward toward him, Mikawa aimed at its edge and blew with all his might.

Imbued with Divider's power, the blade sliced through the torrential rain as it drew nearer.

In turn, imbued with Mikawa's freezing power, the raindrops froze into ice instantaneously as they hit the sword's edge. The blade sliced these in two and flung about half the frozen droplets away, but the rest stuck to the sides of the metal. These pieces of ice piled up quickly as the blade cut through the air, and in moments, the blade was coated with ice on either side, making it not so much an edged sword as an icy pole.

Divider's power could work only with a weapon that had an edge. The sword had lost its cutting ability before it reached Mikawa, but Divider carried on, swinging it toward him anyway. However, the strength of his Third Eye–enhanced body and the knife-proof undershirt were enough to defend against a strike from a simple blunt weapon. Blocking it with his right arm, Mikawa aimed the rest of the air in his lungs at Divider's face. At this short distance, he could easily target his opponent's eyes.

This was just like their previous encounter. *Is this loser so confident in his own victory that he couldn't bother to protect his face with a waterproof mask while he was at it?* Mikawa thought.

But in that instant, the other side of the long sword he had repelled with his arm came back around, slicing neatly up from Mikawa's abdomen to his right shoulder.

Mikawa didn't register any pain or even the impact of the attack, but he knew at once that the depth of the cut was fatal.

His sword held high in the air, Divider grinned savagely.

"Tough luck, pal. Unlike ol' Masamune, Excalibur here is a double-edged sword."

* * *

When Minoru got off the bus at the stop nearest to his house, it was still raining steadily.

Minoru looked at his running watch as he opened his umbrella. The digital face read 6:15 p.m. He would be just in time for dinner.

He hadn't heard anything from SFD Headquarters…meaning that the traffic accident in Akasaka probably wasn't the work of a Ruby Eye after all.

So why do I still feel so worried? Maybe I should call and ask them about it…but if I were going to do that, I probably should've done it while I was still at the train station.

Minoru was still dwelling on these thoughts as he walked quickly down his street toward home. Still, when he saw the gentle light streaming out from his kitchen window, he breathed a sigh of relief.

Norie had said this morning that she was making hand-rolled sushi for dinner tonight, he remembered. He had eaten a late lunch when he got back to headquarters earlier, but his energy consumption had vastly increased since he was infected by the Third Eye parasite, and considering that he successfully completed the absurd mission of going into a nuclear containment vessel earlier today, he felt that he had earned the right to overeat a little.

His mind now full of thoughts about his favorite tuna and avocado sushi, he almost didn't notice the car parked across from his house as he walked past it.

Then, suddenly, a nearby voice spoke to him.

"Welcome home."

Minoru jumped, nearly dropping his umbrella. Grasping it tightly, he quickly looked around, but there was no one else in sight. The passenger-side window of the car, a yellow first-generation Daihatsu Copen, was open, but both the passenger's and the driver's seat were clearly empty.

And the car was a two-seater. Was he hearing things?

"You're not hearing things," the voice, a woman's, said with impeccable timing. Reflexively, Minoru prepared to bring up his protective shell, but before he did so, the thin, slightly husky voice continued.

"It's all right, I'm an SFD member like you. I thought I'd take this chance to say hello."

The empty Copen's left-hand door opened on its own, and the voice spoke again.

"Get in quickly before the seat gets wet."

Minoru was unconvinced. What if this was a Ruby Eye trap, or maybe even an actual ghost? But as his mind churned, he suddenly realized that he had heard this voice somewhere before: two weeks ago, in the raid on Igniter's workplace, Ariake Heaven's Shore, over the radio…

"Ah…you're, um, Re…Refrac…?"

"Yes. Hurry and get in, please."

"R…right."

Gathering his resolve, Minoru folded his umbrella and ducked under the low roof of the Copen, sliding himself into the passenger's seat. When he closed the door, the sound of the rain died away.

Minoru took a deep breath and stole a sidelong glance at the driver's seat, but it still appeared to be completely empty. He did notice, however, the faint scent of perfume inside the car. It was different from the kind Yumiko used, but the fragrance was definitely there.

Minoru gulped and cleared his throat nervously. Slowly, gingerly, he started to reach out toward the driver's seat with his right hand.

"While I understand your intent, I would prefer not to be randomly touched."

"O-of course." Minoru hastily put his hand back on his lap. After a moment, the voice from the driver's seat spoke again in a slightly softer tone.

"...My name is Suu Komura. SFD code name: Refractor. Nice to meet you."

"N...nice to meet you. I'm Minoru Utsugi. My code name is Isolator."

"I look forward to working with you."

"Y-yes, you, too."

As they exchanged greetings, Minoru continued to squint at the driver's seat, straining to see the source of the voice. But he still couldn't see her. The faint glow of the streetlights and the shadows cast by the raindrops streaming down the front window fell onto the camel-colored leather seat without the slightest distortion.

He started to wonder if her power wasn't so much invisibility as it was cognitive indetectability, the type of ability like Chief Himi's that alters the minds of others, but that wouldn't explain how he was able to see the parts of the seat and driver's side door that should have been hidden by Suu Komura's bodily presence. Forgetting for a moment that he was inside a cramped car next to someone he had just met, Minoru mumbled to himself absently.

"What kind of ability *is* that? She's... She's *too* invisible!"

"Have you heard of something called negative-index metamaterial?"

His question answered with another question, Minoru blinked with surprise, turning a little red.

"N...no, I've never heard that term before."

"I see."

There was silence for a moment, as though Suu were gathering her thoughts, before she continued in a voice that sounded almost entirely devoid of emotion.

"All materials in existence have a parameter called a 'refractive index.' To put it simply, it's a number that determines how much the angle of light changes when it comes into contact with that material. For instance, water's refractive index is 1.3; in comparison, a glasses lens has an index of about 1.7. In other words, when it penetrates a lens, light is bent more than it would be by water."

"R-right."

It was a bit strange getting a science lecture from someone he couldn't see, but Minoru did his best to keep up.

"A negative refractive index—in other words, a material that when penetrated by light would bend it in reverse—was thought to be non-existent in nature. However, it was recently discovered. Or rather, it was created. A metal with a nanostructure smaller than the wavelength of light…that is what negative-index metamaterial, or NIM, is."

"It bends light…in reverse…?" Minoru tilted his head, unable to picture the phenomenon, but the invisible driver continued indifferently.

"If scientists can control the angle of light both positively and negatively, it becomes possible to prevent light from hitting an object entirely. For example, say we have a ball, and we wrap it in NIM. Light, which should normally reflect off the surface of the ball from all directions, would instead be circumvented to the ball's surroundings. Now, would you be able to see this ball?"

"Erm…" In order for the ball to be visible, some amount of light would have to either reflect off or be absorbed by its surface. If a lot of light reflected off it, the ball would appear white, or if the light were absorbed, it would appear black. But if all the light simply slid onto its surroundings without touching the ball…

"Ah…," Minoru murmured, finally understanding.

"That's right," his invisible companion affirmed quietly.

"Think of my power, refraction, as the ultimate form of this kind of metamaterial. Light completely avoids my body and any objects attached that indicate my body's presence. Thus, nobody can see me."

"Light…avoids you…" Certainly, when a person sees something, they're actually seeing the light that reflects off or is absorbed by that something. If that light were to instead avoid the object, it would essentially be rendered transparent.

He had somehow grasped the explanation, but for some reason, Minoru thought he detected a note of deep loneliness somewhere in her words. After a moment, the reason dawned on him.

"If… If light completely avoids you…doesn't that mean that you can't see the outside world, either…?"

There was a brief delay before his question was answered. "…That's right. When I use my ability to its fullest, not only am I invisible to the world, but the world is invisible to me, too… I'm a bit surprised, though."

"Huh? About what?"

"You're the first person to come to that conclusion so quickly after hearing my explanation."

"Oh…um, I-I'm sorry," Minoru blurted out reflexively, afraid he had said something impolite, but then he heard the invisible girl next to him stifle a laugh.

"There's not really anything to apologize for. I was a bit impressed, that's all."

When Minoru gave no response but to stiffen nervously, she spoke again.

"…Well, now that we've been introduced and all, I should probably be going."

At that, Minoru blinked and opened his eyes wide, staring at the driver's seat. Was she really going to drive with her abilities still activated—in other words, without being able to see anything?

Then he spotted something unusual. At about Minoru's eye level, two tiny black dots were floating in thin air. They didn't look like anything, really—just like two little spots of darkness, perfectly absorbing all light.

What are *those?*

Furrowing his brow, Minoru leaned in to get a closer look. At that moment…

"Are you planning to kiss me good-bye?" The voice came from incredibly close to his ears, so close that he realized what he was looking at. The two dots were Refractor's eyes. More specifically, her pupils— No, even more specifically, the light being absorbed through her pupils into her retinas to be converted into information and transferred to her brain via the optic nerves.

In other words, Minoru's face was currently just five centimeters away from the face of a person he couldn't see—a person who he was 99 percent sure was female.

"Aah!"

With an exclamation of surprise, Minoru jumped backward with such force that he slammed the back of his head into the passenger-side window. "I'm so sorry!" he cried, shaking his head partly for emphasis and partly to clear away the pain of the impact.

"I didn't mean to do that! I wasn't, I, um…"

"Don't worry about it… Well, then."

As she spoke, a key with a cute animal design on it turned right in the ignition, and the starter motor rumbled into action. Though the car was small, Minoru heard a four-cylinder turbo engine start up sharply. His mouth dry, he reached for the door, still apologizing profusely.

"Um, I…I'm really sorry. I-I'll just be going now…" Just then, he realized that he still hadn't heard the answer to the question that he should have been asking from the start.

"That's right…"

He paused, looking back at the driver's seat. "M-Ms. Komura, why were you in front of my house in the first place?"

Her answer caught him by surprise. "This isn't the first time I've come here. When you and Accelerator are out on missions, either my brother or I are generally here keeping watch, to make sure that your sister isn't attacked by Ruby Eyes."

"Ah…"

Minoru was at a loss for words. He hadn't had the slightest idea that this was going on.

Of course, the possibility of an attack on Norie was a worry that was always on his mind. Ever since Biter had raided his house, Minoru had carefully avoided activating his protective shell, so the chances of a Ruby Eye detecting him and finding his home should be very low. Still, if he were on a mission fighting against one and it discovered his identity, it wasn't impossible that the enemy might track down his address…

But he hadn't expected the SFD to go so far as to station a guard at his house. For one thing, its location in the Sakura district of Saitama wasn't exactly close by the SFD's headquarters in Shinjuku. Which meant that Minoru's reluctance to move to headquarters had directly affected Refractor. "I didn't know that… I'm sorry to have caused you so much trouble."

The quiet apology had scarcely left his lips before he heard her response. "It's all right. If a Ruby Eye did attack this place, they would definitely be a member of the Syndicate. If we captured them, we could get a lot of information out of them."

Hearing such frightening words spoken in a soft, deadpan voice almost made the corners of Minoru's lips twitch, but he quickly bowed his head again. "Still, that doesn't change the fact that I'm grateful for what you've been doing. Thank you very much."

Minoru again moved to open the door of the car, but at that moment, he heard a low rumbling noise from the direction of the driver's seat. The starter motor had already been turned on a while ago, which meant... Could that noise have come from Refractor's stomach?

Turning back toward her timidly, Minoru looked at the seemingly empty driver's seat, wondering whether he should say anything. Finally, he gathered his courage and spoke.

"U-um... You've probably been sitting here for most of the day, so... you must be hungry, right...? Would... Would you like to come in and have dinner with us? Norie said she was making hand-rolled sushi for tonight, so it shouldn't be a problem if we have one more person..."

Minoru had only been trying to offer a show of gratitude, but when there was no immediate response, he realized the implications of what he'd said. Naturally, not being a member of the SFD, Norie had no knowledge of Third Eyes and their abilities. In order to sit at the table and eat dinner together, Refractor would have to deactivate her ability and become visible.

But like Yumiko had told him before, Third Eyes' abilities were born of the pain and trauma the host had endured...so Refractor's strong power of invisibility, which she seemed to keep activated constantly, meant that she probably had some kind of fear associated with being seen by other people.

And I just stupidly asked her if she wanted to eat dinner together like it was no big deal...

But as he was opening his mouth to apologize, an unexpected question came from the direction of the driver's seat.

"Hand-rolled sushi... Does that mean there'll be layered omelets?"

What? Minoru thought, but he reflexively answered, "Um, y-yes... they're Norie's favorite, so..."

"And avocado and tuna rolls?"

"Y-yes, since those are my favorite..."

There was silence for a few seconds, and then...

"Then I suppose I'll accept your offer." The key turned back to the left, and the engine fell silent, leaving only the faint sound of the rain washing over them like white noise. Then, to Minoru's amazement, a petite young woman appeared in the driver's seat out of thin air.

As he watched, dumbfounded, he suppressed a single bemused thought:

Was that seriously a good enough reason to show yourself?

* * *

He had no time to guess at just how deep the damage he'd received was.

The sword raised before him flipped around with a *clink*. The edge that he'd frozen over with ice faced away, revealing the still-sharp blade on the other side as it came down toward him. In this situation—especially with the large gash along the right side of his torso—it was impossible for him to dodge the next attack.

Hoping to at least neutralize Divider's ability, Mikawa blew sharply with the air that remained in his lungs. As the third slash came toward him, the water in the air again froze into ice around the blade. However, with his perception of time currently accelerated, the growth rate of the ice seemed terribly slow. He had to ice that blade into a blunt weapon before it reached his body, or—

I'm going to lose.

Even though it's raining.

Even though I'm surrounded by all this water.

Mikawa rarely felt intense emotions about anything, but right now, a strange fire was welling up in his chest. It was a sensation he'd felt only once before, in the distant past.

It was a cold, rainy day like this, too. All the adults were moping around in raincoats… None of them made any attempt to look at us.

That's why nobody could blame us for sneaking into that place. We avoided the eyes of the men steering the forklifts, crept across that huge lot, opened that wide metal door, and went inside. In that big, dark place, there were boxes everywhere, stacked up to the ceiling. Every time we breathed, the insides of our noses stung.

My friend and I headed deeper into the maze of boxes, undetected by anyone. It was like we'd been teleported into the future, surrounded by incredible new technology.

We didn't know.

When water freezes, its volume expands. We didn't know that such a trivial phenomenon could cause something so terrible.

"......!!"

The floodgates of his memories had started to open, but Mikawa did his best to freeze them shut. As if in response to his powerful feelings, the sphere embedded over his left lung pulsed intensely.

As air flowed from his tightly pursed lips, he saw that it was glittering like diamond dust. It flooded fiercely over the blade that was rushing toward him, freezing it whiter and whiter.

Whack! The strike came crashing down on Mikawa's right shoulder. A shock of pain like a silver spark shot through his brain as the attack smashed into his clavicle. But the sharp cut that he had expected to divide his body in two didn't seem to have occurred.

Fighting against the searing pain, Mikawa struggled to refill his lungs with a bit of air and blow it back toward his opponent's face. Divider quickly defended himself by throwing up his left hand, which was instantly coated in a thin membrane of ice.

Seizing this chance, Mikawa twisted his body to the side and used his left foot to kick at the surface of the flagstones with all his might. At the same time, he blew cold air toward the stones a little ways ahead of him, sliding with his left foot along the newly formed ice like a skater.

As the air in his lungs ran out, he whirled back around. Now about fifteen meters away, he saw that Divider was breaking the ice off his hand. Then, grasping his long sword with both hands once more, the Jet Eye charged forward, a glint of killing intent in his decidedly foreign-colored eyes.

At this point, the deep gash from Mikawa's abdomen to his right shoulder finally made itself known with a flood of white-hot pain and a frightening amount of blood that soaked straight through his jacket, dyeing it black.

Struggling to bear the pain, Mikawa focused on the wound and blew hard.

Kshh... The noise rippled through his body as the streaming blood froze into white ice. The mixture of heat and harsh cold doubled the agony, sending fresh sparks of pain before his eyes.

He could still breathe well enough, so it seemed that the wound hadn't reached his lungs, but it was probably safe to say that at least two or three of his ribs were broken. To continue to fight in this condition would be extremely difficult. Unfortunately, even fleeing would be risky at this point.

Watching Divider slice through the ice toward him at a rapid pace, Mikawa made a snap decision. He could no longer afford to hold back his power.

The second doctrine of the Syndicate: Do not reveal all your power to the enemy.

The power source of Third Eye abilities is the inner pain of the host. In other words, by looking at a Third Eye host's abilities, one could form a conjecture about that person's suffering. One of the black ones had a terrifying deduction-based ability on their side, so once they knew about a red power, they could determine the source of that person's trauma with astounding accuracy.

Of course, in addition to being the source of their power, a Third Eye's inner pain is also their greatest weak point. The black ones had defeated many of Mikawa's comrades by mercilessly targeting that weakness. Once they learned that his power was separating water into hydrogen and oxygen, Igniter, one of Liquidizer's favorite recruits into the Syndicate, had been captured by the Jet Eyes without taking a single one of them down with him in the explosion he caused in a theme park pool.

So far, the only power Mikawa had shown the black ones was turning water into ice. Thus, they had no way of figuring out the trauma and fear that nested deep in his heart.

The pain in Mikawa's heart wasn't just directed toward ice.

Freezing, melting, evaporating, and solidifying again. Mikawa loved these transitions, and feared them deeply.

If he showed them another one of his powers, they would have new material with which to try and dig up his traumatic past. And then, while he wanted to believe this was impossible, they might even use that information to try and track *her* down, as deeply hidden in the city as she may be.

But in this situation, he no longer had the luxury of hiding his powers. The last time things had gotten dangerous, Liquidizer had been there to come to his rescue, but that was only because he'd still been in training. Now that he was independent, if she found out he was captured or even killed, she would scarcely even spare him a sigh.

As Mikawa watched the furiously charging swordsman, a thought flashed into his mind.

Divider...I wonder what the source of your suffering is...? Why do you need to cut things up to be satisfied?

Fighting to ignore the pain, Mikawa filled his lungs with air, but instead of pursing his lips and blowing a thin stream of air, he exhaled in a huge huff. Unlike the sparkling blue of his previous breaths, this one was a thick white.

The white breath diffused outward into the air. And then—*whump!* A sound like the impact of a heavy blanket echoed through the graveyard.

That was the sound of all the water in front of Mikawa being transformed instantly into water vapor—in other words, steam.

Mikawa's ability to manipulate the phases of water didn't just go in one direction. With a long, thin breath, he could transform steam into water and water into ice, both resulting in a lower temperature. But with a big, thick huff, he could turn ice into water and water into steam, the latter meaning that the water's temperature would rise to one hundred degrees Celsius.

The high-temperature steam that Mikawa had created spread about eighteen meters in front of him.

Of course, the heat was immediately sapped away by the surrounding air, and the water vapor resolidified slightly, turning into a thick fog. But Divider, in the middle of his high-speed dash, would still have been surrounded by one hundred–degree steam for several seconds, most likely breathing it into his lungs as well. No matter how good he was at cutting things up, he couldn't cut vapor.

Mikawa hesitated, wondering whether he should close the gap between them and finish him off instead of waiting. After all, he had been forced to reveal the ability he'd successfully kept a secret from enemies and allies alike until now. At the very least, that should earn him the right to his bitter enemy's life.

But Mikawa's mind was quickly made up for him when another bullet flew at him from the southern side of the cemetery. It was probably only thanks to the visibility-obscuring fog around them that the shot narrowly missed his left arm and hit the flagstones. Looking at the bullet, Mikawa hunched down and aimed another wide breath behind him, creating more thick fog that covered the entire center of the cemetery.

I suppose this is my chance.

Shaking off a bit of lingering regret, Mikawa began to run toward the west side of the cemetery. Since he had only frozen up the wound on his abdomen as a styptic, if the ice melted, he would probably start to bleed profusely again. He had to get to the Syndicate safe house as quickly as possible and have the wound treated or even his Third Eye–enhanced stamina wouldn't be able to save him.

"Well, I guess we'll have to call this a draw for now, Divider," he grunted, pressing his left hand against his wound as he ran. Trying to ignore the pain, he forced a smile to his lips.

From increasingly far away, he heard Divider yell after him, his voice raw, "Hey! You're just gonna run away, Trancer? Get back here and fight me!"

The shout echoed through the graveyard, making the fog quiver. But of course, Mikawa kept running west, creating more fog to cover him as he went. *Is he able to yell like that even after cooking his lungs with hot steam because of his stamina as a soldier? Or is it because he just has that much inner rage...?* Through his huffing and puffing, Mikawa managed a weak chuckle.

"Don't be so ill-tempered, Divider. We're taking very good care of your beloved princess..."

* * *

How on earth did the SFD get her a driver's license?

This was Minoru's second thought as he looked at Suu Komura, code name Refractor, for the first time with her ability deactivated.

After all, now that he saw her, there was no way this woman—no, this girl—was older than him. In fact, she looked no older than a middle schooler.

Suu was barely 150 centimeters tall, with fluffy, tawny-brown hair cut just above her shoulders. Her porcelain skin was paler than the average Japanese person, and her face could easily be called otherworldly.

Minoru caught himself thinking that someone so lovely couldn't possibly exist in the real world.

Her facial features were small and delicate like a doll's, the bridge of her nose straight, her lips a captivating cherry blossom pink. Her irises were a mysterious color, a deep violet blue he had never seen before, even in photos or movies.

They're like the sky at dawn...

...Minoru thought, gazing dazedly into her amethyst eyes.

For just a moment, Suu Komura returned his gaze rather nervously, but she quickly looked away and spoke in the same flat tone as ever.

"...I'm very hungry."

After another short moment of absentmindedness, Minoru abruptly came back to his senses.

"Ah, I'm sorry...! Okay, um, let's go, then! M-my house is right over there."

"I know."

Refractor removed the key from the ignition with a practiced motion and got out through the car's right-hand door. Minoru clambered out on that side, too, smacking his head again in the process. He opened his umbrella, and after locking her car, Suu joined him underneath as if it was the most natural thing in the world.

How am I going to explain this to Norie?

In fact, shouldn't I have thought a bit more about the implications of inviting a girl over for dinner?

As all this occurred to him far too late, Minoru paced awkwardly over the last thirty or so meters to his home with Suu in tow.

"So, ummm... This is my friend Suu. I ran into her on my way home, so I may have sort of invited her over for dinner... I hope that's all right...?"

Upon hearing Minoru's slightly clumsy explanation, Norie froze in the middle of stirring the sushi rice with a wooden spoon, blinking at him in astonishment. Then her face suddenly broke into a joyous smile the likes of which he had hardly ever seen, like a sunflower in bloom, and it was his turn to stare at her with surprise.

I know it's pretty rare for me to bring a girl home, but still, you don't need to look that *surprised...*

But as he thought about it, Minoru realized it was more than just rare—

It was the first time ever. In the eight years since he'd moved in,

Minoru had not brought a single friend home. As it dawned on him, he was surprised to find that he, too, was a little shaken.

I, of all people, brought a girl home right after meeting her, without one thought of the consequences? Even though such a singular event is guaranteed to be etched into my brain as an unforgettable memory? Did it not occur to me that later I might regret this, stress out about it, and end up writhing around, agonizing over it for all eternity?

What have I done?

As Minoru stood frozen in complete shock, Norie, still positively sparkling with glee, gripped the wooden spoon with both hands. "Well!" she said loudly. "Well, now... My little Mii's brought a friend home!"

Oh god, please stop calling me that! Minoru inwardly screamed, but before he could make a sound, Refractor stepped forward. Her hands placed neatly above her knees (on the leggings under her white dress), she bowed deeply.

"Good evening, ma'am. My name is Suu Komura." Her voice was as quiet as ever and even more polite than usual. "I hope my unexpected visit isn't too much of a bother. Are you quite sure you don't mind?"

Norie shook her head so quickly, her short bobbed hair flew back and forth. "Oh my goodness, of course not! Welcome, Miss Komura, welcome! I'm sorry—I was just a little surprised. My little Mii's never invited a friend over...never mind a lovely young lady like yourself...!"

Hearing Norie blurt out these far-too-honest words, seeing her eyes brim with genuine tears of joy...the frozen Minoru mentally sank through the floor. *I felt bad that she was watching the house all day in the rain to protect it from a Ruby Eye attack, so I just invited her in! Without thinking!* But he couldn't say that, of course. To start with, he couldn't even tell Norie about Ruby Eyes and such.

Minoru—rooted in place, messenger bag still slung over his shoulder—heard Suu mumble something to herself.

"I'm...the first..."

Then, with a somewhat apologetic look on her face, the beautiful young woman bowed to Norie again. "...I'm very sorry, Ms. Norie, but I am not Minoru's girlfriend or anything."

Minoru was now strongly considering dashing up the stairs, flinging himself into his room, and cowering in the closet with his protective shell around him, possibly never to leave again. But again, there was nothing he could do but grin and bear it.

About thirty minutes later, the two large platters of sushi on the dining room table had been utterly wiped out, leaving behind not a single grain of rice.

Norie had a habit of making too much food anyway, and tonight's dinner, complete with rice, seaweed, and other accompaniments, was no exception. The meal could have easily fed four people, and while Minoru had certainly eaten his fair share, Suu had packed away so much food that he had to wonder where it all went given her thin frame. All the while, Norie looked on smilingly as Suu gobbled away.

Eating her last sesame and plum sushi, Suu finished her plate at the same time as Minoru, took a large gulp of green tea, and gave a long, satisfied sigh. Then her lilac eyes widened.

"Ah...I'm so sorry, I got completely carried away and ate too much... even though I'm not even his girlfriend..."

Side-eyeing her as she bowed apologetically, Minoru groaned. "... Enough about that already..."

Norie simply giggled. "It's fine, really! Please come back for dinner again anytime... Oh, the tea! I'll go make some more."

As she stood up to leave, Minoru and Suu both bobbed their heads, thanking her in unison. Then, once she was out of the room, they cautiously exchanged glances. Minoru was quick to avert his eyes, but then he heard Suu murmur something to him softly.

"I'm...the first...?"

Don't tell me she could be... No, she's definitely making fun of me. Why are all the members of the SFD like this?

As Minoru groaned again, Suu stood up, trotting briskly over to the kitchen. After another moment of hanging his head, Minoru heard the Refractor's voice.

"Excuse me, Ms. Norie? Would you mind terribly if we had the tea in Minoru's room instead?"

If there was any small comfort to be had in this uncontrollable situation, it was that Minoru's kindly older sister was always cleaning his room for him. So at least it would be tidy, the furniture free of dust, and there wouldn't be anything lying around that he didn't want Suu to see (at least on the surface).

And so, balancing a tray with two small teacups and some tea cakes, Minoru resignedly walked up the thirteen steps to the second floor and his room as if being escorted to the gallows. Suu followed close behind him, her footsteps scarcely making a sound.

What on earth is she trying to do here?

Minoru was wondering, too late to do anything, as he awkwardly turned the doorknob with his wrist and stepped into the darkness of his bedroom. Then, nudging the switch on with his shoulder, he waited for the LED ceiling light to illuminate the room before placing the tray down on the low table in the middle of the floor.

The only major furnishings in Minoru's four-by-four-meter room were his computer desk, his bed, and a few bookshelves, so the floor was fairly spacious. "Please have a seat," he said stiffly, motioning to one of the two round cushions that sat on either side of the table.

The Refractor closed the door with both hands, then nodded, sitting down on the cushion with her legs out to the side. Minoru knelt stiffly on the opposite cushion, lifting one of the teacups off the tray to place it in front of Suu. He put the cakes and other teacup on the table, set the tray aside on the floor, then carefully lifted his cup with both hands and took a sip.

"...This feels like a marriage interview."

Caught off guard by Suu's quiet, unprompted remark, Minoru practically choked on the hot tea and swallowed it painfully in silence. He returned his teacup to the table—having nearly dropped it—and took a deep, ragged breath. "So...," he said weakly, "what exactly is going on here?"

"What's going on...? Well, you're the one who invited me over for dinner..."

"I-I guess so, but...I didn't think it would end up, you know...like this."

"I should hope not. If you had, it would seem like you'd invited me with the ulterior motive of luring a girl into your bedroom, now wouldn't it?"

"Ah...right, that's true."

Minoru nodded absentmindedly, then hurriedly switched to shaking his head rapidly as his mind caught up to him. Throughout all this, Suu paid him no mind, calmly and quietly taking a sip of her tea. She gave another little sigh, then abruptly ducked her head.

"But really…thank you for inviting me. I can't remember the last time I had such a delicious meal. You have a wonderful older sister—I can understand why you're so reluctant to move to SFD Headquarters."

Blinking in surprise for the umpteenth time today at Suu's serious face, Minoru nodded slowly and responded in a small voice, "Um, you're welcome…"

Speaking with her up close like this, it was even harder not to notice her overwhelming beauty. She definitely had some amount of foreign blood. There was a golden tint to her tawny-brown hair that didn't look artificial, and her skin was snow-white to the point that the whites of her eyes looked faintly blue by comparison. Among these pale colors, the violet blue of her irises stood out brilliantly.

Nearly getting lost in those eyes, with the color of clouds at dawn and the jet-black of her pupils, Minoru quickly came to his senses and looked away. The silence between them was as complete as if he were inside of his protective shell, until it was broken by Suu's quiet voice.

"Minoru. Do you believe in the existence of 'sight lines'?"

"…Huh?" Minoru looked up blankly, not understanding the meaning of the sudden question. Turning the phrase over in his mind a few times, he attempted to formulate a response. "Sight lines… You mean like, um…a line that connects a person's eyeballs to whatever they're looking at…?" he asked, drawing a line in the air between his right eye and Suu's face as he spoke.

Suu, however, shook her head lightly, her expression as hard to read as ever. "No, not exactly. More like the sort of thing that makes you turn around because you felt someone looking at you from behind. A sort of signal or energy that emanates from someone's eyes when they look at something."

"What…?" This time, it was Minoru's turn to shake his head. "That's more of a figurative concept, right? After all, human eyes are like camera lenses that take in light…um, electromagnetic waves? So they're receptors, not transmitters. So there's no such thing as a physical sight line…at least, I would think so…," he mumbled awkwardly, again looking into Suu's violet eyes.

Even those beautiful eyes wouldn't be able to emit some kind of energy or anything, right? And yet...why does it feel like it's harder to breathe when I meet her eyes, then? It's like she has enough power to look right through me...

Suu nodded slightly, maintaining eye contact with Minoru. "Right. That's what the doctor who examined me said, too, a long time ago."

"What? A doctor...?"

"I can see other people's sight lines. I've been able to for a long time... ever since I was a child."

Hearing this explanation in a small, wavering voice, Minoru took a full five seconds to process her words. "Since you were a child...?" he asked uncertainly. "Komura, you're in middle school, right?"

"Yes. I'm a third-year."

Only a year younger than me... Wait, that's beside the point.

The appearance of the mysterious spheres that infected human hosts had been just three months ago, meaning that this ability Suu was talking about wasn't one that came from a Third Eye. In other words...

"So...it's a real psychic ability?" Minoru asked hoarsely.

"That, or a mental illness." Suu lowered her long eyelashes, barely moving her lips as she spoke. "The doctor said that scopophobia—the fear of being seen—is fairly common in Japanese people. However, there are aspects that a phobia doesn't explain. For instance, I can see someone's sight line even if I don't know that person is there."

"If you don't know they're there...? You mean, you'd see a sight line first, follow it, and then see that there's a person looking at you?"

She nodded. "Yes."

Certainly, if that were true, a simple diagnosis of neurosis wouldn't explain that phenomenon. At a loss for words, Minoru simply nodded back, and Suu continued with words that were even more startling.

"There's another thing, too. The sight lines that I can see have colors."

"Colors...?"

"It's very pretty. They're thin, colorful beams of light that sparkle in the air. So when I was young, although I didn't understand them, I wasn't afraid or unhappy. It was only when I became older, and realized that the colors had meaning, that I became afraid..."

Raising her head, she stared straight at Minoru with her lilac eyes. He looked back reflexively, but of course, he couldn't see any lines or colors emanating from her eyes. Her lips moved slightly as she continued in a quiet voice.

"...When I was small, most people looked at me with a yellow sight line. But around when I started middle school, most women started to look at me with blue lines, and most men's lines were a shade of red. At first, I thought it was just based on the person's gender. But there were still people whose lines were other colors—yellow, green, orange—so I tried to think harder about the differences."

Suu paused for a moment, her slender frame trembling ever so slightly.

"Then, one day, something happened that made me realize the truth. The colors of the sight lines change based on the individual's feelings toward me. Yellow means they feel love and affection. Blue is the color of hatred. And red is the color of lust and desire."

"...!"

Minoru breathed in sharply.

In other words, that meant that most women hated Suu, and most men lusted after her.

Well...in a way, it wasn't entirely surprising. By nature, both Suu's appearance and her disposition were very out of the ordinary. And human beings were programmed by society to instinctively want to either reject or possess anything unfamiliar.

But to be able to visibly detect that kind of negative emotion would certainly be nothing less than terrifying.

As if detecting Minoru's thoughts in that moment, Suu shrugged lightly, trying to bring the mood back to normal.

"...At this point, I understand that feelings like that can't really be helped. But...what I really couldn't take was watching my mother's sight line turning from yellow to blue, little by little...and my father's... slowly but surely turning red." She glanced at Minoru, who had frozen in place again, and continued with deliberate indifference.

"If that black sphere hadn't come down from the sky three months ago and given me the ability to hide from the gaze of others...I think I might have committed suicide by now."

With that, Suu stood up abruptly, walked over to the wall behind them, and flicked off the light switch.

The room was plunged into darkness. For a moment, Minoru could see nothing, but his Third Eye quickly went to work enhancing his vision, so that he saw everything as if through a dark gray curtain. Through the haze of darkness, he saw Refractor walk back over, come around the table, and kneel down to sit close beside him. Minoru couldn't say a word as he strained to see in the dark.

Suu's voice rang out through the heavy silence. "The reason I wanted to come to your room is so that I could clearly see your sight line again."

Hearing this, Minoru finally recognized how stupid he'd been. Suu had been able to see his sight line this entire time and, with it, the color that revealed his emotions. Realizing this far too late, Minoru squeezed his eyes shut. As soon as he did, he heard Suu whisper into his right ear:

"Don't worry. In the car, your sight line wasn't red or blue. If it was, I would've declined your invitation. Now...open your eyes and look at me."

I can't, Minoru thought immediately.

Minoru had never been able to show his true emotions to anyone, even his beloved older sister Norie—perhaps not even his real parents, when they were alive.

Through his entire life, there was only one person who had been able to completely break down the wall around his heart: his older sister Wakaba. Though she had been three years older than him, they had laughed together, cried together, and occasionally even fought together. She was the only person in the world whom he hadn't even remotely seen as a stranger. Ever since she'd passed away, Minoru had been determined to never again let somebody else into his heart.

However...

"Look at me."

Suu's words seemed to be casting a spell on Minoru's eyelids. Somehow, something about the flat tone of her voice—even though all emotion seemed stripped away, or perhaps because of it—was shaking his resolute refusal.

Having squeezed them shut for as long as he could, Minoru finally eased open his now-stiff eyelids.

In the dim light, just barely a foot away, Suu stared back with violet eyes under thick eyelashes, her face almost inhumanly expressionless. She was so close that he could count every lash, trace every patterned line in her irises.

Minoru could almost feel his sight line being sucked into Suu's dark pupils as if they were two black holes. For a moment, her violet-blue irises widened, then quickly returned to their usual aloofness.

"...So..."

Even though he'd just finished drinking his tea, Minoru felt hoarse as he uttered the question almost unconsciously: "What color is my sight line...?"

Suu didn't answer for a moment, opening and closing her eyes twice, then three times. Finally, her lips parted ever so slightly, and she murmured words that for once had a faint tint of emotion. "...It was difficult to make out your sight line in the light, and now I see why. Minoru, your sight line... It almost doesn't have a color."

"What...?"

"It's thin, weak, almost transparent... I've seen one like this only once before... It's the color of apathy."

Minoru's eyes opened wider despite himself.

"The color of...apathy?"

"Yes. You feel no desire toward me, certainly no hatred, and maybe not even any human interest at all," she stated bluntly. For some reason, as she spoke, there seemed to be the faintest, softest hint of a smile on her lips.

Minoru stared once more at the girl sitting stiffly before him, then slowly shook his head again. "That can't be... Of course I feel interest toward you! At least, it seems that way to me..."

"As a fellow Third Eye host, maybe. But as Suu Komura, I don't interest you at all."

Her retort caught Minoru off guard, leaving him at a loss for words. As much as he instinctively felt that to be a ridiculous assertion, there was still a part of him that thought it just might be true. Her ability to see others' sight lines, and the ability to avoid that sight through refraction, certainly fascinated him. But as for the girl in front of him who held that power...

Could he really say that he hadn't questioned whether there was any point in getting to know her?

Minoru's left cheek prickled with pain. It was the spot where the Divider, Olivier Saitou, had slapped him a week earlier.

Olivier had accused him of not feeling anything toward the taxi driver who had fallen victim to the Ruby Eye Igniter.

And he was right.

Of course, Minoru couldn't forgive the Ruby Eyes for targeting inno-
cent people, and he truly did want to work with the SFD and put a stop to
their murders—but he couldn't say he felt any real pain over the deaths
of the victims. After all, they had been strangers, with no connection to
him. This applied to the Ruby Eyes and their victims alike.

Was there some sort of defect in his heart that made him this way?
And his colorless sight line just proof of that warped part of him?
Minoru bit his lip and looked down, but Suu's voice immediately
addressed him again from nearby.

"Don't make that face. I'm not accusing you of anything."

"But..."

"If anything, I'm happy about it, because I don't need to be afraid of
your sight line. And besides...I probably feel the same way."

"Huh?"

Raising his eyes to glance at her, Minoru saw that Suu was smiling
faintly again. "I'm sorry. But I'm also more interested in your ability
than in you yourself. I have been ever since I heard about you at headquarters. Because...our powers are similar, but they're also opposites."

Unable to understand her meaning right away, Minoru furrowed his
brow. Then, after a moment, he realized what she was trying to say.

They were similar in that they both isolated the user from the outside
world.

And they were opposite in that Suu's power blocked out visible light,
while Minoru's power blocked out everything *but* visible light.

Shuffling closer to Minoru so that their knees almost touched as they
knelt next to each other on the floor, Suu continued, "The sources of our
powers seem as though they would be quite similar. And yet, why does
your power spare only visible light? To me, the eyes of other people are
the most frightening things of all. Is it different for you?"

It was a question that Minoru had no reason to be able to answer.
After all, it was the Third Eye in Minoru's chest that had formulated his
protective-shell ability, not Minoru himself.

And yet Minoru felt compelled to answer. For Suu, who could per-
ceive other people's emotions through their sight lines whether she
wanted to or not, it must have been terrifying to enter this house—no,
even to have just deactivated her ability in the car. And yet she had

pushed ahead and done so, most likely for the sake of asking him this question.

"I..."

Minoru gave up on deciding which parts needed to be said and dove right in. "I'm afraid of other people, too. But it's because they'll start to have memories of me, and I'll have memories of them. I think what I'm really afraid of is those memories—inside others and inside my own mind... But lately, I've realized that might not be the source of my power. If it was, I probably would've gotten a memory-altering ability like Chief Himi, after all..."

At this point, Minoru was addressing his own concerns as much as he was addressing Suu's.

"Ever since I got this power, deep down I've been thinking...this isn't the absolute solitude I wanted. If it was based on that desire, I don't think what happened last week would've been possible... Bringing another person into my protective shell, that is."

"The Professor told me about that. You protected Accelerator from an explosion in your fight against Igniter, right?"

Suu's voice startled Minoru out of his brooding, and he nodded.

"...Right. But I was able to do it only once. We tried to re-create it in experiments recently, and when I couldn't make it happen again, Yumiko was furious with me."

"Hmm..." Suu tilted her head thoughtfully, gazing off into space.

"...Minoru. Is it okay if you can't see me?"

"Wh-what?"

"If you can't see the other person, would you still be able to bring them into your protective shell?"

Minoru was stunned into silence for a few moments, then stammered out a flustered response. "I...I can't! Even if I couldn't see the person, I could still, um, f-feel them...and besides..." He continued as if frantically firing off excuses. "When it fails, the other person gets pushed away super quickly! Even in the experiment room, where there's mats and meter-thick foam padding on the walls, Yumiko's nose was turning red after a while!"

A soft giggle escaped Suu's lips at that. "I bet she got really mad."

"Yeah...I mean, of course she did. I don't want to try that experiment again for a while... I mean, the point is, it's too dangerous to try it no matter who it's with!" Feeling a cold sweat on his back for some reason, Minoru was breathing heavily as he finished his messy statement.

However, Suu responded quite casually.

"We have a mat right there."

"H-huh?!"

Suu's slim index finger was pointing straight at the wood-frame bed up against the far wall. After another few seconds of shocked silence, Minoru shook his head rapidly, his back stiff. "Wh…? No! I mean, technically it's a mat or at least a mattress, but, um…there are other problems with that… I mean, er…"

Minoru gulped and looked at Suu.

"Wait…are you just messing with me?"

"…I just wanted to know more about both our abilities…"

The Refractor's elfin face clouded with disappointment.

"A-ah, um, I'm sorry!" Realizing his mistake, Minoru apologized reflexively. Suu had just admitted earlier that she was terrified of men looking at her with lust. It was absurd to think that she would joke about that sort of thing for fun.

She really does just want to learn more about her powers and help me figure out mine, he thought, chewing his lip and looking down again as he reproached himself. *And I responded so rudely…*

"Let's try it, then," Suu said casually, her face instantly returning to its usual aloof expression. "See if you can bring me into your protective shell."

…But how am I supposed to do that?

As if seeing the question in his eyes, Suu answered calmly, "I'll lie down on the bed, and you can activate your powers above me."

"Uhh…"

As Minoru sat dumbfounded, Suu stood up coolly, walked over to the bed, and casually stretched out on top of the blankets.

"Uhhh…," he repeated.

Suu flicked her violet-blue eyes toward him. "It's all right. I'll activate my ability to its full extent, too, so you won't be able to see me at all, and I won't see you, either. That should lessen your fear of us creating memories of each other." With that, Suu's Third Eye power went into action, just as promised, and her delicate form vanished into thin air with the same faint sound as before.

The light from the streetlamps that streamed in through the window was simply curving around her body, rendering her perfectly invisible. But unlike the firm leather seat, the soft blankets on Minoru's bed wrinkled underneath her weight, showing a vague outline of her body.

"All right, go ahead."

Suu's voice came from the indented outline on the bed, but Minoru didn't move right away.

I know she's invisible, but...

He stared uncertainly at the seemingly empty bed. Thinking about it, Minoru decided this was at least as stressful as when he'd had to stand behind Yumiko and press up against her. Minoru doubted he had the self-possession to practically lie on top of a girl on his bed, much less to bring her into his protective shell.

Minoru opened his mouth to apologize and say that he couldn't do it after all, that it was bound to fail anyway, but then he paused, Suu's words from a few minutes ago playing back in his mind.

"It's the color of apathy... I don't interest you at all."

Those words, coupled with Olivier's accusations from the previous week, weighed down on his heart painfully. Being afraid of others and being apathetic sounded similar, but they weren't really the same. The latter, after all, implied that he didn't care whether other people lived or died. What if the source of his power was not really fear but apathy? Had he gained the ability to create a protective shell because, deep down, he didn't care about anyone else as long as he himself was safe?

...That's not true!

Minoru gritted his teeth, steeled himself, and walked over to the bed with new resolve. If his power had really been born from a selfish desire to protect himself, he wouldn't have been able to bring anyone else into his protective shell. But he didn't want what had happened at Ariake Heaven's Shore to be his only proof that his power had come from somewhere else.

Minoru put both his knees down on the bed, avoiding the area that most likely contained Suu's legs. Cautiously confirming the location of Suu's upper body with his fingertips, he placed both hands approximately above her shoulders.

"...Okay, h-here goes," Minoru mumbled. Taking a deep breath, he cautiously lowered his body toward the bed.

The wooden bedsprings creaked quietly and lightly as he felt something soft against the front of his body. It was a very strange experience: There was definitely something underneath him, but it looked as though he were simply floating above the bed. No matter how hard he squinted at the now slightly deeper indent on the bed, he could see nothing but blankets.

Detecting the faintest scent of shampoo, Minoru swallowed and spoke with a dry mouth.

"U-um...a-am I too heavy?"

"It's fine," Suu responded, her voice as level as ever. "I'm a Jet Eye, too, after all." She had a good point—to a Third Eye host's enhanced physical strength, the weight of one person was no big burden.

But what about mentally speaking? Minoru thought, despite himself. No matter how scientific the goal might be, technically speaking, he was still on a bed pressing down on a person he had just met today. "Um... you're not scared?" he blurted out half unintentionally.

"Only a little," Suu admitted, her voice close to Minoru's ear as she continued on. "...I'm sorry. I said I just wanted to know more about our powers, but the truth is, that was only half my reason. The other half was...to test the limits of my own fear."

"To test the limits...?"

"Yes. Of all the men I've met, you have the least threatening gaze I've ever seen. I thought, if I can be near this person without being afraid, then maybe someday..."

Trailing off, Suu lightly touched Minoru's hands with her transparent fingertips.

"There, see? I'm not scared. So you shouldn't be scared, either, Minoru... Whenever you're ready."

In truth, Minoru had only half understood the meaning of Suu's explanation at best. But for just a moment, the warmth of her fingertips on his hands made him forget his negative thoughts.

"...Here I go." Without a second thought about what might happen if he failed, Minoru activated his protective shell.

The room had seemed quiet enough before, but only when it disappeared completely did the volume of the background noise that had previously been audible become apparent. The sound of cars passing on the road in front of the house, the low hum of the ventilation system, the voices from the TV that Norie was watching in the living room—all of them vanished at once, leaving behind a profoundly complete silence.

Immediately, though, that silence was broken by the sound of shallow breathing.

Minoru had expected the invisible Suu to be repelled by his protective shell and pushed farther into the bed, but in his now blue-tinted field of vision, he saw no such thing. The blankets on the bed had only shifted ever so slightly. Which meant...

"...Did it...work...?"

The fact that he could hear Suu's quiet whisper was another surprise.

"Y-yes...it looks like it did," he replied in an equally hushed tone, realizing he had been holding his breath.

Why he had succeeded on the first try now when he had failed so many times in the experiment room was a complete mystery to Minoru. All he knew for sure was that he really did have the ability to bring other people into his protective shell. In other words, this power hadn't come from fear or apathy toward others at all.

But in that case, what was the source—the emotional trauma—that *had* created this invisible barrier? As Minoru contemplated this thought, Suu once again spoke near his ear.

"Amazing. There really is a barrier there. It doesn't feel like anything... No texture, no temperature or friction, yet it's completely solid..."

"Ah...Suu, you can feel the shell?"

In response, he felt her nod, her hair brushing invisibly against his cheek. "Yes, I feel it. Which means its shape must be dependent on your posture."

"Th-then that means that if I'm not careful about how I move..." Minoru gulped. Usually, the shell projected about three centimeters around Minoru's body and adjusted to match his movements. So right now, it must have expanded just enough to encompass Suu's body as well.

So it'd probably be impossible to walk around or run like this..., Minoru thought.

At that moment, Suu said something to even further startle Minoru to his very core. "Also...what's that noise?"

"Wh...?" Minoru had gotten so used to it that he had completely forgotten about it. When he produced his shell and cut off all outside noise, those sounds were mysteriously replaced by a low, rhythmic thudding.

Over time, he had come to assume that this was produced by the Third Eye in his chest, indicating that it was working and that he could hear it pulsing through his body. However...

"Y...you can hear this noise, too, Suu?!"

"Yes. It's a very mysterious sound..."

"D-does it sound to you like it's coming from my chest?"

"No. It's...closer than that. I wonder... It almost feels like I've heard it before somewhere..."

Minoru sank into uncertain silence, but before long, Suu spoke again. "Minoru. I can't really move right now, so I need you to reach into my breast pocket and pull out my smartphone."

"Huh?" Minoru squeaked, then shook his head quickly and lightly. "I-I-I can't!"

"I'm not asking you to do anything difficult. Come on, hurry."

"Th...then at least deactivate your ability so I can see your pocket..."

"If I do that, then this whole phenomenon might fall apart. It's not as if I'm expecting you to enjoy it, so calm down. We have to record this sound and bring it to the Professor so she can analyze it."

Two minutes later.

"U...um..." Sitting on the edge of the bed next to Suu, who had deactivated her ability and was once again visible, Minoru was keenly aware that he was sweating profusely. "Now that I think about it, wouldn't it have been easier for me to just deactivate the shell for a moment and borrow your phone so I could record it myself...?"

Holding her ultrasmall phone to her ear, Suu blinked for a moment as she processed Minoru's words. "...You're right," she muttered. "But it's better that we avoid activating our powers too frequently. Keeping it to a single time was for the best."

Only as he heard these words did Minoru realize he had forgotten himself and activated his shell in his own home. Not only that, but Suu had used her ability, too. If any Ruby Eyes had been nearby, there was a chance they'd been detected.

Noticing Minoru's anxiety, Suu put her smartphone back in her pocket and turned to him. "Don't worry. I've been monitoring this neighborhood all day, and besides, my ability's detection radius is extremely small."

"D-detection radius?"

"Yes. It's the range of how close a Ruby Eye would have to be to pick up the scent of a Jet Eye's ability or vice versa."

Minoru was already quite familiar with this phenomenon. Whenever a Ruby Eye used their ability near him, he smelled an intense, almost animalistic scent of dirt and iron. He didn't know what it smelled like for them, only that Ruby Eyes could detect Jet Eye powers in the same way.

However, he hadn't realized that the range of this effect could vary depending on the individual.

"The detection radius of a Third Eye user's ability varies based on the nature and scope of that ability," Suu explained to a blinking Minoru. "To put it simply, the bigger the effect that the atom manipulation has, the wider the radius. In the SFD, members like Divider and Accelerator have a detection radius of about twenty-four meters. By contrast, Speculator's and Searcher's radii are close to zero."

"I see..." Thinking about each of the mentioned SFD members' abilities, Minoru nodded. Certainly, Divider (Olivier) and Accelerator (Yumiko) had abilities that affected their whole bodies or the area around them, while Speculator's (Professor Riri Isa) involved only her own brain, and the power Searcher (DD) used had virtually no effect on reality at all.

But by that logic, a powerful effect like Suu's invisibility seemed like it would have a very large detection radius. As if reading his thoughts, Suu shrugged lightly. "It's not as though I turn my body into glass or anything. I cause the light around me to alter for only a fraction of a second at a time... In fact, in a battle a little while ago, a Ruby Eye didn't even notice me until I was less than sixty-one centimeters away."

"Sixty-one centimeters... So that's your 'detection radius,' then?" Minoru thought some more. *Where does my protective shell fall in this equation? Creating an impenetrable wall around me certainly seems like it's having a major effect on reality. Does that mean I would have a wide detection radius like Olivier and Yumiko?*

"According to the Professor," Suu said, her brow furrowed as if she, too, were thinking about something, "your isolation power *should* have an enormous effect on the environment, with a detection radius several times that of Divider, but...according to the data from your encounters with Biter and Igniter, it most likely goes up to only about nine meters. She thought it was very strange..."

Suu fell silent for a moment, looking at Minoru with her mysterious lilac eyes.

"...But after entering your protective shell earlier, I think I might understand. I believe your ability gives off a scent only in the instant it's activated. Once the shell is completely formed, it blocks out even its own detection radius... It really is the ultimate form of isolation. In that moment, it was as if you and I were alone in our own separate world... Maybe that is the source of your power."

Suu stood up smoothly and walked toward the door. As she grasped the doorknob with her slim white hand, however, she paused, and spoke without turning back to face Minoru. "Be sure to report the results of today's experiment to the Professor for me... I enjoyed talking with you today, and the sushi was delicious. Thank you, and I'll see you later."

She turned the doorknob, pushing open the door. As she turned her head ever so slightly on her way out of the room, Minoru thought he saw a faint smile on her lips.

2

Two days later, December 30, 2:00 p.m.

Standing in Toyama Park in front of the path that led to SFD Headquarters, Minoru hesitated.

When Suu Komura had told him two days ago that he should report their experiment to the Professor, he had nodded—but now, he wasn't sure how he was going to tell her. He'd met Suu for the first time, invited her in for dinner, chatted with her in his room, and ended up conducting a test on his bed to bring her into his protective shell and succeeded on the first try... No matter how he phrased it, it wasn't going to sound good.

"...Why am I the one who has to report this, anyway?" Minoru grumbled into the scarf that covered the bottom half of his face, his hands shoved into his pockets.

Still, if it was only the Professor, it wouldn't be that bad. The real problem was what he was going to say to Accelerator, Yumiko Azu, after having attempted the same experiment with her a few days earlier and failing so repeatedly and spectacularly that she ended up skinning the tip of her nose.

...But I'm sure she'll be taking today off or else be out in the field somewhere, so I won't have to see her. Yeah, definitely.

Reassuring himself with this groundless line of wishful thinking, Minoru began to walk down the path into the forest.

Arriving outside the seemingly run-down apartment complex that housed SFD Headquarters, Minoru stepped into the ancient elevator. When the doors creaked open on the fifth floor, he stepped out into the spacious room that made up the entirety of the floor.

Minoru crept quietly into the room, but as he looked around, he saw that his prayers had been answered. Sitting cross-legged in front of the big-screen TV was Olivier Saitou, and Professor Riri Isa was holed up in her research booth, peering at a monitor. Nobody else seemed to be around.

Secretly breathing a sigh of relief, Minoru then took a deeper breath to steel himself before venturing to greet the two. "H...hello."

The Professor gave him a quick wave, but Olivier remained hunched over without so much as a twitch in response; he was probably wrapped up in level grinding in another old-school RPG. With a rueful smile, Minoru was changing out his shoes for a pair of slippers when the Professor called to him from her small room on the west side of the floor.

"Sorry, Mikkun, but our meeting's going to be delayed by fifteen minutes or so."

"Ah...sure." Minoru nodded, then glanced around the room uncertainly. For the time being, he decided to settle on the sofa behind Olivier.

Looking over Olivier's shoulder at the TV, Minoru saw that Divider was playing a JRPG series that even he was familiar with. Judging by the quality of the graphics, Minoru had to wonder if this game had come out near the beginning of this century. Tense, urgent music played through the sound bar that was set up underneath the TV as a giant monster rampaged around on the screen.

At least I'll have a boss fight to entertain me while I wait for the Professor, Minoru thought, already leaning forward in his seat.

Then he noticed something odd. The boss monster was unleashing deadly attacks, but the party of heroes facing it wasn't moving in the slightest. The game had a real-time battle system, so the player had to enter commands or the protagonists would simply stand there being hit by the enemy's attacks. In fact, of the three-member party on the screen, two of the members had already run out of HP and fainted.

And the remaining member's HP was already in the red. Minoru leaned over on his side to look at Olivier's hands, and sure enough, he wasn't moving a single finger on the controller. Maybe he had some strategic reason for not attacking the boss, but at this rate, he was going to get wiped out. Concerned, Minoru timidly called out to the motionless back in front of him.

"Um...Oli-V?"

There was no response.

Minoru tried again, a little louder this time. "Oli-V, your party's going to lose..."

At his words, Olivier's broad shoulders jerked suddenly. "Huh? Wh... aaah!" At the exact same moment as Divider's shout, the last remaining protagonist cried out in unison and collapsed with a thud. The screen faded to a dark gray, the GAME OVER text mercilessly large in the center.

"Ah...ahhh..." The crestfallen Divider's shoulders sagged as he let the controller fall from his hands. For a moment it looked like he would stay that way indefinitely, but then he shook his head and groaned.

"And I was almost at the final boss, too..."

Heaving a sigh, he reached out and ejected the game disc from the system, which brought the screen back to the game system's menu. Then, putting the disc back into its case, he turned to Minoru with a strained smile.

"Yo, Mikkun. How's it goin'?"

"Ah, um...very well, thank you."

Now that he could see all of Olivier's handsomely featured face, Minoru noticed that there was a flesh-colored hydrocolloid bandage over his right cheek, as well as what looked to be some blisters hidden by his bangs and blue-framed glasses. He seemed to be ignoring Minoru's gaze as he looked down at the game, but eventually he raised his head.

"Hey, Mikkun, do you have this console?"

"Huh? Y...yes, I think so..." In his current state of affairs, Minoru couldn't even remotely afford any of the current-generation consoles, but this older system had been one of Norie's favorites when she was younger, so there was one tucked away on the AV shelf in the living room.

"Cool, then play this." Olivier unceremoniously dropped the game into Minoru's lap.

"Huh...?!" Minoru looked up at him, eyes wide. "But you're still playing it, aren't you? You said you were almost at the last boss!"

"Yeah, well..." Olivier shrugged casually. "When I get a single game over, I stop playing that game for good."

"Game over...? But you must've saved your game, right? Why wouldn't you just start over from your last save...?"

Looking as though he didn't know how to respond to Minoru's automatic question, Olivier stood up and sat down next to him on the couch.

"...Hey, Mikkun. What do you think the SAVE function in an RPG is, really?"

"What is it...?" Minoru mumbled. Unsure what was meant by the question, he went with the most obvious answer: "It's a function that stores your progress in the game on a memory card, right...?"

"Well, yeah, sure. But that's just what it means to us when we're playing a video game in the real world. What I mean is, what do you think that SAVE means to, say...the hero and the demon lord and the world they're fighting in?"

"Ahh..." Finally grasping the meaning of Olivier's words, Minoru tilted his head and responded more thoughtfully.

"I guess...it'd be like magic or some kind of miracle? Like in older games, when you entered a password instead of being able to save... didn't they call those passwords 'resurrection spells' sometimes?"

"Yeah, exactly. But y'know..." Olivier paused, and for a moment, there was a hint of intensity in his expression. "If that's the case, why can't the demon lord save, too?"

"Huh...?"

"I mean, he's doing his best, too, in his own way, right? Coming up with battle tactics, sending his minions after the hero, that kind of thing. And sometimes, he does really well and wipes out the hero's whole party. But does he get to celebrate his victory? No! Because the hero alone has the power to turn back time for the whole world. And he'll do it, over and over for eternity, until it finally ends in the demon lord's death. Man, if I were that demon lord, I'd get pissed off and quit right away."

Dumbfounded by Olivier's speech, Minoru waited a few moments after he'd finished before venturing another question.

"So when you said you stop playing a game for good once you get a game over, that's not because it'd be a pain to start over from the last SAVE point, it's because, um…it seems unfair to start over? So in the game world when you're playing, as soon as the hero's party is defeated, it means…the demon lord has won…?"

Olivier grinned wryly, sinking deeper into the couch.

"Yeah, it sounds pretty silly when you put it that way. But I'm not the one who came up with this whole 'saving is unfair' thing, just so you know. But, like…once the idea got into my head, I couldn't stand seeing a hero who just starts over whenever he loses, y'know?"

"Um…I do kind of understand where you're coming from, I guess…," Minoru murmured, examining the hero and heroine in the game's box art with somewhat mixed emotions. Olivier snickered and elbowed him lightly.

"I'm not saying you now have to play like that, too, or anything, Mikkun."

"R-right… Oh, but I guess that explains why you're always grinding levels way more than necessary. So you won't get a game over…"

"Pretty much. It is crazy boring, though… But you can actually learn a few things from playing permadeath-style."

"Huh…?"

Shifting his gaze off to the right, Olivier looked up at the high ceiling and answered with a sigh.

"For one thing, even if you max out all your levels and prepare everything to a T, all it takes is one moment of spacing out for you to lose everything. And another thing… At any given moment, even the smallest action can turn into something that you can never take back."

Divider stretched out his legs and stood up, returning to his usual nonchalant self. "Hey, looks like the meeting's gonna start. C'mon."

Minoru tucked the game into his messenger bag and followed after

Olivier, though there was one more question he wished he could have asked.

Who was it who first told you that saving is unfair?

In the research room, several folding chairs had been lined up around the 203-centimeter monitor, one of which was already occupied by Denjirou "DD" Daimon. As Minoru walked in, Searcher glanced at him from under his trademark camouflage baseball cap and gave him a brisk wave. Minoru returned the greeting and sat down next to Olivier. *I guess Yumiko really isn't here today,* he thought.

At that moment, there was the sound of the door suddenly bursting open behind him, and he turned, only to see a familiar gray pleated skirt fluttering in the doorway.

"Sorry I'm late."

Accelerator (Yumiko Azu) bowed her head promptly and sat down in the chair on Minoru's right, casting a quizzical glance at his frozen expression. "What're you making that face for?"

"I…it's nothing, really," Minoru mumbled, shaking his head stiffly. Mercifully, Professor Riri then clapped her hands together quickly, positioning herself near the monitor.

"Okay, looks like we're all here! Everyone, I'm sorry to call you in to headquarters so close to New Year's Day, but it seems like the Ruby Eyes have no intention of taking the holiday off, either. So, let's begin with a report on yesterday's battle, shall we?"

"Yeah, sure," DD responded in his usual bored drawl, his fingers tapping across the smartphone already in his hands. A full-body image of a person promptly appeared on the large monitor next to the Professor. It appeared to be a low-light photograph taken at night and then digitally enhanced; the quality was a bit grainy, but the person's features and physique were clear enough at least.

Above the photo was a caption that read "Identified Ruby Eye Host No. 11: Trancer." As Minoru recalled, Igniter's number had been nineteen, so this "Trancer" was a Ruby Eye who had appeared earlier than Igniter—a veteran, so to speak.

After waiting a moment for Minoru to get a good first look at the image, DD spoke up.

"…Since it was raining yesterday afternoon, Oli and I went out on patrol, as usual. After about fifteen loops around our route, we caught wind of his scent. Since we were in Otemachi and Trancer was in Akasaka, he was real close by."

What? The moment he heard that, Minoru half rose to his feet. "Yesterday…in Akasaka?! Th-then that traffic accident really was…?"

"Mm-hmm. It was the work of this man." The confirmation came from the Professor, who was sitting next to the monitor as if she really was teaching a class. The expression on her small, childish face was extremely grave. "A Ruby Eye who can manipulate water… His code name—the one he's given himself, anyway—is Trancer. He's a well-known enemy of ours…a big-shot veteran Ruby Eye who's been around for quite a while."

As he listened to the Professor's explanation, Minoru stared at the photo again. Descriptions like "big shot" and "veteran" hardly seemed to suit the subject, who looked to be only around Minoru's age. The half of his face that was visible looked rather meek, and his straight-fringed hairstyle was more typical of an honors student than a hardened Ruby Eye criminal.

This young man really caused that much destruction…?

As if sensing Minoru's skepticism, the Professor continued her explanation.

"Trancer froze the entire Aoyama exit ramp into ice, sending ten vehicles or so sliding into the Akasaka intersection, including a trailer truck. A tanker truck that was at the intersection was struck and exploded, a disaster that killed seven people and injured eleven more. Apparently it took a lot of pushing from the National Police Agency Security Bureau's Public Security Division to get the investigators at the scene to declare it an accident… At any rate, that just shows how dangerous this man is. It's not just that he has a very powerful ability—he's also very adept in how he uses it."

"How he uses it…?"

"That's right. All of us Third Eye holders, both Jet and Ruby Eyes alike, came into our powers only just three months ago. I don't think even we SFD members have fully mastered our abilities yet. And our enemies are the same: Igniter, for instance, was still developing his ability to divide water into hydrogen and oxygen when we fought him not long ago. I might even go so far as to say that that's the reason we were able to beat him…"

The Professor looked up at the monitor and tapped the image on the screen with her finger. "However, Trancer here is different. I believe that at this point in time, he has already completely perfected his abilities… DD, please continue." She took a step back to allow DD to take the floor.

"Sure. So, uh…obviously, by the time we got to Akasaka, Trancer had already fled, but we managed to catch a whiff of him. We pursued him by car, and luckily he went into Aoyama Cemetery. I figured with my rifle and Oli's sword, it was the perfect situation to go after him, but…"

DD trailed off, his eyes shifting toward Olivier's seat next to Minoru, but Divider simply continued sitting with his arms crossed and head angled downward, not moving a centimeter. After a short sigh, DD cleared his throat and continued. "Oli was wearing the waterproof suit the Professor made him after our last fight with Trancer. The suit worked great, and Oli managed to injure him pretty badly. But…then he busted out a trump card of his own…"

This time DD glanced at the Professor and ducked his head like a sheepish student making an excuse to a teacher.

"Just like the Professor predicted, we found out that the reason he'd rejected our nickname 'Freezer' to go by 'Trancer' is that his power isn't just to turn water into ice—he can also turn water into steam. We were ready for that, but what caught us off guard was that the steam he made was extremely hot, and Oli got hit with it face-first. While I was busy getting Oli out of there, Trancer ran away, and we lost him… Um, that's the end of my report."

"…Hmm." The Professor planted her hands on her hips, her pigtails bobbing from side to side. "Well, it is my fault that I didn't predict that the steam he produced would be so high in temperature. However, DD— No, let me ask *you*, Oli-V. Why didn't you report to me at any point from the time you detected Trancer in Akasaka to the point where you lost him in Aoyama Cemetery?"

The Professor stared at him piercingly, but the tall swordsman was silent for a long moment. Finally, he stood up slowly and bowed low as he answered, "I'm sorry. I decided that DD and I could handle it on our own."

"Well, next time report it anyway and just include that assessment, then," the Professor snapped.

Though she looked to be only a little girl of around ten years old, the withering glare her dark brown eyes emitted was more intimidating than that of any teacher at Minoru's school. "Oli-V, you didn't really decide that you and DD would be able to handle the situation; you just wanted to take care of it yourself. And you didn't report to headquarters because you didn't want anyone to get in your way... Am I right?"

Olivier stood still without a word, and the young commander turned her gaze away from him, softening her words slightly as she continued.

"The Industrial Safety and Health Department, Specialized Forces Division... We may have an elaborate name, but all we really are is a reserve force chosen by the government to deal with situations related to Third Eye phenomena. I still don't know all the details about the 3E Incident Countermeasure Committee, but it seems that they're currently divided between two options: continuing to keep the Third Eyes secret until we fully understand them or releasing the information to the public and passing related bills for the complete neutralization of all Third Eyes. If they were to choose the latter, we would all most likely be forced to undertake compulsory surgery to remove our Third Eyes."

Minoru's breath caught involuntarily. The Professor glanced at him, a cynical smile forming on her tiny lips.

"The only reason our department is able to act relatively free of the 3E Committee's interference in the first place is that there are bureaucrats and big politicians in the Ministry of Health, Labor, and Welfare who think they can use the SFD as a tool in some political conflict. The Self-Defense Forces' Special Task Squad, who worked with Mikkun and Yukko the other day, are the same way, but we never know if our budget or authority might be taken away without warning for any number of reasons. That's why, at least among our own members, I think it's of vital importance that we maintain a relationship of mutual trust. That's why, if anything, I'm more upset that you didn't report to HQ than I am about Trancer getting away, Oli-V."

The Professor fell silent, and DD stepped in, speaking with another sigh. "She's saying to quit being so damn standoffish, Oli. C'mon, don't you think you could at least tell us by now why you're so obsessed with catching Trancer?"

There was another long silence, broken only by the distant sound of cars passing on Meiji Street some ways away. Finally, there was a louder clatter as Olivier placed his hands on the back of his chair and bowed his head deeply. "...I'm sorry," Divider said in a subdued voice, without lifting his head. "I still can't tell you. It's as important to me as my SFD duties... No, it's even as important as stopping the Ruby Eyes from killing people. But I'll at least stop trying to take him down by myself. 'Cause...it seems like I'm not strong enough to beat him on my own yet."

Minoru's eyes widened. Hearing those words from Olivier Saitou, who was always overflowing with confidence in his ability to cut through anything, was something of a shock. Straightening up and catching Minoru's gaze, Olivier shot him a bitter smile and said something that shocked Minoru even more.

"C'mere, Mikkun. Hit me."

"Um...what...?!"

"I punched you out the other day because I said you didn't have enough resolve, right? 'Cause you didn't feel anything toward the Ruby Eyes' victims and stuff."

Instinctively, Minoru touched his left cheek, then quickly lowered his hand. "I mean...you were right to hit me for that, so..."

"But I'm the same way. Trancer is even more dangerous than Igniter, but I just charged in after him for my own reasons and ended up letting him get away. If he kills somebody else now, it's gonna be on me. I had no right to say anything to you when I'm just as bad, so...hit me."

Minoru swallowed. Averting his eyes from Olivier's intense gaze, he shook his head again. "I can't. I...I can't just hit somebody."

I'm afraid that the feeling of it would never leave my hand, the same way that punch won't leave my left cheek.

"...Gotcha. It's cool, I didn't mean to make things weird." Olivier turned back toward the Professor and bowed again.

"I'm really, really sorry. I'll be more careful from now on."

"All right."

The commander's answer was short. Her face said that she was resigned to the fact that there was nothing else she could say about the situation.

"Well then, that concludes our discussion of yesterday's incident. I'm sure Trancer will show up again on another rainy day. We'll utilize the data we gained from this encounter to its fullest so that he won't get away next time."

The meeting moved on to topics like the SFD budget and countermeasures against the mass media, so Minoru was only half listening as he reflected on Olivier's words.

Something that's as important to him as his SFD duties.

In other words, there was some circumstance that was equally significant to him as his mission to stop the Ruby Eyes from murdering people.

In all honesty, the weight of this mission still didn't feel entirely real to Minoru. He was here now only because, in exchange, Chief Himi had agreed to erase all memories of him from other people's minds once the Third Eye calamity was resolved.

Is there anything so important to me that I would throw away that deal?

Minoru wondered for a moment. *It would probably have to be something like Norie's life*, he thought. Did that mean that Olivier's secret situation was something along those lines? Was there someone so important to him that, for whatever reason, he had to fight Trancer alone for that person?

The only scenario he could come up with to fit that hypothesis would have to be revenge. That had been the case for Yumiko, who had been bent on defeating Igniter after her previous partner, Sanae Ikoma, was left in a coma in room 404 downstairs after a battle with the Ruby Eye.

Stopping at that conjecture for now, Minoru glanced over at Olivier again. However, his downturned expression didn't reveal any trace of emotion.

"Well, that brings our last meeting for the year to an end. Group dismissed." No sooner had the Professor finished her brief statement than Olivier stood up and strode quickly toward the elevator, DD following close behind him.

Those two sure are close, Minoru thought vaguely, but he was startled back to reality when the Professor called his name.

"Mikkun, Yukko, I hate to ask, but do you think we could spend another hour or two on that thing from the other day? I have a few more ideas I'd like to try."

"Certainly. I brought my motorcycle helmet with me today for that exact reason."

The Professor smiled wryly.

"Don't you think that'll just increase the sense of distance between you and Mikkun?"

"Well, I don't want to skin my nose again, that's for sure!"

As he watched the pair's spirited exchange, Minoru searched frantically for a way to explain what had happened. Finally, he raised his right hand nervously.

"So…um…is…is Komura going to be here at all today?"

"Hmm? Komura? Do you mean the older brother or the younger sister?"

"Ah, um…the s-sister."

"Oh, Hinako? She's probably in her room. She usually just watches the meetings via relay broadcasting."

"U-um, Hinako…? I was talking about, er, Ms. Suu Komura…"

At this, the Professor laughed and shrugged. "Oh, sorry, that's just the nickname I call her. The kanji for her given name is written like 'hina,' so I call her Hinako… Wait…come to think of it, Mikkun, have you been introduced to her?"

"No, um… Actually, two days ago, I had a chance to greet her while she was watching my house…"

At this, Yumiko, who had been listening in silence until now, spoke up in a surprised voice. "What? I'm sure she was using her invisibility, though, right? And you still noticed her?"

"Ah, no, I had no idea she was there. I just thought there was an empty car there, so I went to walk around it, and then she called out to me from inside the car…"

"What?!" both Yumiko and the Professor cried out in unison. Then, while the Professor crossed her hands over her lab coat and blinked in undisguised amazement, Yumiko hastily masked her surprise with a tiny frown.

"W…well, that's a surprise. I can't imagine Refractor giving away her presence to someone she'd just met," Yumiko added quickly.

Mentally scrambling for a way to smoothly explain what had happened from that point to the experiment and Suu's departure, Minoru continued cautiously:

"So…then, um, well. I didn't know that she'd been watching over my house while I was out on missions, and, ah, one thing led to another, and so I ended up inviting her in for dinner…?"

"Ah, well, I'm sure that didn't go well."

Professor Riri nodded sagely, a rueful smile on her small face. "I'm sure it got awkward there, right? I'm sorry. That's why I've been putting off introducing you to her. But see, Hinako has her reasons for—"

"Oh, ah, th-that's not it, exactly... She, um, she did come in and have dinner with my sister and me, so..."

"HUH?!"

Once again, the two voices rang out at the same time, albeit with slightly different tones.

"Wait a second, Utsugi. If she ate dinner at your house...does that mean she deactivated her ability...?"

When Minoru nodded affirmation to Yumiko's dumbfounded question, both of the girls lapsed into stunned silence for several long moments. Finally, the Professor spoke up, her voice a bit low. "But Mikkun...besides Hinako's ability, refraction, she has...other circumstances that predate her Third Eye..."

Uncertain whether it was all right to talk about it, Minoru chose his words carefully. "You mean...about sight lines, right?"

"What? Hinako told you that much...?"

"Yes..." The surprise on their faces continued to escalate. At this rate, Minoru realized he would never get through his explanation, so he took a deep breath and finished the report in one go. "So then, Komura wanted to see if her refraction power and my isolation power could be related and said she thought maybe I'd be able to bring someone into my shell if I couldn't see them... So, uh, we ended up testing it out in my room. And when we did that, um, I don't know why exactly, but it may have somehow succeeded on the first try? And then Komura recorded a sound that she heard inside my shell, and she said she'd bring it in for you to investigate, Professor, so she told me I should explain what happened. So, um...there you have it."

He had gotten increasingly flustered and incoherent by the end, but Minoru had somehow managed to say everything he needed to, so he took in a long, deep breath as he wiped the sweat from his brow with the cuff of his shirt.

The ensuing silence was at least five seconds long.

Finally, the Professor raised her right hand slowly, extended her index finger, and pushed it down repeatedly as if buzzing in on an imaginary button. "W...wait a minute. Let me make sure I've got this right first. Mikkun, you said it 'succeeded,' right? Does that mean you were able to bring Hinako—Refractor—into your protective shell? And on the first try, too?"

"Err..." Suddenly, Minoru hesitated, getting the feeling that confirming this would set a series of events into motion that he wasn't at all sure would be favorable. But it was too late to take it back now. Slowly, reluctantly, he nodded. "...Yes, I...I guess you could put it that way..."

Another long silence settled over the western side of the spacious fifth-floor room. Finally, the Professor dropped her hand back to her side and groaned. "Geez...I can't believe it! Did it succeed because you couldn't see Hinako, or was there some other factor? We'll have to run lots of experiments..." Still mumbling to herself, she started to pace back and forth in front of the monitor. Looking away, Minoru nervously turned his gaze toward Yumiko, who was still sitting in a folding chair with her legs crossed.

Still in her black school blazer despite the fact that winter vacation was well under way, Yumiko maintained the same expression of surprise for a while, even when Minoru's eyes met hers. Then, blinking suddenly as if she'd just realized something, she turned to face straight ahead. From this angle, her expression almost looked crestfallen. She suddenly squeezed her eyes shut as if something had frightened her. Her hands, clenched in her lap, trembled slightly.

However, her visible reaction told Minoru next to nothing about what she was actually thinking. Within seconds, she had straightened up, opened her eyes, and turned toward him with a smile.

"Well, that's a relief! I guess I won't be scraping up my nose today after all!" she said lightly, briskly clapping her hands and turning to the Professor. "That being the case, I suppose I can tap out and let Komura take over as your lab rat, yes?"

"Hmm? Ah, right, yes..."

"Well, then! I'll be heading back to my room. I'm still a high school student, after all, so I ought to study once in a while! Great work today, everyone," Yumiko said smoothly, and she stood up and walked toward the elevator without another glance at Minoru. There was the tap of footsteps, and the elevator doors creaked open, then shut.

After a few moments, the Professor let out a long sigh. Minoru, having blankly watched Yumiko leave without thinking to say good-bye, snapped out of his daze and turned around. Meeting his eyes, the elementary school–aged commander smiled somewhat bitterly.

"See, this is why I'm not qualified to be a leader."

"H…huh?"

"I can recite the digits of pi for eternity, but when it comes to the human heart, I can't predict what they're going to do even if it's just one second into the future. I guess no amount of research and secondhand information can replace life experience…"

"Um…what do you…?" Minoru tilted his head. In response, the Professor hoisted herself onto the edge of her desk and sat there, still smiling wanly, as she asked him an unusual question.

"Hey, Mikkun, have you ever been in love?"

At first, Minoru thought she was joking, and he opened his mouth to make some light joke in response, but he closed it when he realized he was meant to answer seriously. Waiting a moment, he slowly shook his head from side to side.

"No…I don't think so."

He had adored his late sister, Wakaba, and deeply admired his step-sister, Norie, but of course, that wasn't romantic love. There was a girl from the Yoshiki High School track and field club, Tomomi Minowa, who he went on morning jogs with from time to time, but if he was asked whether he was in love with her, he couldn't see himself saying anything other than no.

"I see." The Professor inclined her head slightly at Minoru's answer. "Neither have I. More accurately, I do seem to remember having some interest in a boy in my class up until three months ago, but once I received a Third Eye and my speculation powers, I forfeited those feelings."

"Wh…why is that? It's not as though your feelings for someone caused the trauma that fuels your Third Eye's power, right…?"

"Yes, that's true. But I got carried away with the thrill of having an intellect that no ten-year-old should have by rights. I wanted to come up with the answers for everything, even things I didn't need— No, that

I *shouldn't* have thought about. The result is that I've lost the chance to find within myself any real answers about the hearts of others..."

Minoru could only half follow the meaning of the Professor's muttered words. Looking at the pigtailed girl as she sat on the edge of her desk, still wearing a white lab coat over her jeans and sweater, he opened his mouth slowly. "Um...in other words, is that because you learned the 'meaning of life,' like you mentioned before...? Since you managed to come up with the answer to such a hard question, now it's pointless to try to understand how something like love works, or...?"

"I guess. Well, it's not so much that it's pointless as that I just can't bring myself to want to know the answer, I think. Or...I want to know, but my interest is only scientific, a matter of data. I figured I could at least hear about your experiences, but I guess I'm out of luck, huh, Mikkun?" She grinned, and Minoru ducked his head apologetically.

"I'm sorry I couldn't be more useful. But...what made you bring that up all of a sudden?"

"Well, I'm trying to figure out which I should prioritize—learning more about your ability or the mental health of the SFD's members."

"S-sorry? Mental health...?"

"Yeah. But I already know the answer. Mikkun, I'm changing your mission for the evening. We're going to put off the experiments for now. Instead, I need you to go to Yukko's room on the fourth floor and buzz in on the intercom."

Thrown off by the unexpected order, Minoru automatically repeated it. "B-buzz in...? Should I just come back here once I've done that?"

"Uh, no. What is this, ding-dong-dash? No, once you press it... Well, good luck, anyway. I'm sure you'll figure it out."

3

Following the Professor's vague instructions, Minoru took the elevator down one story to the residential floor.

Walking eastward down the old-fashioned outside corridor, Minoru passed by the room that would be given to him if he decided to move here temporarily, room 403, and stopped in front of room 404, where

Yumiko and her currently comatose partner, Shooter (Sanae Ikoma), lived.

Certainly, Yumiko's response when she had left the fifth floor a little while ago had been out of character for her. In fact, Minoru didn't think he'd ever seen such a distinct smile on her face. But what had caused the issue—and why the Professor had sent him here—was utterly unclear to him.

Of course, he couldn't imagine Yumiko was satisfied with the fact that after their experiment with his protective shell had failed so many times, it succeeded on the first attempt as soon as he tried it with Suu. But since the reason it had worked was probably Suu's invisibility, he didn't see any point in getting hung up on it.

So what does the Professor want me to talk to Yumiko about? Still at a loss, Minoru timidly pushed the buzzer on her door.

Ding-dong. The old-fashioned chime rang out loudly, but it wasn't until at least ten seconds after the sound had died away that a curt voice emitted from the speaker.

"Yes?"

"Ah, um, it's Utsugi…"

"…What is it?"

"Well, I…um…," Minoru stammered, unable to come up with a reason for his visit right away. The only instructions the Professor had given him beyond this point were "good luck." And Minoru wasn't feeling very lucky, since he still hadn't figured out why he was here at room 404.

As he stood hesitating, he heard a small sigh from the speaker, and the door unlocked with a click. Hanging back in the dim light behind the slightly opened door, Yumiko was still in her uniform. "Well? What do you want?"

Wilting under her glare, Minoru opened and shut his mouth a few times before settling on explaining the situation honestly. "Um, well… the Professor sent me here to talk to you."

Inhaling deeply, Accelerator let out a rapid stream of words that was true to her code name. "I see. Well, you've already accomplished that, then, haven't you? Go back to the Professor and tell her for me that I said there isn't a problem. See you later."

As soon as she finished her statement, Yumiko moved to close the door. Panicking, Minoru automatically took a half step back. When he did, the light that he'd been blocking from the north side of the hallway flooded into the darkness of the half-closed doorway. And that was when he noticed.

Yumiko's eyelids were red and puffy, and there were traces of still-wet tears on her cheeks.

Without thinking, Minoru reached out and grabbed the edge of the door that she was trying to shut, firmly holding it open. At the same time, Yumiko, apparently realizing what he'd seen, quickly turned her face away, covering her eyes with her free hand. Her voice cracked sharply in the dry winter air.

"What are you doing? I said I'm fine! Just go back upstairs!"

"B-but…"

"I said go away! Leave me alone!" she shouted, but her voice was trembling. Apparently giving up, she let go of the doorknob and gave a loud sniffle, rubbing her eyes furiously. "…I'm sure you're getting the wrong idea about this," she said finally.

"Huh…?"

"And I'd rather not let you continue to misunderstand."

"Huh?"

"Come in, then. I'll give you the briefest explanation possible."

This time when he entered, she ushered him into a room partway down the hall. The room was about thirty square meters, with a writing desk, a single bed, and a large beanbag cushion. It appeared that this was Yumiko's room, though the decor was exceedingly plain. With a small dresser, plain horizon-blue curtains, and not a single poster or photo to be found on the walls, the room gave little evidence that it was home to a teenage girl. The one exception was a large, possibly deerlike stuffed animal lying on the bed, but its goofy face and black nose gave Minoru no clues as to what it was supposed to be.

"Is that stuffed animal a…reindeer…?" Standing by the bed, unsure of what to do next, Minoru ventured what seemed like a safe question. Yumiko glanced over, her eyes staying on the mysterious creature as she answered.

"It's a pronghorn. Also known as a pronghorn antelope or a prong buck."

"Pronghorn… Where does it live?"

"Midwestern America. It's the fastest herbivore alive," Yumiko explained shortly, then pointed at the beanbag cushion on the floor. "Sit there."

As Minoru gingerly settled into the round cushion, Yumiko sat on the bed and pulled the stuffed pronghorn over to her, hugging it on her lap. She remained silent for a while and Minoru stole an upward glance at her.

Just as he'd thought, her eyes really were red. What's more, her voice seemed hoarser than it had been back on the fifth floor.

Does she have a cold? Or maybe an unseasonable case of hay fever?

Minoru came up with various possibilities, trying to be optimistic.

Shooting him a glare, Yumiko cut right to the heart of the matter.

"All right, I'll admit it. I was just putting on an act when I left the fifth floor. Once I got down here, I ran straight to my room and cried like a baby."

"L…like a baby?"

"That's right. And I whacked this stuffed animal around while I was at it, too."

"You…wh-whacked it?"

Try as he might, Minoru just couldn't picture the self-assured Yumiko Azu bawling her eyes out and venting her anger on a stuffed animal. And he still didn't quite understand the reason…

"But that's where you've got the wrong idea!" Yumiko proclaimed abruptly.

"P-pardon?"

"I know what you're thinking. You think I was crying because I felt like Komura stole you away from me, right?"

"Huh?! Uh, no, I didn't—"

"Well, you're wrong!!" Yumiko slammed a fist into the pronghorn's stomach, then pointed at Minoru as if targeting the tip of his nose. "The reason I was crying is that I was frustrated with my own failure. It had nothing to do with you whatsoever, that much is for sure."

"Failure…? But it was my fault the experiment kept failing the other day, not yours…"

"That's true. It was absolutely your fault." Yumiko rested her chin on the stuffed animal's head. "But the reason I couldn't help feeling disappointed and angry with myself wasn't about the experiment. It was

just that I always end up comparing myself to her. I'm sure I've never even crossed her mind, yet here I am, making comparisons, coming up short, and getting depressed all of my own accord... Really, I feel like such a fool."

Her voice gradually lowered as she spoke, ending in a quiet murmur. Minoru, unable to respond, sat in silence, and she shot him another look.

"Utsugi, you saw Komura in the flesh, right?"

"Y...yeah."

"Then, did she tell you what color your sight line was?"

"Yes...it was colorless, apparently. Su... Komura said it was 'the color of apathy.'"

"Apathy, huh...? You're consistent, at least." Brushing away a black strand of hair that had fallen over her cheek, Yumiko gave a faint, bitter chuckle. "She finally showed herself to me, too, about a month ago. I think you and I might be the only ones who have seen her face aside from Chief Himi and Professor Riri. However...Komura wouldn't tell me what color my sight line was."

"Ah..."

"I'd imagine it was a color she didn't want to talk about...but I can hazard a guess. My sight line toward her was probably purple...the color of jealousy."

"Jealousy...?"

"That's right. I am jealous of Komura. But...that started way before I had ever even seen that outrageously pretty appearance of hers."

Yumiko sighed, her eyes wandering toward the window in the south side of the room. Tomorrow was New Year's Eve, and so at this point in the late afternoon, the sun was already tumbling down toward the horizon, dyeing the light that streamed through the window a deep orange. Looking at Yumiko's face as the sunlight illuminated it with golden edges, Minoru couldn't help thinking that she was perfectly beautiful herself. Then, realizing this line of thinking was just comparing Yumiko and Suu, he quickly looked away. Yumiko glanced at him and continued her explanation in a low, quiet voice.

"The SFD began its activities about a month after the Third Eyes came to Earth... In other words, we started about two months ago, with only Sanae, DD, the Professor, and myself. Olivier joined shortly after, and then after that came the Komura siblings."

Looking again at Minoru, who was listening attentively, Yumiko traced numbers in the air with her finger. "Sanae and I paired up and brought down seven Ruby Eyes together. But Suu has secured at least as many as that all on her own. She can serve as both backup and offense... the strongest Jet Eye in the SFD."

"The...the strongest?!" Minoru repeated, his memories of Suu Komura flashing through his mind's eye. Sitting in the car after she revealed herself for the first time, averting her eyes as if she was afraid of him. At his dining table, spreading rice and garnishes onto a piece of seaweed in her left hand with a look of intense concentration. And in his bedroom, sitting face-to-face, quietly explaining about sight lines.

Suu Komura, the middle school girl who always looked as if she could vanish into the air at any second—and had the power to literally do so... Yumiko was saying that this girl was the strongest fighter in the SFD?

"Your face says you don't believe me," Yumiko said, a thin smile on the edges of her lips. "But if you think about it a little, it makes sense. When she uses her powers almost to their fullest, all you can see are two tiny black pupils. And her detection radius is only about one meter. Which means unless they're surrounded by something like water or mud, or they have some kind of strong sensor that doesn't rely on sight, an opponent won't notice her until she's at point-blank range."

"...And from that range..."

"That's right. Whether she uses a Taser, an anesthetic injection, or, of course, a gun, she's sure to hit her target." As she fell silent for a moment, Yumiko's smile shifted into one of self-deprecation. "The only reason the Professor put me into the battle last week against Igniter instead of Komura was that it was taking place at a pool... That, or she was just humoring my grudge against Igniter. Although, in the end, all I really did was nearly die and get rescued by you, huh?"

"What?" Minoru shook his head earnestly. "No...that's not true. My power is useless on its own for anything but defense. If you weren't there with your acceleration, we never would have beaten Igniter."

Yumiko looked at Minoru keenly, a serious look suddenly coming into her eyes. "...I'll be honest. Ever since we combined my ability with your protective shell and defeated Igniter in one blow, I've been thinking...if we could use that incredible power at any given time, I'd be able to win against Komura."

"Ah…"

"The mission at the Tokyo Bay Nuclear Power Plant just proved that your shell is invincible against any attack. In which case, it wouldn't matter whether the enemy detects us or not. We could neutralize any Ruby Eye just by charging in and body slamming them. For that matter, if we can confirm where the Syndicate's base is, you and I could march right in and take them all out."

The Syndicate… That's a group of Ruby Eyes, right?

But Minoru was too distracted by the intensity of Yumiko's words to focus on that question. Taken aback by her fervor, Minoru responded instinctively.

"W:…win against Komura? Is there really any point in competing against another SFD member…?"

For a moment, he thought he saw a sharp flash in Yumiko's eyes. However, it quickly disappeared, her shoulders sagging as the rueful smile returned to her face. "…You're right. Our goal is to neutralize Ruby Eyes and protect people from becoming their victims. It doesn't matter which of us individually has the most victories."

"R-right…"

"Yes. It's absolutely right, beyond a shadow of a doubt. But you know, Utsugi…the only reason you can say that so easily is that you don't yet know how it feels to truly hate them."

Though Yumiko's voice was quiet, Minoru could sense an intense fire behind her words. "Hate…?"

"Yes. If they ever take away someone you care about, give you a personal reason to truly despise them…I'm sure you'll understand then."

Minoru glanced toward the southern wall of the room, thinking of Sanae, the Shooter, asleep in the living room on the other side. "But…," he murmured. "You've already beaten Igniter. The Ruby Eye who put Sanae into a coma…his powers and memories were taken away, and he's back to being an ordinary person. Doesn't that mean your revenge is over?"

"So I should retire from the front lines, is that it? Are you saying I should just settle for being a backup and let Olivier and Komura and the others handle the real battles?"

"Wh… No, of course not…"

"You know…" Yumiko's eyes glittered as she stared Minoru down, speaking almost in a whisper. "On its own, my power isn't all that useful in battle. Sure, I can use my acceleration to get close to an enemy regardless of their speed or distance, but since I can't become invisible like Komura, they usually see me long before I'm within range to use a weapon against them. That means I can't do anything against Ruby Eyes who use long-distance attacks or transform their bodies. You've seen that firsthand—I couldn't win against Biter one-on-one... Without Sanae's shooting to back me up, I'm as good as useless."

But...that's not true! Minoru wanted to cry out. Yumiko's acceleration ability was plenty frightening on its own. With her ultrahigh speed, it would be difficult to pinpoint her even in close-quarters combat. She could use her ability on a knife for a powerful attack or extend it into her beloved motorcycle to make it move at over 483 kilometers per hour, jumping over dozens of meters with ease. How could someone with those abilities ever be useless?

But as if she were reading his thoughts, Yumiko shook her head lightly. "Sure, I can speed up my motorcycle, but I have to have a motorcycle handy to use that ability...I'm so dependent. On Sanae, on my bike...and now I'm trying to lean on you, too.

"...I bet the only reason Sanae's Third Eye is hanging on and keeping her alive and breathing is that she's worried about me. She's probably trying to stay by my side because she knows I can't fight on my own... I have to prove myself. I have to show her that I can get by without her now... But now I'm just trying to use you to do that. I...I'm so..."

Silently, fresh streams of tears formed on Yumiko's cheeks. Burying her face in the stuffed animal on her knees, Accelerator began to sob quietly.

Her antagonism toward Suu Komura. Her intense hatred of the Ruby Eyes. Finally, Minoru understood that the state of her partner, Sanae Ikoma the Shooter, was at the heart of all these emotions.

When she had first brought Minoru into room 404, she said that she and Sanae had been the ultimate combination of offense and backup. However, Igniter's oxygen deprivation attack had fractured one of their wings. Ever since, Sanae had been in a vegetative state, continuing to breathe only because of the Third Eye in her body. Yumiko believed that this was because of her own weakness. What's more, she believed that Sanae remained in this state somewhere between life and death because

Yumiko couldn't fight alone to her own satisfaction, lagging behind Suu Komura in her ability to succeed in battle.

And now she was tormenting herself with the belief that she had to defeat a multitude of Ruby Eyes on her own in order to resolve Sanae's worries.

Of course, Minoru had no way of knowing the cause of Sanae's comatose state. Yumiko's guess could even be correct, though it could just as easily be wrong. But it pained him to see Yumiko feeling that way—to see her crying like this in front of him.

She's hurting, he realized somewhere deep in his mind. *I'm not the only one in pain. Yumiko... No, Suu, Olivier, and the Professor, too...all of them carry the pain of their own wounds. All of us.*

This concept was incredibly foreign to Minoru. For as long as he could remember, he had seen other people only as potential threats who held the ability to hurt him.

But maybe he had been wrong. Maybe everyone carried a fragile heart inside a protective shell, sometimes colliding and hurting one another. At the very least, he knew that he had caused the tears that Yumiko was now crying in front of his eyes. And in that way...

This person isn't a stranger.

The feeling rose up in his heart out of nowhere, then faded as quickly as it came. Minoru held his breath, trying to hold on to the lingering traces of that feeling.

This is it.

This was what he'd felt in his heart the time he protected Yumiko from the explosion or when he and Suu attempted the experiment in his room. It was quiet and invisible, yet seemed to contain within it some strong desire.

"Yumiko...," Minoru said quietly. The crying girl's shoulders twitched, and her weeping abated slightly. "I think...if we tried right now..."

Yumiko raised her head slightly, her cheeks wet with tears, and Minoru looked steadily into her eyes. But before he could continue, the sound of a buzzer blared sharply through the speaker in the wall. Then it was quickly followed by DD's voice, which sounded full of tension.

"This is DD. Oli and I were just out patrolling the city, and we detected a Ruby Eye scent on Kasuga Street!"

"Is it Trancer?!"

"N-no. I've sensed this Ruby Eye only once before... I think it's her. *Liquidizer*..."

"What?!" The Professor's voice cut in over DD's, sounding strained. "Be careful—don't get any closer to her! Just keep plenty of distance between you and follow her scent. Don't let her notice you! Yukko, Mik-kun...and Hinako, please come to the fifth floor at once!"

* * *

"How is your wound doing, boy?"

In response, Trancer gave a strained smile. "Please refrain from calling me that. We're not master and apprentice anymore, you know."

"Oh? But you must still be a novice to have gotten such a deep wound, ah...Mikawa." A sarcastic smile painted on her red lips, Mikawa's visitor—the executive of the Syndicate, Liquidizer—paused a moment before calling him by his name. However, the smile was quickly replaced with a frown. "Goodness, though, why did you choose such a flashy name?"

"Flashy? That's harsh. *Mi* as in 'three' and *kawa* as in 'river'; it's a reference to the River of Three Crossings, which the dead cross to get to the afterlife. Haven't you heard the phrase 'raindrops fall from the Sanzu River'?"

"Hmm... No. What is that supposed to mean?"

"It means that as soon as you take a single step outside, you never know what dangers await you."

"I see. Well, you've certainly demonstrated that with this little incident."

With another cynical smile, Liquidizer tossed one of the two paper bags she was carrying onto Mikawa's bed. A bundle of gauze, a roll of bandages, and a small bottle of ointment rolled out onto the blankets.

Returning the sarcastic smile, Mikawa picked up the items and looked down at his own body. Bloodstained bandages were wrapped tightly around his bare chest. That was the spot where Divider had opened up three of his ribs two days ago. Fortunately, his lung hadn't been torn, but it was still an unquestionably serious wound; even two days later, his chest still ached with every breath he took.

Unwinding the bandages with his left hand, Mikawa glanced at Liquidizer. "...This is going to be pretty tough to replace all by myself."

"I'd imagine so."

"...I'd certainly be very grateful if you helped me with it."

"I don't wanna. It'd be a pain."

Having expected that response, Mikawa smirked again. He couldn't really complain. After all, when he had come crawling pathetically back to the hideout from Aoyama Cemetery, the enigmatic woman before him had treated his wounds, even using her liquefaction ability and medical adhesive to temporarily repair his broken ribs.

Crumpling up the used bandages and tossing them into the trash, Mikawa peeled the clinging gauze away from the wound, causing fresh blood to ooze forth. However, the wound had already healed considerably in just two days. This was probably thanks to his Third Eye enhancing his body's healing abilities, but the admirable precision of the cut he'd received from Divider's ridiculous sword probably helped, too.

Mikawa slathered antibiotic salve onto the wound, applied the gauze, and began with some difficulty to attempt wrapping the bandages. Then, Liquidizer shot him a bewitching smile.

"Oh yes...but I suppose if you'll do me one small favor, I could be persuaded to help you."

Without waiting for a response, she strolled over to the kitchen in the corner of the drab room and produced a mineral-water bottle from the fridge. Taking a crystal glass from the cabinet nearby, she poured the water into it.

"If you would be so kind."

Mikawa looked at the glass and shrugged slightly. Pushing down the pain as he sucked in air, he puckered his lips and blew a light, thin breath toward it. There was no apparent change to the water inside, but a distinctive *kshhh* resounded in the air.

"...Done."

At Mikawa's words, Liquidizer tilted the glass in her left hand over the sink. The water flowed out in a thin stream, and she skillfully flicked the glass upright before the rest of its contents could be emptied. What remained at the bottom was a handful of perfectly round, transparent spheres about five centimeters in diameter. Mikawa had frozen them into ice.

Using one's abilities carelessly ran a risk of attracting the attention of the black ones, but the handful of safe houses they had in the metropolitan area were exempt from that rule.

Liquidizer looked satisfied as she held the glass up to the light, watching it play over the spheres of ice for a moment. Then, she reached back into the cupboard, this time producing a bottle of Scotch whiskey, and poured the amber liquid over the ice in the glass. Leaving the kitchen, she sat in the single chair in the room, crossing her long legs. Mikawa forgot the pain of his wound for a moment as he watched his former master.

It was impossible to guess her age. With the dark eye shadow she wore and her red-stained lips, and the proportions of her body that was at least 173 centimeters, one might guess that she was in her late twenties, but her carefully controlled words and mannerisms suggested the maturity of someone slightly older. With her light brown hair done up in a bun, Liquidizer wore her usual suit jacket and tight skirt that were undoubtedly from a high-class brand.

Apparently heedless of Mikawa's gaze, she looked thoughtfully into her glass for a while, then finally brought it to her lips and took a long swig, swallowing the dark liquid down her slim throat. Then she gave a long, contented sigh.

"Delicious. Really, nothing else compares to the ice you make for me, boy. Maybe the shape of the spheres prevents bubbles from forming?"

"I wouldn't know the first thing about what makes alcohol good or not," Mikawa answered with a shrug, turning his back toward her. "More importantly, you'll help me out now, right?"

"Don't be such a wet blanket. This is thirty-year-old Dalmore Scotch, you know."

Liquidizer huffed, but as promised, she walked over to the bed and began to wrap his bandages around for him. Each time her soft, cold fingertips touched his bare skin, a shiver went up Trancer's spine. But it wasn't a shiver of desire by any means. It was his instincts—or perhaps his Third Eye—warning him how dangerous she was.

Hypothetically, if I had to fight Liquidizer right now, how would I do it?

The thought came to him unbidden as he lay with his back exposed to her.

Mikawa's weapon of choice, water, was readily available in the form of the plastic bottles of mineral water that sat in cardboard boxes in the corner of the kitchen. First, he would convert all of it to steam and disperse it through the room. Then, if he froze the vapor that was touching her, he could encase her in a solid shell of ice...

He had thought it through only this far before Liquidizer reached the end of the roll of bandages, tucking it in lightly at the center of his chest. Then, with one smooth stroke, the end of the bandage vanished, perfectly fused into the bandages below at a molecular level by her liquefaction ability.

"There, all done."

As she pulled away, Mikawa watched her retreating back with a grim smile.

I would lose. At this range, she would surely manage to lay a hand on him before he could finish sealing her into a block of ice. In that instant, Mikawa's body would be liquefied, a level of damage that would make Divider's near-fatal cut seem like a scratch in comparison.

What was truly frightening about Liquidizer's ability was that it worked on everything—even the human body.

Although Mikawa's ability was manipulating the phases of water, he couldn't use it on the liquid content inside a human body, since that did not exist as its own separate entity. He had to be able to recognize the individual water molecules in order to be able to influence them. By the same token, he couldn't use the moisture in soil or anything along those lines. Most likely, these same restrictions had applied to Igniter's manipulation of oxygen as well, since he hadn't been able to use the dissolved oxygen that exists in people's blood.

But Liquidizer was different. With a single touch, she could liquefy any solid object, whether the target was inanimate or a living thing. In other words, she could turn any part of a human body into protein soup just by touching it. If it was an arm or a leg that she touched, the target might be able to survive, but if she were able to melt even part of their head or torso, it would mean instant death.

Thus, in order to stand a chance in battle against her, one would have to maintain a safe distance at all times so as to avoid being touched. In this small room, victory would be impossible. The ideal battlefield would be a large, open space with plenty of water around. *Like a beach, for instance...*

"Would it kill you to at least thank me, boy?" Liquidizer smiled as she returned to her chair. Immediately putting aside that line of thought, Mikawa returned the smile and bowed his head.

"My apologies. Thank you very much for your help."

"It'll take more than a glass of Scotch on the rocks next time, understand?"

"I guess I'll have to learn some new tricks, then... Anyway, I've been wondering, what's in the bag?" Mikawa pointed at the second paper bag that Liquidizer had with her, hoping that perhaps she'd brought him a get-well gift of pastries from a famous bakery or the like.

"Oh, this?" Instead, what she produced from the brown bag was a large, battered old video camera.

Mikawa frowned. "What do you have that for? Do you have a secret filmmaking hobby or something?"

"Don't be ridiculous. As a matter of fact, I made a quick stop at the hospital before I came here today."

"The hospital...?"

"That's right. I was paying a visit to that old man who sadly missed his chance to join our ranks not long ago."

Mikawa's eyes widened. "Igniter...?! B-but why now? He's lost his Third Eye and all his memories of being Igniter, hasn't he...?"

"Really, it's cruel of them, those Jet Eyes. Turning our people back into helpless, purposeless humans... It would be far more merciful just to kill them."

"...Don't tell me you...killed him...?"

Liquidizer gave an uncharacteristic laugh in response to Mikawa's nervous question. "Ha! Of course not. Why would I do something so utterly pointless? No, I went with Empathizer to see if there were any traces of his memories left in some corner of his mind."

Upon hearing that name, Mikawa instinctively grimaced.

"That Peeping Tom? Sounds pointless to me. There's never been a case of a former Ruby Eye retaining their memories after undergoing the black ones' treatment, right?"

The ends of Liquidizer's red lips turned upward in a mysterious smile, and she tossed the video camera over to Mikawa, who barely managed to catch it in midair. Surprised by its heaviness, he checked the logo and realized that, far from being a digital camera, it was a long-outdated Hi8 camcorder, which used an analog tape.

"Play it and have a look."

Mikawa cocked his head doubtfully as he opened up the LCD video panel and pushed the playback button. At first, all that appeared was a sandstorm of gray. Occasionally, the grains would clump together as if about to form a shape, but then they would turn back into noise.

"I don't see anything…," Mikawa began, but at that moment, a noise rang through the tinny speakers and a faded image came into view on the screen.

The light swayed unsteadily. It was a body of water. Reflected in its surface, a sandy beach and a few somewhat shoddy palm trees could be seen. But this wasn't a tropical island. Judging by the metal beams and glass barriers in the background, it was a pool meant to look like a beach.

On closer inspection, about half the palm trees were broken in the middle, and most of the glass was in pieces as well. It looked like the aftermath of a huge explosion.

Suddenly, a man's voice cried out hoarsely, "UNFORGIVABLE!!" A cut and bleeding left hand came into the frame. Its clawed fingers were outstretched toward two hazy figures standing huddled together some distance away.

The owner of the hand was most likely Igniter. And the two he was aiming his finger at must have been the black hunters.

A red light surged out from the center of his outstretched hand. The steam that surrounded the two figures was pulled away in an instant. This was Igniter's ability to manipulate oxygen; he had taken away all of the oxygen molecules from the air surrounding the two black hunters. In seconds, they would collapse to the floor, suffering in agony.

However…

"…Why?" Igniter growled, speaking the same question that was on Mikawa's mind.

Surrounded by the shallow water, the two black agents were still standing, undisturbed. There should have been no breathable air around them, yet they didn't show the slightest sign of discomfort.

"WHYYY?!" Igniter's voice rose to a scream of rage. He clenched his outstretched hand, fresh blood spurting from countless wounds.

At that moment, one of the two black hunters took a single step forward.

It was just one motion, and yet it sent both of the black agents, now holding on to each other, flying straight toward the screen at a terrible speed, as if propelled by boosters in their shoes. The pool water was scattered to their left and right, forming a tall column of water. Despite the fact that he was watching this on a tiny screen, Mikawa instinctively leaned away.

The image was too blurry to distinguish facial features, but the pair of hunters appeared to be a young man and woman. Approaching at breakneck speed, their shoulders slammed into Igniter, and the video immediately cut to black.

"...Is this video...?" After a long silence, Mikawa finally spoke. "Is this what they call 'psychic photography'? Empathizer can not only see people's memories, but he can do *this*...?"

"That's right. Although it doesn't work with digital cameras, for whatever reason. You wouldn't believe what a pain it was to track down this ancient thing."

Mikawa nodded slowly, looking at the Hi8 in his hands. Then he rewound the tape to watch Igniter's memories again from the beginning. One-sided though it may have been, Mikawa had felt kinship and respect toward him because of their similar abilities, and so hearing Igniter's bloody scream made his own heart ache with pain.

If only I had been there...

With that much water at his disposal, Mikawa could have taken on any number of black agents.

But the same should have been true of Igniter. It was clear that the explosion at the indoor pool at Ariake Heaven's Shore had been the work of his oxygen-manipulating powers. How had those two black hunters survived such a powerful explosion?

"We won't be able to say much until we've analyzed that footage at the hideout...," Liquidizer commented in a somewhat sultry voice, as if sensing Mikawa's misgivings. "But what do you think? There was something awfully strange about the way the water moved when those two were charging, don't you think?"

"Ah...really?" Knitting his brow, Mikawa squinted at the blurry images. Now that he looked again, the water at the black agents' feet during their high-speed approach did seem to be spraying out far higher than it should. Yet their feet, which should be splashing through the water, didn't seem to be making contact with it at all.

"…It's wind pressure, right? Like a hovercraft…"

"That's right. Or possibly some kind of barrier…"

"Barrier…?" Mikawa tilted his head uncertainly, trying to grasp her meaning.

In response, Liquidizer swirled her now-drained glass, the still-solid ice clinking against the sides. "An invisible wall, like this. It could be made of something transparent, like glass or ice…"

"It's probably not either of those, if this barrier protected those black hunters from Igniter's explosion."

"Well, like diamond or orichalcum, then."

Liquidizer spoke as she poured herself another glass of whiskey.

"But whatever the case may be, let's assume the male hunter is the one who made this barrier that was strong enough to withstand the explosion at the pool."

Mikawa raised his hand slightly. "The male? Why him?"

"The girl with the long hair most likely has a movement-related ability. The Jet Eye who stabbed Mr. Igniter with a knife fairly fit her description. And if it was her ability that launched them forward with a single step, the barrier must be his ability… At any rate, Trancer, how do you suppose you would fight a Jet Eye with the ability to create a barrier as strong as diamond?"

Mikawa thought for a moment, then gestured with his left hand dismissively. "I wouldn't. If he can make diamond out of the carbon in the air whenever he likes, I'd join forces with him and make a killing in the diamond industry."

"Oh my. You'd come up against the De Beers company, then."

"Sounds like fun to me… All jokes aside, well…assuming we're in a place with plenty of water around, I suppose I'd bury him under ice, barrier and all, and wait for him to run out of oxygen?"

"Hmm. And what if he had a high-capacity oxygen cylinder with him?"

"I'd wait for that to run out, then. Or for him to die of thirst or starvation."

Liquidizer raised her glass wryly. "A toast to your remarkable patience, then, boy. But I suppose burying him in ice does sound like it would work…"

"You know, master, I can't help but detect a note of reluctance in your voice," Mikawa commented with an equally wry smile. "I mean, if it was you fighting him, it'd be over once you touched the barrier whether it's diamond or anything else, right?"

"As long as it's a solid material...yes." Liquidizer's eyes narrowed, and she brought her glass to her lips, downing the rest of the amber liquid in one go. Then she carelessly held it away from her body.

Splish. With a little noise, the glass melted into a transparent liquid and dripped down onto the floor. Mikawa watched with a shudder as the pool of liquid immediately solidified back into a pane of glass.

Afraid Liquidizer would sense the fear oozing from his heart, Mikawa quickly snapped the camcorder's screen into place. "This thing is a pain to close," he complained. Liquidizer only smirked in response, so he attempted to change the subject. "So, in order to get this footage, you and Empathizer must have used your abilities in Igniter's hospital, correct? Is that going to be all right? They might sense you were there and use that to come after us..."

"The information we gained was worth the risk. Besides, I left some bait for those Jet Eyes elsewhere. I'm sure those little dogs are sniffing around in the wrong place even as we speak."

* * *

Yumiko had informed him that she would catch up after washing her face, so Minoru left room 404 on his own.

The curious feeling that had been born in the depths of Minoru's heart shortly before they'd received DD's communication had vanished, leaving only the faintest echoes behind. As he walked toward the elevator, Minoru struggled to remember that moment.

She's not a stranger.

Those few simple words seemed to reverberate through his mind. But the more he tried to grasp their meaning, the further away he seemed to get from the revelation he'd had just a few minutes ago.

A person who's not a stranger.

Certainly, he now knew about Accelerator Yumiko Azu's secret pain, which she'd kept locked away in her heart all this time. In that respect, Yumiko was far from being someone unfamiliar. But what did that make her, then? A friend? A partner? A comrade?

None of those words seemed to capture the feeling he was looking for.

Perhaps he would have been able to explain it at that moment, but right now he couldn't put it into words at all.

However, there was one thing he knew. The key to his ability to take someone into his protective shell lay in Minoru's perception of that person. It could be that the moment his emotions were synchronized with the other person's, they would stop being a foreign substance that the shell inherently rejected.

"My emotions..."

Minoru murmured while pressing the elevator's up button. In other words, taking something into his heart and reacting to it...which would also mean the creation of new memories. Ever since his family had died eight years ago, he had stubbornly avoided making any new memories with others, keeping his distance from everyone and refusing to even look people in the face when speaking with them.

The reason for this was that he was afraid of the thoughts of him that would be created in others' minds and the memories of others being created in his own. Just imagining feeling strong negative feelings toward others, or being scorned, ostracized, or hated by them, was enough to make his limbs go cold and his chest tighten. Some adults might say that this was just human nature and it was best not to worry about it, but Minoru knew there was no limit to the malice that can be born in a human heart.

As the elevator doors slid shut and it began its ascent, Minoru clenched his sweating hands. Other people were terrifying. It was impossible to know when they might turn on you.

And he was afraid of himself, too.

At any moment, his human heart could give in to those same malicious impulses.

Therefore, Minoru fundamentally wanted to avoid having any feelings at all toward other people. He didn't want to know anything about them. He didn't even want to be in the same room as them. That private desire may very well have been the source of his protective shell ability. Not fear or rejection of others, but the desire to be separated from them.

But if that was the case, what was the feeling that arose when he was able to bring another person inside the shell?

Minoru was still wrapped up in his anxious thoughts as he arrived at the fifth floor, changed into slippers, and walked toward the west side of the room. Passing by the TV area and the bookshelves, he walked into the research area where Professor Riri Isa was waiting.

"...Yumiko will be here shortly," he said to the Professor, who was staring at the monitor. Walking over to the eight folding chairs lined up in the room, he sat on the only one that had a pink cushion on the seat.

"...?"

Something felt strange. For a cushion, the surface was strangely elastic; the back of the chair was extremely soft. On top of all that, the chair was giving off a faint, sweet scent. One that he felt like he'd smelled somewhere recently...

"Hello, Minoru."

A voice spoke from directly behind him.

Minoru sprang out of the chair with an unbecoming shriek, stumbling as he turned to stare at it. At the same time, a faint whooshing noise came from that direction. As if materializing from thin air, Refractor Suu Komura suddenly appeared in the chair that Minoru had plunked himself onto just moments ago. A startled Minoru toppled backward and landed on his rump on the floor, where he sat staring.

Suu was again dressed in a one-piece and leggings, similar to her outfit from the other day, but with her hair tied up in a dainty ribbon. Her face, as lovely and elfin as ever, showed the faintest smile for just a moment as she spoke. "This cushion is meant to indicate where I'm sitting. Please keep that in mind in the future."

"R-right." Minoru nodded automatically, then finally realized what had just happened: He'd sat down with all his weight on Suu's lap. His nodding immediately switched to a rapid shake of the head, his hands flailing frantically. "S-s-s-s-sorry, I'm so sorry! I should have noticed... Um, please forgive me!" He apologized profusely, his voice shrill, but Suu simply shrugged noncommittally.

"Don't worry. The weight was nothing compared to when you got on top of me in your bed before."

"...Oh?"

The Professor raised her eyebrows, turning from the monitor. Minoru felt the blood draining from his face, and he shook his head hurriedly.

"D-d-during the experiment!" he explained fumblingly. "We had no choice...for safety...um—"

Suu cut in smoothly. "Also, compared to the forty-plus seconds it took you to get my smartphone out of my breast pocket, the amount of time was nothing, either."

"...Oh-ho?"

Get me out of here!

Minoru screamed silently, about to instinctively activate his protective shell, when the elevator creaked behind him. Instantly, there was another whoosh as Suu vanished into the air. Now that he knew she was there, he could see an indent in the pink cushion where she was sitting.

"...What are you up to now?"

"N...nothing, really...," Minoru mumbled sheepishly, slinking into a different chair.

Glancing to his right, Yumiko caught sight of the pink cushion and gave a slight nod, her expression steady. "Hello, Komura."

A response came immediately from the seemingly empty air above the cushion. "Hello, Azu." Looking away, Yumiko took the seat to Minoru's left. Immediately, as if he'd been waiting for the three to assemble, DD's strained voice came through the speaker.

"This is DD. We've arrived at the area where Liquidizer seems to have used her power. She's already long gone. But...it's very strange."

"What is?" the Professor asked quickly, speaking into the microphone on top of the desk. After a moment, a response came not from DD but from Olivier.

"...Nobody's been killed."

"What...? It wasn't a murder?" The Professor's pigtails swayed as she spoke slowly and dubiously. "Then what did they do...?"

"It was a robbery. In fact, it looks like something out of a Hollywood heist movie. Looks like that woman used her liquefaction ability to melt a giant hole in the wall of a bank and enter the vault."

Olivier's words stunned all of them into silence, their eyes wide, with the obvious exception of Suu, whose expression wasn't visible.

"So does that mean...they stole a bunch of gold...?"

"Well, about that..."

DD's voice returned to continue his report. "The site of the robbery was the Yamato Bank branch near Ootsuka Station, but of course it was already all blocked off by the police...though we tapped into the police radio and heard them say that none of the money was missing.

Apparently they just went through the safe-deposit boxes and stole some of their contents."

"Safe-deposit boxes, huh…? Hmm. Then it'll be tough to figure out what exactly they stole."

"Yeah. Even the bank staff don't usually know what the customers are keeping in their safe-deposit boxes…"

"Hmm…" The Professor folded her arms over her lab coat and leaned back in her high-back chair, closing her eyes. Behind her smooth forehead, her speculation ability was likely hard at work. Her eyes still closed, the ten-year-old commander spoke as if thinking out loud. "Liquidizer was probably after just a single item and used the other safe-deposit boxes for a diversion. And if she was willing to risk us detecting her use of her abilities, the item was probably very important to the Syndicate's goal of a widespread attack on humanity…or was something to help them exterminate the SFD."

The Professor's eyes snapped open, and she shifted her gaze to the round analog clock on the wall. "But wait… Why now? It's not even four o'clock yet. There would still be the risk of passersby seeing them, and bank clerks, too. Why would they break in at that time?"

"Maybe it's just their Ruby Eyes arrogance…?" Yumiko spoke up, her eyes narrowed and her voice quiet and hard. "They don't even see ordinary humans as people anymore. Couldn't it be that they just didn't care if there were eyewitnesses, since they could kill anyone who got in their way…?"

"Hmm…I'm not so sure about that. Judging by the data we've collected so far, Liquidizer is a coolheaded pragmatist. She would have everything planned to a T, without a single unnecessary action. It would obviously be much easier to break in to a bank at night than during the day. That woman would surely have known that, so deliberately choosing daytime—and the fact that she made a hole in the other wall to begin with… There must have been a reason. Which means…"

The Professor pressed her middle finger to her temple, then continued in a more forceful tone. "Which means it wasn't every safe-deposit box but one that was the diversion… They *all* were. This entire break-in was meant to distract us—it was bait to attract DD's senses!"

Everyone in the room, as well as DD and Olivier over the speakers, was shocked into silence. After a moment, Minoru ventured a dumb-founded question. "You mean...at the same time, the Ruby Eyes were up to something else in some other place?"

"So it would seem. And I'm willing to bet that what they did there wasn't a murder, either. If it was, I doubt they would've gone so out of their way to distract us from it." With her speculation ability at full throttle, the Professor rattled off deductions:

"Whatever they were doing, and wherever they did it, they didn't want us to find out about it. And it was something they could do only during daytime. No...most likely, a place that they could get into only in the daytime." She whirled in her chair to face Minoru and Yumiko. "What sorts of places come to mind that you can enter only until about three or four p.m.?"

"Other banks," Yumiko guessed immediately.

"The post office," Suu suggested, still invisible in her seat.

"...School?" Minoru offered uncertainly.

I feel like there's someplace else...

As he racked his brain, the young women to his left and right continued firing off ideas in succession:

"A ward office."

"Museums."

"Art galleries."

"Hospitals."

"That's it!" the Professor shouted, half leaping out of her mesh chair. "There was a report a while ago that one of the former Ruby Eyes who'd undergone Third Eye removal surgery and was in rehabilitation had been contacted by someone possibly from the Syndicate. If that's what happened here, then the target must have been..."

The Professor grabbed the receiver of the landline phone off the desk, hitting a speed-dial button. As soon as it connected, she fired off a rapid question, then snapped her fingers when the person on the other end responded. With a hasty thank-you, she hung up the phone, the traces of a triumphant smile on her lips.

"Bingo. Today at three thirty p.m., at the Harbour Ward Hospital, the patient Yousuke Nakakubo—in other words, the former Igniter—had a visitor for the first time."

"What?" This time it was Minoru who half rose from his seat. "Don't tell me they…k-killed…"

"If that were the case, they'd have no reason to cover their tracks. No, Nakakubo is safe. However, one of the nurses witnessed something strange. Apparently, the man who visited Nakakubo was recording his face with a video camera while he slept. I'm not sure why, but that recording must somehow contain information valuable enough that Liquidizer staged a bank heist in order to acquire it in secret."

The Professor then leaned over and spoke into the microphone, her voice full of conviction. "DD, Oli-V. Forget about the bank. Sorry, but can you head straight over to the hospital where Nakakubo is being kept? I need you to get a hold of the surveillance camera footage. I'll make the arrangements with the Ministry of Health, Labor, and Welfare now."

* * *

Walking out of the building that served as a Syndicate safe house, Mikawa paused and looked back for a moment. It really did look like a harmless five-story building. Rain stained the concrete outer walls black, and there was a dust cloud gathered at the entrance.

However, the inside bore no resemblance to the decrepit exterior. For reasons unclear, one could use Third Eye abilities inside the building as much as one pleased without fear of detection by the black hunters. Presumably, this was thanks to some kind of device set up in the walls.

At one point, Mikawa had asked Liquidizer how it all worked. But a knowing smile had been her only response.

There were still many things he didn't know about the Syndicate. He had been a part of it for about two months now, yet he didn't even know how many members it had, and he'd never met the group's leaders.

However, none of that ultimately mattered to him. The Syndicate provided Mikawa with shelter and information, without even asking for anything in return. Now that he was independent, they wouldn't come to his rescue if he got into battle with the Jet Eyes, but he was thankful just to have a place like this to nurse his wounds.

Apparently, Igniter had rejected the Syndicate's invitation because he hadn't liked their strict limitations on murder. Mikawa felt the same way, but he also knew that going around killing recklessly was a surefire way to get sniffed out by the black dogs.

Two days ago, he had obtained plenty of kills thanks to an unexpectedly heavy downpour. Even now, if he closed his eyes, he could picture perfectly the sweet spectacle of countless cars crashing into one another and going up in flames. This memory alone could likely sustain him for the next month; he needed time to let his chest wound fully heal, anyway.

And once January came, there would surely be plenty of snowstorms. Snow would mean a much larger buildup on the ground than any rain. If he could come up with some creative new ways to use his power, he was sure he could have even more fun than two days ago. And the humans, who would assume that the havoc he caused was brought on by water's natural phase transitions, would learn just how terrifying and merciless those phenomena could be.

Just as I once learned it firsthand.

And just as my friend continues to experience it, somewhere in the recesses of this city.

Abruptly, Mikawa turned his back on the building and began to walk unhurriedly toward the nearest station, mindful of the wound on the right side of his chest.

✳ ✳ ✳

"Okay...here goes nothing."

"Go ahead," a quiet voice responded from behind Minoru's back.

Minoru glanced briefly at the silently watching Professor Riri and Yumiko, then activated his protective shell in despair.

It's just going to fail again. Suu's going to get thrown into the wall, just like Yumiko did before. The fact that it succeeded in my room was definitely a one-time-only stroke of luck. And my mind is so preoccupied right now...

His head full of such thoughts, Minoru waited a moment in the newly created perfect silence before he slowly, fearfully looked over his shoulder.

But as he looked at the polyurethane foam padding through the pale blue haze, he didn't see a single dent.

"Um…did it…?" he started in a whisper.

Immediately, a voice responded so close to his ear that he jumped.

"Yes, I'm here, Minoru. No matter how many times I experience this…it's still very strange."

"Ah…um, that is… Yes."

Why did it work?!

In his mind, Minoru practically screamed. True enough, he couldn't see Suu Komura right now with her refraction ability activated. And after taking into consideration the failures from a few days ago, they had changed positions so that Minoru stood in front of her instead of behind. But with her pressed so close to his back, he could still feel her body heat and hear her breath by his ear. It could hardly be said that he wasn't aware of her presence.

Could it be that the success or failure of these experiments isn't based on my mentality at all, just on the random whims of my Third Eye itself? …Hey, that's what's going on, right?

He addressed his thoughts toward the Third Eye parasite embedded in his chest. At the same time, he cast a sidelong glance toward his left. Professor Riri was standing by the recording equipment with a look of intense interest on her face, while Yumiko sat a little ways away, fixing Minoru with a bit of a glare.

This in spite of the fact that she herself had suggested they attempt to re-create the experiment while they waited for DD and Olivier's reconnaissance report. And directly beforehand, she had whispered privately in Minoru's ear, "It's not as though I'm hoping for you to fail or anything."

So while he didn't expect her to be thrilled about the experiment's success or anything, he would've appreciated it if she would at least refrain from directing a piercing ice beam at him from her eyes. As this thought was running through his mind, the Professor picked up a small microphone from the desk and spoke into it. The same light-wave communication system they had used for the nuclear power plant mission a few days before was again set in Minoru's left ear, and she made no effort to hide her excitement as her voice flowed through.

"All right! Now please proceed to the second stage of the experiment."

"Huh? Second stage…?" Minoru tilted his head, puzzled.

"That was directed at me," Suu said quietly behind him, equipped with the same communication setup. "The Professor and I made some arrangements earlier."

"Huh…? Suu, what are you…?"

Without answering his question, Suu suddenly wrapped her invisible arms around Minoru's torso. The body heat he could feel on his back intensified, and he stiffened up immediately, only to feel Suu's breath on his right ear as she whispered softly:

"Minoru. I don't know why, or maybe there are a lot of different factors, but…whatever the reason might be, I don't feel afraid of you. Even though I couldn't even show my real appearance to Chief Himi, who I trust and respect…"

"Um…right…," Minoru responded stupidly, unsure how to react to this sudden confession.

Suu continued calmly. "So you shouldn't be afraid of me, either."

"Huh…? Of course I'm not a-afraid…"

"The day before yesterday, I said that your sight line was transparent. But to be honest, it did have a very slight hint of color…the faintest tint of gray. Black…is the color of fear. I think that if I could see my own sight line, it would be as black as ink."

"…Black…," Minoru repeated dazedly, forgetting all about the Professor and Yumiko watching them nearby. But it made sense. There was no doubt that Suu Komura was still a stranger to him. No matter how similar their abilities were or how much he sympathized with her pain, he still couldn't read her thoughts and feelings. For all he knew, underneath her cool facade, she could secretly be laughing at him, scorning him, despising him—

"…!!"

Minoru gritted his teeth, forcibly cutting himself off from that line of thought. If he was doubting whether Suu might secretly hold malice toward him, that was virtually the same as having malicious thoughts toward her himself.

"…I'm sorry. I don't know if I can stop being afraid of you…of *anyone* entirely," Minoru murmured dejectedly into the silence that was otherwise broken by only the mysterious, rhythmic noise. "But…for what it's worth, I believe you. That you're not afraid of me."

"Thank you."

Suu's quiet words were carried into his ear on a warm breath. Then she spoke more loudly into the headset. "All right, I'm going to start now."

Whoosh. Minoru heard a quiet noise like static. Then he saw his body—from his head to his feet, complete with his hooded jacket, jeans, and all—vanish into thin air. "Wh...wha—?!" he yelped, waving his right hand in front of his face, but he could see nothing there, no matter how hard he focused. He could feel the wind pressure when he blew on his hand and his skin when he touched his nose and cheeks, but he definitely couldn't see any part of his body at all.

"Did you... Is this..."

"Yes, it's my refraction ability. The visible light all around you is avoiding your body, making you completely transparent. Aside from your pupils, that is."

"You mean... Suu, you can apply your ability to other people, too...?" Minoru asked in a hushed voice, but he felt Suu shaking her head by his right shoulder.

"No...not just anyone. Until now, the only other person I've been able to make vanish with me is my brother."

"Your brother...?"

Minoru repeated what she said, realizing that although he knew that Suu had an older brother, he didn't know anything about him: his name, his age, or his ability. However, this must mean that Suu didn't feel any fear toward her older brother, either. This seemed like it would be natural, but she had said a few days ago that she was even afraid of both her parents.

Minoru's thoughts were interrupted by a movement on his left, and he turned to look. The Professor was smiling complacently, giving them a thumbs-up.

"...Well, I'll deactivate my ability now. We'll just have to look forward to finding out what happens when I activate it fully next time."

As Suu spoke, Minoru's body came back into view. He deactivated his protective shell as well, and exhaled deeply when he felt Suu's body heat pull away from his back. Just as he looked up, he heard the Professor shout.

"All right! Mikkun, Hinako, great job!"

"Ah...um, thanks..." Minoru nodded absently, shifting his gaze to her left to see Yumiko, her expression even more dangerous now. The Professor seemed to have forgotten all about the situation from just two hours ago, in which Yumiko had stormed out and she herself had sent Minoru after her.

"Ah...errr, um..."

I have to do something about this.

He racked his brain desperately, a stiff smile on his face as he fumbled for words. "U-um, but this combination of isolation and refraction isn't really all that useful, right? Suu's ability on its own is enough for surprise attacks and stuff without mine..."

"Not at all, Mikkun!" the Professor responded excitedly, obliviously dashing Minoru's efforts. "Now we'll be able to enact a mission that's been impossible until now!"

"Huh? A...a mission?"

"That's right! A while ago, we were planning to have Hinako go invisible and do some intelligence gathering about the Syndicate. But even though Hinako's detection radius is pretty small, there's still the risk of someone noticing her if she gets too close... But with your protective shell thrown in the mix, it's another story entirely. Your protective shell even cuts off the scent that would allow others to detect you, and even if you're found out, you'll be able to escape safely. In other words, with both your powers working in tandem, you can sneak into a Syndicate safe house and find out where their headquarters is. It's a reconnaissance mission!"

As the clock's hand turned past five, DD's worn-out-sounding voice finally came in through the speakers.

"Ahem, this is DD. It was a bit tough, but we finally managed to get copies of the surveillance footage for the day from Nakakubo's hospital. The problem is that the guy who visited him was in disguise... He was wearing a hat, glasses, and a mustache. We can barely make out his face at all."

"Hmm. Well, I suppose that's to be expected," the Professor responded through the desktop microphone. "But having an idea of his height, physique, and gait will still make for very useful data."

Minoru watched the Professor intently, his hand pausing midair with a piece of pancake impaled on a fork. As usual, he'd been coerced into making snacks per Yumiko's orders. They were just simple pancakes using a store-bought mix, but there was a trick to cooking them. As soon as you dropped the batter onto the pan, you had to turn up the heat or else there wouldn't be enough gas and the pancakes would cook into uneven, hard discs instead of fluffy round perfection. It was a technique that Minoru had perfected over years of pancake making.

As he finished up, Yumiko and Suu each took a stack of four pancakes, adding their butter and maple syrup with looks of serious concentration. Though of course, Yumiko's expression was the only one actually visible, since Suu had reactivated her refraction ability, her pancakes seemingly cutting themselves up with an invisible knife and fork.

As Minoru watched in amazement, each portion of her pancakes disappeared as soon as the invisible fork stabbed it. Apparently Suu's ability could even extend to the tools she was using and the objects those tools made contact with.

"...These are delicious. Minoru, you'll make an excellent housewife someday."

"Utsugi's code name is Isolator for a reason, you know," Yumiko countered, already finishing her first pancake.

At that moment, the communication system showed an incoming signal from DD. Apparently unwilling to let her pancakes get cold during the exchange, the Professor took a huge bite before speaking into the microphone again, chewing away as she talked. "Whah abouh the pharking phwot footage?"

"Uh...it kinda sounds like you've got something tasty going on over there."

"Ho-ho!" the Professor exclaimed, gulping down her food. "You've got sharp hearing as well as a good nose, huh, DD? Mikkun made us pancakes!"

"What?! No fair! Why do you guys get homemade snacks when I'm not around?!"

"Fine, I'll save you a bite. So, did you get any more information?"

"...Yeah. The guy's license plate number apparently showed up for a fraction of a second when he drove away."

"Great! It's probably a fake number anyway, but we should be able to track his movements from today at least with the N System! What's the number? Okay...okay...yep, got it! Thanks for going to all that trouble!" Ending the call, the Professor continued eating with the fork in her left hand while skillfully manipulating the keyboard with her right.

Minoru's brow furrowed, and he leaned over to Yumiko to reluctantly ask yet another stupid question. "Um...what's the 'N System' again?"

"It's a network set up by the police that monitors the main roads in the city and automatically records the license plate numbers of the cars that pass by. Even if the number in question is fake, it should be recorded by the system anyway, so that we can track where it went and what roads it used."

"Ahh...I see. So we can use that to figure out where Igniter's visitor came from and where he went...?" Instinctively, Minoru looked over at the Professor's back as she tapped away at the keys. It was hard to tell as her pigtails bounced around on her small back, but their tiny commander's speculation ability really was incredible. She had guessed correctly from a tiny hunch that the bank incident had been a diversion, figured out that their enemy had actually been visiting Igniter, and now she was even able to track that enemy's movements.

Just as Minoru thought this with a small, private sigh of admiration, the Professor suddenly waved her fork in the air without looking up from the monitor.

"Mikkun, more pancakes!"

"I agree."

Startled, Minoru turned to see Yumiko assenting with a deadly serious expression.

"It's really one of the greatest benefits of the Third Eye that no matter how much you eat, the extra calories will all be consumed by the parasite instead of turning into fat."

"You're absolutely right," a quiet voice agreed from a seemingly empty chair, and a single now-empty plate floated over to Minoru all on its own.

4

It was the morning of December 31, New Year's Eve, and Minoru was already getting rattled about on the JR Saikyou line train.

He had a feeling that Norie was growing suspicious about his frequent trips into Tokyo, but for whatever reason, she had seen him off with a smile and a "Have a good day!" without questioning him about where he was going. *Maybe she's got the wrong idea about me and Suu and thinks that has something to do with it...*, he thought, hanging on to one of the overhead straps.

Technically, he *was* going to see Suu, so that made him feel a little less guilty. Still, he got the feeling that letting Norie carry on with her misunderstanding was setting himself up for an eventual catastrophe.

I guess I really should consider moving to headquarters...but how would I explain that to Norie? Minoru worried to himself as he got off at Nishiwaseda Station, walked along Suwa Road to arrive at SFD Headquarters, and took the elevator to the fifth floor.

He still couldn't believe his orders.

"Huh?! Sneaking into the enemy's base...?!"

Minoru nearly stumbled backward in surprise, but the Professor just smiled and nodded.

"Yup. It's the reconnaissance mission I was talking about yesterday. We got a perfect hit on the number we got from that car in the N System. Using security camera footage, we've tracked him to a specific parking lot. The company that was registered as owning the lot was totally bogus, but there was a building nearby registered under the same company name. Most likely, that building is the Syndicate safe house we've been looking for!"

Her voice full of excitement, she snapped her fingers and rapidly continued to explain.

"The timing of this with the fact that we just successfully combined your and Hinako's powers has got to be some kind of divine intervention. As long as you activate your powers some distance away, you should be able to totally avoid the detection-radius issue. Then, you can stay invisible as you approach the building in question, sneak inside, and gather as much information as you can! If we're lucky, we might even find a clue that'll lead us to their headquarters!"

"Uh...I see...," Minoru mumbled, thinking hard. *So, in other words, Suu and I would have to be practically glued to each other the whole time? And one of us would have to cling to the other from behind for...minutes? Hours?*

"Um...wait a second...," he said aloud, suddenly frantic, but then an invisible hand clapped him on the shoulder and a voice spoke up from behind him.

"Very well. Let's do our best, Minoru."

It seemed as though Suu was already on standby for the mission. Her voice was as level as ever, without a hint of enthusiasm or trepidation.

"'Do our best'...? But..." Alarmed, Minoru looked over his shoulder to face the spot that the voice had come from, gesturing frantically.

"But if we're going to go in without being detected, we'll have to activate the shell far away from the building...wh-which means you'll have to stick super close to me the whole time! Ah, I mean, um, not that I mind, but, uh..."

"I don't mind, either."

"..." Minoru was flummoxed for a moment before he rallied his thoughts and tried again. "B-but, um, the protective shell's shape adapts to my movements, so...even if you're staying close to me, you wouldn't be able to walk. In fact, I think maybe the pressure from the shell could end up injuring you... I-it's just too dangerous!"

"No, I think it should be fine." This time, it was the Professor who countered him. "I'm still in the process of analyzing the data we gathered yesterday, but to give you an idea...I don't think your shell is the super-hard, solid physical barrier we thought it was."

"Huh? It's...not hard?"

"Of course it is. But it also has a certain level of elasticity. And it's restricted to only one direction."

Minoru blinked, not understanding, and the Professor shuffled closer and held out her right hand. "Listen. When you activate your protective shell, some invisible thing is produced around you, a little over two centimeters away from your body. This barrier is literally impenetrable from the outside. Not even a diamond drill could pierce it, and not even a hydraulic cutter could cut through it."

The Professor waved her hand around near Minoru's body, pretending to be repelled by an invisible barrier, then lightly brushed her hand against him. It tickled a bit, but he did his best to endure it and listen to the rest of the explanation.

"But if something makes contact with you from inside that barrier, those limits don't apply. When you produce your protective shell, your clothes are included inside the three-centimeter space... Remember when I had you try activating your shell with a baseball in your pocket?"

"Y-yes..."

"That ball had a diameter of almost eight centimeters. I was expecting it to be violently ejected from the shell to the point where the seams would be shredded up, but..."

Grinning as Minoru's jaw dropped, she continued, "But that's not what happened. It seems like there was a little pressure, but not nearly enough to damage the ball significantly. So...I tried touching the barrier around the ball, and sure enough, that part of the barrier alone was jutting out. Which means that your shell has a certain amount of elasticity if pressure is applied to it from the inside."

"Elasticity...from the inside...?" Minoru repeated. With the barrier activated, he cautiously attempted to move his right hand outward, but since the shell adapted to his movements, he wasn't able to touch it himself.

"Ah...I think I understand," Suu said abruptly from close behind him.

"When I enter Minoru's barrier, I do feel a slight amount of pressure. It's like being wrapped in some kind of stretchy fabric... Well, no, not exactly. When I touch it from inside, it doesn't stretch at all. It's very hard."

"...What? It doesn't move if you push on it from the inside, Hinako...? How strange. I was sure it would stretch a bit like rubber if you touched it..."

The Professor crossed her arms and started to pace back and forth.

"Um..." Minoru spoke up timidly. "In that case, wouldn't it be better to postpone this 'reconnaissance mission' until we know exactly how it works...?"

"Hrmm...so it's not a property of the shell itself...? Does the elasticity fluctuate...? But what are the parameters for that change? It's not time... Is it the hardness of the object being brought into the shell? I don't think so..."

Realizing it would take some time for her to work her way through her thoughts, Minoru attempted to sneak away, but a polite tap on the shoulder from an invisible finger stopped him. "Professor," Suu said quietly.

The lab coat–clad elementary school student looked up and clapped her hands together, apparently remembering the situation at hand. "Oh, right! Well, whatever the exact nature of the shell might be, if Hinako's body stays in a fixed position relative to yours, it shouldn't be a problem. And so..."

The Professor strolled into the research booth and produced a strange object from the desk, stretching out what looked to Minoru like a heap of tangled cords. It had a series of wide belts that intersected in complicated-looking ways, with padding thrown in somewhere in the mix. There were also several sturdy-looking buckles attached. Overall, it looked like a device for somehow attaching something to something else, but Minoru had no idea what its practical use might be.

"...Um, Professor? What on earth is that?" he asked nervously.

The Professor grinned. "It's a product developed especially by the SFD Equipment Department—the back-mounting harness!"

"The back...what?"

"It's incredible! The belts are all made with military-grade aramid fiber, and the pad uses moisture-wicking materials that won't get all sweaty. And the carbon-made buckles are ultrahigh quality and ultralightweight..."

"But...what *is* it?"

"Of course, more primitive versions of this tool have been used in Japan since ancient times. I guess back then they would've called it a baby carrier!"

Minoru was silent for a moment. Then, he made another attempt to escape the room, this time at full speed, but he was stopped again by Suu's hand.

Lane six, South Aoyama, Harbour Ward, Tokyo.

That was the location the N System had pinpointed as a Syndicate safe house.

Leaving SFD Headquarters, Minoru was now sitting in the backseat of a black Delica D:5 as they drove south down Gaien Higashidori, intently holding his breath.

Eighty percent of the reason he was sweating it out was, of course, nervousness about the reconnaissance mission. However, half of the remaining 20 percent came from the new equipment he held in his hands, the...whatever-it-was harness. And the other 10 percent was thanks to the silent figure in the passenger's seat—Accelerator, Yumiko Azu.

I mean, I understand that we need to have a backup for this kind of mission. But why Yumiko of all people? Wasn't it the Professor who told me to look out for Yumiko's mental well-being in the first place?

The fact that Minoru was now partnering up with Suu Komura certainly couldn't be helping matters there. After all, Yumiko already viewed Suu as her chief rival, and this was being majorly intensified by the fact that Minoru could bring Suu into his protective shell and not her.

So why would the Professor have Suu and me form a team together? What was she thinking...? —Actually, it's entirely possible she's just doing this for her own amusement...

As Minoru was caught up in these thoughts, the Delica came to a stop. For a while now, they had been trapped behind a terribly slow-moving BMW, and as a result, they had been forced to stop at every single traffic light. This was probably not helping the temper of the speed demon Yumiko, and finally, unable to take the atmosphere of persistently rising tension, DD spoke up from the driver's seat.

"Uh, so how about this... Maybe after the recon mission, Utsugi can carry Yumiko piggyback, too?"

OH GOD, WHAT ARE YOU SAYING?!

Minoru screamed inwardly. At the same time, Yumiko simply reached over to the steering wheel and pushed on the horn, producing a long *hoooooonk*.

This was directed at the BMW, which hadn't moved despite the light turning green, but instead of prompting the car's swift departure, it resulted in the BMW's side doors flying open and a group of angry-looking men charging toward the Delica.

"Yeeek!" DD yelped, cutting the steering wheel sharply to the right as he pushed down on the gas pedal. As the car screeched past the men, a series of shouts along the lines of "HEYGETBACKHEREWHERE-DOYOUTHINKYOU'REGOINGYOUASSHOOOOOLE" was audible through the car windows. Accelerating and weaving through traffic, DD didn't slow the car until the BMW had vanished from the rearview mirror. Then he unleashed another shriek.

"What the hell was that, Yumiko?! Those guys were totally Japanese mafia!! That might've been the heir to the family learning how to drive or something!!"

"Well then, they should've put a new-driver sticker on the car,"

Yumiko retorted sullenly. Then, glancing into the backseat, she gave a calm smile.

"I'm sure this goes without saying, but no, there is not a single atom in my body that wants you to carry me on your back."

"R...right."

"Besides, you already basically carried me like a baby in our fight against Igniter, so I have no reason to want you to do such a thing now. Obviously."

With a huff, she faced forward again. Then Minoru heard Suu's quiet voice murmur next to him:

"...Is that true, Minoru?"

"Huh? Um...'like a baby'...? I mean...," he stammered, sure that anything he said could trigger another crisis. Luckily, as he was desperately shifting his gaze back and forth, the Professor's voice came in through the headset in his left ear.

"If we could end this little comedy skit there for now, I'd like to begin preparations. Now, the door to the building we're targeting will most likely be locked, but as long as it's nothing terribly elaborate, the lock-picking gun I set you up with should be enough to open it."

"U-understood," Minoru responded, looking at the building's floor plan that each of them had been given.

The Professor's instructions continued. "Of course, you should be able to confirm any Ruby Eye presences in the building beforehand with DD's ability. I think it should be virtually unmanned, but if that's not the case, we'll change our strategy from reconnaissance to observation and shadowing."

"Gotcha," DD answered.

The car had by now left Shinjuku and entered Harbour Ward; they were probably only a few minutes away from the enemy's location. Minoru glanced out the side window.

Under the cloudy gray sky, the town was virtually deserted, as it was early afternoon on New Year's Eve. Although the heat was on in the car, Minoru still felt a bit of a chill, and he rubbed his hands over his sleeves.

Somehow, Minoru had expected South Aoyama to consist of tidy streets lined with stylish, trendy shops, but as the Delica slowed, all he saw was a slew of gray multitenant buildings. A little farther south, he could see the overhead structure of the Route 3 Shibuya Line, and he heard the distant rumble of cars passing by.

"All right, I'm going to bring us past the building now, so try to remember the way," said DD.

"Right," Minoru responded, turning to watch attentively through the front windshield. The car passed slowly along the two-lane street, which was lined with parking meters. On the large screen of the car's navigation system, the map scrolled along at the same pace, until finally a red marker appeared to indicate their destination.

"That's it on our right. The concrete five-story building there."

DD pointed at a very mundane, commonplace-looking apartment building. It didn't seem to be occupied by any tenants, and there were no signs on the walls. All the windows, too, had the blinds closed from inside. Overall, it was as if the building was hidden away between the slightly larger ones on either side.

"...Since the Professor called it a safe house and all, I was kind of expecting something more...like a fort or a stronghold, I guess," Minoru mumbled.

DD laughed drily. "Wouldn't it defeat the purpose of a safe house if it stood out? Our headquarters don't exactly look like a secret hideout, either, right?"

"It's just a shabby apartment complex," Yumiko added. With her trademark expression of slight irritation, she looked over her shoulder. "Listen. The Professor said to focus on intelligence gathering and avoid combat if possible. Safety is the highest priority here, got it? If you sense even the slightest bit of danger, you're to stay in the protective shell and escape as quickly as possible—jump through a window if you have to."

"R...right, of course." Minoru nodded apprehensively.

"I don't think there's anything to worry about," DD drawled easily. "There aren't any Ruby Eyes within a ninety-one-meter radius of that building. If there were, I could sniff 'em out from this distance whether they used their powers or not."

"And yet you can smell food from a mile away," Yumiko observed mercilessly. Meanwhile, the car passed by the front of the building and stopped in front of a parking meter, just about ninety meters away.

"We'll be on standby right here, and Oli is already in the area keeping watch on the building. If there's an emergency, use the light communicator...or, well, I'd like to say that, but I guess it doesn't work very well when there's stuff in the way of the line..."

"Well, we couldn't very well have set up transmitters all over the place. Apparently the Professor is researching miniaturization technology right now, but...for now, we'll just have to use our phones for communication."

Minoru was only half listening to DD and Yumiko's exchange. He was more worried about his most difficult mission yet, and that wasn't referring to the reconnaissance. It was the SFD-made "back-mounting harness" in his hands. Staring down at it, Minoru mumbled a bit hoarsely, "...Um. Couldn't we, like...tie our legs together like a three-legged race...or like a centipede race or something?"

"I'm not good at either of those," Suu responded coolly.

Minoru's mind was still churning as he clambered into the back of the Delica. In the driver's seat, Yumiko was in her usual blazer, but Minoru and Suu had changed into black jackets reminiscent of some kind of military special-ops uniform. Reluctantly, Minoru fixed the front half of the harness around his shoulders and waist, clicking the buckles into place.

"Go ahead, M-Ms. Komura..."

He turned his back toward Suu's direction, and she responded with a dry "Pardon me," soon followed by a faint, sweet scent, the feeling of something soft, and finally a moderate amount of weight on his back, the three-way assault forcing Minoru's thoughts to grind to a halt—

"Need some help there, Utsugi?" Yumiko inquired sweetly. Minoru flinched and shook his head.

"N-no, thank you! Um, K-Komura, can you get the buckles all right?"

There was an additional round of clattering sounds, followed by a small voice. "I can't reach the ones near your waist."

After two tension-laden minutes, the setup was finally complete, all the belts fastened tightly. Tentatively, Minoru shifted back and forth. The high-tech harness held Suu firmly in place, even without her hanging on.

"O...okay, I'm ready."

"Me, too."

Looking sour as ever, Yumiko nodded and got out of the car first, checking their surroundings. Then she pounded on the rear door, signaling Minoru and Suu to activate their abilities.

"Um…after you, then, Komura," Minoru said, trying to calm down. Near his right shoulder, he felt Suu nod.

"Very well."

There was a whoosh of static, and Minoru's body disappeared from view. Even though he'd experienced it before, it was still very bizarre. He had to reach out with an invisible hand and pat his body to assure himself that it still existed before he spoke again. "O…okay, um…here I go."

But he hesitated for a moment before activating his ability. So far, he had brought Suu into his protective shell only under experimental circumstances, with very little consequences if he failed. This would be the first time they'd attempted it in an actual mission—one that could involve combat with Ruby Eyes.

If he failed now, the barrier would probably break the harness and send Suu flying. If she was thrown into the side of the car, Third Eye user or not, there was no way she wouldn't be injured. In other words, failure was not an option from here on out.

Minoru's back stiffened as the sudden surge of stress overwhelmed him. At that moment, he felt warm breath on his right ear, carrying a quiet voice.

"Don't worry."

It was just two words, but it was enough. Minoru nodded, shook off his hesitation, and activated his protective shell.

The world around him turned blue and silent, and his body floated ever so slightly. To his relief, he could still feel Suu's weight on his back. Minoru tapped on the back door of the car, and Yumiko opened it and took a step back.

With both their powers activated, Suu and Minoru were completely separated from the outside world. Yumiko couldn't see, talk to, or touch Minoru. And yet, Accelerator seemed to look straight into his eyes as she mouthed two words:

"Be careful."

Reading her lips, Minoru nodded. "I will," he said, though he knew she couldn't hear him. Then he began to walk north along the road.

Though it was a walk of only about ninety meters, it was a very strange walk, indeed.

Naturally, Minoru had never gone anywhere while carrying a girl on his back before. It would probably have made a very strange sight, but nobody they passed on the sidewalk so much as glanced at them. Of course, the other pedestrians made no effort to avoid them, either, so Minoru had to give them an extra-wide berth to avoid brushing against them. And out of fear that a bicycle or something might suddenly come up behind them, he looked over his shoulder frequently as well, adding even more time to what should have been a fairly brief journey. Despite all this, they managed to make it to the front of the building without incident, other than a quizzical look from an alley cat.

"...This is the place, right?" Minoru whispered.

"It should be."

Doing his best to ignore the strange feeling of the girl shifting around on his back, Minoru examined the building's rather dark entryway. There was nothing particularly suspicious about it. On the left was an elevator door, and on the right was a staircase.

"I'm going in," he announced shortly, gathering his courage and walking in.

Glancing to the left and right, he decided to start by exploring the first floor.

"...Huh?"

There wasn't one. Aside from the elevator and the staircase, there wasn't a single door or hallway in sight. He thought there ought to be some kind of entrance in the front wall, but there was nothing but a blank concrete surface.

As Minoru looked around uncertainly, he heard Suu's voice behind him. "Minoru. The wall in front of us...it seems different from the walls on the left and right."

"Huh? Really?" He squinted, but as everything was tinted blue by his barrier, it was difficult to tell. Drawing closer, he cautiously pushed on the wall through his shell, but this brought him no closer to any kind of revelation. "You don't think...they figured out that we found this place and sealed off the entrance with concrete or...?" he murmured uncertainly.

"We just found it yesterday, so I don't think they would've had time for that."

"R...right."

"I'm sorry. It must have been my imagination. Let's try the second floor."

Still feeling a bit uncertain, Minoru withdrew from the wall and headed up the dimly lit staircase, emerging into a hallway on the second floor. This time, there was a metal door in the sort of wall he'd expected to see downstairs, and he cautiously approached.

Before they'd entered, DD had confirmed with his prized nose that there were no Ruby Eyes in the building, but it was possible that people unrelated to the Syndicate could be inside. In order to verify that and to unlock the door, he would need to deactivate his ability. Minoru checked that there were no security cameras in the stairwell.

"I'm going to turn off the shell for a moment," he announced as he did so. His body sank back down, the soles of his shoes landing on the floor. Suu, too, deactivated her ability, and the two of them became visible again.

For a moment, both of them focused all their senses on the incoming temperature, sounds, and smells. They felt only the midwinter chill, the noise from the street, and the dry, dusty air of the building; the wild, beastly smell of the Ruby Eyes was nowhere to be found.

Breathing a quick sigh of relief, Minoru pulled out a small mobile phone from his jacket and pressed the speed-dial button that would connect him simultaneously to the waiting car outside and SFD Headquarters. Holding it to his ear, he whispered into the receiver.

"This is Isolator. Refractor and I are now infiltrating the second floor."

There was a short "roger" from the Professor and a "no Ruby Eyes detected" from DD. Minoru promptly ended the call. As he was doing this, Suu, still strapped to his back, was pressing a stethoscope-like device to the wall with her right hand.

"No sounds from inside," she reported, pulling it away. "I don't think anyone is there."

"Ah...all right. I'll open the door, then...," he whispered, reaching into a different pocket. This time, he produced a lock-picking gun and held it to the keyhole. When he pulled the trigger, the gun unleashed a barrage of complexly shaped needles into the hole. After a bit of resistance, he felt them slide all the way through and gently turned the gun to the left.

Click!

The door opened, and Minoru breathed another short sigh. Putting away the gun, he reached out with a thinly gloved hand and turned the doorknob. The door opened away from him surprisingly smoothly.

The other side was shrouded in darkness. All he could see was a faint stream of light from a window much farther down the hall. As the air from inside drifted over him, Minoru caught a faintly familiar scent. It was heavy, sort of like rust...

"...I smell blood," Suu said quietly.

Minoru felt a knot forming in his stomach, but they couldn't very well turn back now. He walked into the entrance hall, closing and locking the door behind him. At the same time, both of them reactivated their abilities, and the metallic smell vanished.

Trying not to think about where that smell had come from, Minoru turned on the small high-luminance LED light in his left hand. A dim circle of white light appeared in the murky darkness.

"It's...sort of like a pretty normal home...," Minoru observed, his voice a low whisper despite the fact that his barrier would lock in any level of noise.

"Like a two-bedroom apartment," Suu agreed on his back. Perhaps sensing his anxiety, she continued, "Don't worry. Nobody's going to ambush us. If anyone was here, I would've seen their line of sight."

"Ah...that's true." Minoru nodded, took a deep breath, and continued into the hallway. This building still had three more floors above this one. There was no sense in wasting too much time on the second floor.

The layout of this floor was that of an ordinary apartment, but it didn't seem very lived in. There wasn't a single pair of shoes or slippers by the entryway. Minoru peeked into the bathroom on the left of the hall, but it didn't appear to be used, either.

Next, he carefully opened a door that was about halfway down the hall. Fortunately, it had a push handle instead of a knob, so he was able to open it without deactivating his shell. This room seemed to be about forty square meters. The first thing his LED light illuminated was a simple pipe bed. There were blankets folded on top of the bedsheets, but in a somewhat disorderly fashion. Unlike the bathroom, it seemed like this room had been used.

Moving the light around the room, Minoru saw a small sink and refrigerator in the corner and a pile of cardboard boxes nearby. When he approached the refrigerator and opened it with some difficulty, he was a bit taken aback by its contents. Bottles of mineral water lined the door, but more oddly, the shelves were full of nothing but glass jars. The jars were painstakingly labeled, but Minoru had no idea what the words meant. As he furrowed his brow, Suu spoke quietly over his shoulder.

"Antibiotics...styptics... They're all medicine. And all of them are for external wounds."

Minoru straightened up and looked in the cabinet above the sink, finding neat stacks of gauze and bandages. The one object that seemed out of place was a small bottle of what looked like whiskey, but he supposed this could also be for disinfecting.

"So this room is...a sickroom...? Or a treatment and recovery room, I guess...?"

"So it seems. It may very well be a place for treating wounds they've incurred in battle with us."

"Then...the blood we smelled before must have come from here..." Instinctively, Minoru pointed his light at the floor, but the smooth resin tiles appeared to be devoid of bloodstains. However, he suspected that if he were to use some sort of powder that reacts with blood like a TV detective might, it would light up the room.

Minoru shuddered a little as he continued to search, but this medical treatment room didn't seem to contain any documents or computers, so they soon moved on to the next room. Minoru was terrified, convinced that the next door would surely lead to a gruesome scene of blood-stained floors or even a corpse. However...

"...Huh?"

The room was almost disappointingly normal. Or more accurately, it was empty.

The thirty-by-thirty-meter room didn't even have a tiled floor, just gray concrete that was beginning to peel. The walls were in a similar state, too, with concrete and exposed plasterboard. The only furnishing was a single LED light that hung from the ceiling.

Minoru gingerly stepped inside, pressing his foot down on various parts of the ground through his shell, but the floor seemed to be of uniform firmness, with no secret hatches or the like to be found.

"...I'm moving on to the next room."

"Go ahead," Suu responded after a moment. It seemed as if she, too, had a gut instinct holding her back, but since the room was clearly empty, they couldn't afford to spend any more time there.

Returning to the hallway, Minoru opened a glass door toward the back end. The interior was very spacious, possibly as much as ninty-one square meters, suitable for use as a living room. However, this room, too, was mostly unfurnished. Light slanted into the room through the blinds of the windows on the south wall, enough so that Minoru decided the LED was unnecessary. He switched it off and put it away, then scanned the room quickly.

"Ah..."

"Ah."

The pair reacted in unison.

Against the western wall of the room, there was a simple desk and chair. And on top of the desk, at last, was what they had been searching for: a slim rectangular shape that was undoubtedly a notebook computer. In addition to the power cable sticking out from the side, there was a LAN cable connected to a port in the wall.

"...We...have to take a look inside, huh?" Minoru commented nervously.

"Of course."

He nodded somewhat reluctantly. In order to operate the computer, he would have to drop his barrier.

Glancing back toward the entrance to confirm there was no movement, Minoru again deactivated his ability. The soles of his sneakers made a soft thump as they came back down to the floor, and the sounds and smells of his surroundings all rushed back in.

It didn't seem like anybody was going to rush in and attack them. He reached into his pocket for the cell phone, but since Suu's ability was still in effect, he couldn't see the screen or his own hands. Luckily, since it was an old flip phone and not a smartphone, he could manage by feeling around the buttons, but it still took him three tries before he managed to call the SFD line again.

"This is Isolator. We've successfully infiltrated the second floor, and we found a laptop. It seems to be connected to the Net."

"Great!" the Professor responded immediately. "Plug the flash drive I gave you into the USB port and boot it up. It should automatically copy all the data and then return the laptop to its regular state. Once the program starts, you'll be able to close the lid without affecting it."

"R-roger."

Wow, I feel like I'm in a movie, Minoru thought, taking the black USB flash drive out of his pocket and inserting it in the port on the side of the laptop. He eased the lid open carefully, causing the LCD screen to light up automatically. It appeared the laptop had only been in standby, not powered off.

With an apparently fast CPU and an advanced SSD, it took only a few moments for the machine to load the desktop. The background was solid black, with only the drab default icons visible. A progress bar appeared automatically, and the light on the flash drive began to flash rapidly.

"Um...copying is under way," Minoru reported. He was closing the lid of the laptop when DD's voice suddenly cut in.

"Ah...oh, shit!" His voice was low and tense through the phone's speakers. "There's a Ruby Eye approaching from the northwest! I can't tell who it is...but they're giving off crazy pressure—my nose is burning up! Isolator, activate your shell right now! They're gonna reach the room you're in in less than a minute!!"

"B-but the data is still..." The small blue light was still flashing frantically. If he activated his shell, he wouldn't be able to collect the drive—and if he pulled it out now, it wouldn't be able to set the PC back to its original state, and the enemy might realize the computer had been tampered with.

"...It doesn't matter; your safety is our top priority. Turn it on now!" ordered the Professor.

"Roger," Minoru responded, immediately activating his protective shell.

Based on the data from their previous battles, Minoru's detection radius—in other words, the range from which a Ruby Eye could smell the activation of his abilities—was about nine meters. If this Ruby Eye was walking toward the living room from the north side of the building, they should be well outside that distance. Thus, the approaching Ruby Eye should still be unaware of Minoru's and Suu's presence. Nonetheless, Minoru headed over to the southwest corner of the room in the blue-tinted silence of his shell.

"...Crouch down, so we're in the shadow of the wall," Suu said unexpectedly. Puzzled, Minoru did so, and she explained, "You and I are mostly invisible right now, but our pupils aren't. If we're up against a light background, it's possible that someone could notice them."

"I-I see…" At this, Minoru's heart began to pound even faster. Just then, Suu reached around from his back and pressed her hands over his heart.

"There's nothing to be afraid of. If it comes down to it, we'll fight. There's no power on earth that can beat ours when we're working together."

"…Yeah." Even through the sturdy harness, Minoru could feel the warmth of Suu's hands, slightly cooler than his own. As if her hands were draining away his anxiety, he felt his heartbeat slowly settling down as he nodded.

A few moments later, the doorknob on the living room's glass door turned slowly.

The only Ruby Eyes Minoru had ever faced down directly were Biter and Igniter. Their ages, physiques, and personalities had been very different, but they'd shared one trait in common: hatred. Both of them had held a seemingly endless level of hatred toward other humans that radiated from them like a poisonous cloud. Even through his protective shell, Minoru had been able to feel that hate.

But the Ruby Eye who was coming through the glass door now was completely different from both Biter and Igniter. Their movements and even the atmosphere they projected were perfectly controlled, not revealing a single hint of information about the Ruby Eye's thoughts.

And there was one more obvious difference: This Ruby Eye was a woman.

"…?!" Minoru let out a loud gasp, then instinctively covered his mouth in a panic before remembering that there was no way for her to hear him through the shell, anyway. Taking a deep breath, he looked at her more closely.

The woman walked toward the sofa on the opposite side of the room from their hiding place as if gliding across the spacious wooden floor. Placing the tote bag she was carrying on the floor, she stretched and gave a long sigh, then walked over to the window and opened the blinds. Light poured into the room, illuminating her body.

She was fairly tall, at least 170 centimeters. Her light brown hair was gathered up in a bun, and she wore a stylish blue-gray suit with a tight matching skirt. Her long legs were clad in glossy tan stockings, and her lovely face could only be described as bewitching. She wore rather heavy makeup, with a long nose and double eyelids rarely found on a Japanese person. She seemed to be in her late twenties, but it was difficult to say for sure.

She's no ordinary person, Minoru's instincts told him, but he was unable to tell what kind of threat she might pose immediately, so he whispered hoarsely to Suu, "Is that…the Ruby Eye…?"

"…I think so," Suu answered, her voice echoing Minoru's uncertainty. "I've never seen her before… It's too bad we can't photograph her."

"Wh…? Oh, right…" Minoru was about to ask why not, but then he worked it out himself. Suu's refraction ability also applied to the clothes she was wearing and objects she was holding, so a phone or camera would also be affected, meaning the light that should normally reflect off it would avoid it instead. In other words, even if they had a camera, its lens would be unable to capture the necessary light.

In that case, we can at least burn her image into our eyes until smoke comes out of them, Minoru thought, focusing on her.

"Huh?!" he yelped suddenly in alarm. Suu had covered his eyes with both hands. The light that should have been flowing into his pupils was now blocked by her hands, so he couldn't see a thing.

"Wh-what are you doing?!"

"Nnng…"

"…'nng'?"

"Nnng." Repeating her mysterious groan, Suu seemed very reluctant as she let go of Minoru's eyes. The sight that awaited him made Minoru jerk backward, nearly headbutting Suu in the face.

The woman who was presumed to be a Ruby Eye was in the process of unzipping her skirt and tossing it onto the floor. Minoru froze in shock and stayed frozen as she proceeded to unbutton her blouse. Even as the white fabric slipped away from her shoulders, he didn't have the mental capacity to look away, rooted to the spot less than nine meters away from the woman as she stripped down to her black underwear.

When the woman tossed her clothes onto the couch and sat down, pulling off her tan stockings, Minoru finally calmed down enough to avert his eyes, his mouth still hanging open. The atmosphere inside the silent protective shell had become unbearably tense. Feeling that he had to do something about this, Minoru cast around for ideas, for a moment contemplating making some kind of joke before quickly giving up on

that plan. His neck creaked as he turned his head to look at the laptop and finally hit upon something to say.

"Ah…i-i-it looks like the USB drive is done copying the data."

On top of the desk in the north side of the room, the USB flash drive had stopped blinking; it seemed it had finished copying the laptop's data and had returned to a state of hibernation.

"…But if she goes to use the computer, she'll notice it's there…"

"…Probably."

Was it Minoru's imagination, or was Suu's tone a bit chilly as she responded, "We should attempt to retrieve it now if at all possible"?

"Y-yeah. But…in order to take it out, I'll have to deactivate the barrier…"

"You can't do it from inside the shell?"

Relieved at least that the conversation had continued, Minoru shook his head slightly. "I…don't think so. Turning a door handle is one thing, but extracting such a small object…"

"…"

Since Suu had fallen silent, Minoru risked another glance toward the sofa. Her stockings removed, the woman was sitting on the sofa in her underwear, a small mirror now set up on the glass table. She took some kind of cream out of her bag and began rubbing it over her face. It looked like she was taking off her makeup—in which case, she would be occupied for some time, giving them a chance to retrieve the flash drive.

After a moment, Suu spoke up thoughtfully. "…I don't think the coefficient of friction for the shell is fixed at zero. You might be able to change it."

"…Change it?"

"Yes. Think about it… When you walk, your feet don't slide around at all. It's much steadier than I'd imagined. Do you remember what the Professor said before this mission? That the shell's elasticity might be changeable?"

"…Y-yes… I guess so, but…"

"If the same is true for its friction…you might be able to change it to suit your needs, so that we can retrieve the memory stick while still in the shell."

"To suit my needs…" Listening to her explanation, he did feel as if it made some sense. When they had infiltrated the Igniter Yousuke

Nakakubo's former home, Minoru had been able to descend the stairs of the flooded basement while still in the shell. The stairs had been slick and moldy, and in theory he would have likely slipped on them even if he hadn't been in his protective shell, but instead his feet had stuck to the rotting steps like suction cups.

If he focused now like he had then, was it possible...?

"...I'll try." Minoru glanced at the sofa again. The woman was busy rubbing cold cream on her eyes, her face turned away from the computer desk.

Minoru rose into a crouch and slowly began to edge along the wall toward the northern side of the room. Spacious though the living room was, the distance to the desk was still only about forty-six meters, but right now that felt incredibly long.

Arriving in front of the desk after about ten seconds, Minoru twisted his body and stretched his invisible right hand toward the laptop. He spread his thumb and index finger out wide and attempted to pinch the USB flash drive in between them.

As he started to glance toward the woman's back again, he heard Suu's voice. "I'll keep an eye on her. You focus on controlling the shell."

"Ah...all right." Minoru nodded and slowly, carefully moved his fingers until at last he felt resistance on his fingertips. *Stick together. Stick together.* Willing his fingers to hold on to the drive, he pulled back his hand, but it slipped right through, with as little friction as oil on glass.

I knew it wouldn't work, he thought with a sigh, then pulled himself together to rethink the situation. *Okay. When I was walking down those stairs, I didn't have any awareness of feeling the surface of the shell or its friction. If anything, I felt as if the soles of my feet were sticking to the ground. So instead of trying to use the shell to grasp it...if I think about holding it with my fingertips...*

Reaching for the USB again, Minoru focused on the nerves in his fingertips this time. In reality, they were three centimeters away from the drive, but if he focused his mind on reducing that distance to zero...

"...!" He felt resistance in his right hand, stronger this time. "I-I think I have it!" he exclaimed in a low voice.

Suu's reply was immediate. "Good. She's almost done with her lips. Pull it out and put it in your pocket quickly!"

Minoru nodded and quickly but carefully pulled out the USB flash drive. A cheaper connector would have stuck in stubbornly at a time like this, but luckily, the Professor's drive was gold-plated and polished, so it slid smoothly out of the laptop's port.

If that woman was to look this way now, she'd see a USB drive floating above the desk. Minoru held his breath as he pulled the drive away and slipped it into his jacket pocket. Immediately, it entered the field of Suu's refraction ability and vanished.

Exhaling deeply, Minoru started to move back toward the southwest corner of the room, when Suu cried out suddenly. "Ah…the cord!"

Without his noticing, Minoru's right leg had gotten caught on the LAN cable that stretched from the laptop to the wall, and his movement had pulled it ever so slightly. It looked as though the cord had caused the laptop to move a little as a result.

Minoru and Suu wouldn't have been able to hear it, but if it had made a noise, the woman might look their way.

Clenching his teeth, Minoru quickly turned to look at the sofa. The woman had paused her movements, but her face was still pointed toward the mirror. She could just be checking that all her makeup had been successfully removed, or she could have been pricking her ears up to listen.

"…We don't know what that Ruby Eye's power is…," Suu murmured, her voice low and tense. "We'd have to beat her to the punch. If she comes over here, circle around behind her and deactivate the shell. I'll neutralize her with my Taser."

"…Okay," Minoru responded briefly, still crouching and clenching his teeth.

Before long, the lingerie-clad woman rose from the sofa. However, instead of turning to the left toward Minoru and Suu's hiding place, she turned right and walked toward an adjacent kitchen. Leaning over the sink, she turned on the faucet and began to wash her face.

Breathing a small sigh of relief, Minoru carefully eased back into the shadows of the wall. After a minute or so, the woman dried her face with a towel and strolled back over to the sofa. Then she let down her hair, brushed it out for a moment, and parted it into a simple ponytail with a black hair tie.

…That hairstyle doesn't seem like it'd match the suit she was wearing very well…

Minoru thought to himself rather nosily, and indeed, the woman pulled out a new change of clothes from her shopping bag, producing a navy-blue skirt of some kind that she shook out briskly.

In a moment, Minoru's eyes again widened in surprise. His astonishment seemed to be passed on to Suu, who gave a small gasp over his right shoulder.

The outfit the woman had pulled out of the bag was unmistakably a sailor suit—a high school uniform.

The two trespassers were dumbfounded. Unaware that she was being watched, the woman first pulled on the snug top, tugging her hair out of the neck hole, zipping up the side, and fastening the three buttons on the chest. Then she pulled on a pair of black stockings and stepped into the blue pleated skirt, finally taking out a white scarf that she tied around the collar and pulled through the front loop of the shirt.

As she shook out her hair and stood up, she was no longer the young businesswoman they had seen enter the room. Without the makeup, her face looked fresh and clean, and her simple hairstyle and knee-length skirt made her nothing less than the perfect image of a prep-school student. She reached into the bag again and pulled out a pair of black thick-rimmed glasses to complete the look, then neatly put away her chic suit and cosmetics with practiced ease.

"Wh…which one is the real her?" Minoru asked, hoping for some feminine wisdom from Suu, but she simply shook her head.

"…I don't know… Since Third Eyes invigorate their hosts' bodies, it's hard to tell someone's age from their looks…" After a moment, she seemed to pull herself together. "But if she really is in her twenties, I would think it would be intensely difficult to walk around dressed like that, even for a Ruby Eye."

…*Is that right?* Minoru thought drily. Before his eyes, the career woman–turned–high school girl picked up her repacked tote bag, closed the blinds, and at last began to walk toward the computer desk.

If she started up the laptop now, there should be no traces left to indicate it had been tampered with. Despite knowing this, Minoru was still sweating as she approached, but instead of sitting in the mesh computer chair, she simply tore off a single sheet of paper from the memo pad on the end of the desk and wrote something out with the attached ballpoint pen. Then, still holding the note, she strode briskly toward the door to leave the room.

"I-it looks like...she's leaving. I wonder what that memo was..."

"A message for one of her associates maybe?"

"Yeah, it could be... We should probably try to get a look."

As they spoke, the high school girl reached the glass door and walked into the hallway without looking back. Minoru waited about ten seconds, then stood and walked far enough into the room to see into the hallway just as the entranceway door closed. After another few moments, he looked through the blinds and saw the woman leaving the building and walking north. Walking briskly, the woman turned down a side street and disappeared from sight.

"...She wasn't holding the note anymore...," Minoru murmured, and Suu nodded.

"She may have left it in one of the other rooms."

"Right... We should look for it." Checking that the USB flash drive was still securely in his pocket, Minoru opened the glass door and walked into the hallway. Immediately, he noticed that the door to the small, empty side room they'd checked before was now open.

He knew there should be nobody else in the building, but he was nervous nonetheless as he walked to the door and shone the LED light inside.

"Ah..." In the center of the concrete room, there was a white sheet of paper. Without a doubt, it was the memo the Ruby Eye woman had written. Given its conspicuous placement, it must have been meant for the next person who would be arriving at the building. Which meant they couldn't leave without finding out what it was.

As he started to step into the room, Suu suddenly squeezed Minoru's shoulders.

"Wh-what's the matter?"

"...No, it's... It's nothing."

"Okay..." With a puzzled tilt of his head, Minoru took one step forward, then two, until he soon arrived in front of the paper. Crouching down, he attempted to read the dark black letters.

It was only one short sentence, with Roman letters in neat cursive, but Minoru couldn't immediately grasp their meaning. He picked it up, staring at it with intense concentration.

"What does it say? It's...it's not English, right? Um...*A, u, r*..."

He had gotten only about halfway through when Suu cried out sharply, "Oh no...we have to get out...!!"

"Huh…?" Automatically, Minoru half rose to his feet, but he still couldn't take his eyes off the note.

Au revoir.

It was a phrase he felt sure he had seen or heard somewhere. French maybe. As for the meaning…wasn't it…

Farewell?

At that moment, the concrete beneath his feet suddenly lost its solidity.

Although he shouldn't have been able to hear anything, Minoru felt as if he heard a sucking sound. In an instant, his body dropped straight downward, and darkness swallowed his feet, his chest, and finally up to his face, closing out any light overhead.

5

Ultimately, what we call "heat" is really the kinetic energy of molecules.

When an object is hot, its internal components are intensely vibrating. Conversely, in a cold object, the molecules are in repose.

In other words, cold and stillness are essentially the same thing. As the temperature goes down, the world is wrapped in peace. Most likely, if an enormous amount of liquid helium were poured over the Earth, within moments all man-made noise would cease.

It wasn't liquid helium by any means, but the place where Mikawa was currently lying was certainly very cold—negative thirty degrees Celsius.

All around him, the piles of boxes stacked to the ceiling were frozen white. The pipes and ducts that crept around the room were covered in thick layers of frost. In the air, tiny ice crystals sparkled and danced.

Mikawa had been lying on the floor for almost eight hours now, after sneaking into one of the cold-storage warehouses that lined the Tokyo harbor. Of course, even with the enhancement of a Third Eye, there was no way he could simply sleep in these conditions wearing only synthetic jeans and a jacket without freezing to death. Instead, Mikawa was continuously changing the phases of the moisture clinging to his clothes, producing the minimum amount of heat necessary to preserve his body temperature.

However, deep in his heart, Mikawa knew there was a lurking desire to allow himself to freeze here. It wasn't that he wanted to die. He just wanted to...freeze. He wanted to know what it felt like. He wanted to feel that sense of peace throughout his entire body.

Really, living things were so frail.

On the macro level, they needed the phase transitions of water to live—and yet, on the micro level, they couldn't survive at water's freezing or boiling points.

Without moving from his prone position, Mikawa directed a long sigh up toward the ceiling, which crystallized instantly in the air. He watched it glitter as his mind wandered.

The male Jet Eye in the spirit photography that Liquidizer had shown him yesterday...the one who could create an invisible barrier...would that person be able to get closer to peaceful silence than Mikawa was able to? Could he go into some university's ultralow-temperature lab and experience that stillness for himself?

...*No.*

Mikawa quickly rejected that thought. Sealed up inside a barrier, he wouldn't be able to experience the real power of water's phase transitions even if he went to the North Pole. The only way to truly understand it was by feeling the low temperatures with your own unprotected flesh. Of course, it would cost you your life, but as the blood froze in your body, as your breath slowed and your brain cells were destroyed... surely you'd be able to feel it. Perfect stillness, perfect silence, in a moment that would last for eternity.

My friend must have gotten to that level, way back when...

Suddenly, there was a tiny bloom of heat—of movement—in his breast pocket.

Mikawa frowned and reached in to locate the source: a small machine that was vibrating continuously. Cupping it with both hands, he pressed the talk button.

"Hello? This is Trancer."

"It's me, boy."

"...Like I said, please stop calling me that."

Mikawa breathed a small sigh, watching it turn white in the air. "What's this about? It's been a while since you've called me like this, Liquidizer."

"That should tell you just how important this is, then. I need you to come to the safe house in Gotanda at once."

At this, Mikawa's frown deepened. "Gotanda? Not South Aoyama like usual?"

"Don't go anywhere near that location. It may have been infiltrated by the black hunters."

"What?!"

Mikawa sat upright in surprise, the frozen gears of his mind beginning to move again.

"...What do you mean, 'may have been'?"

"I went there earlier to change clothes, but my instincts told me... something was off. And they do have someone with the ability to turn invisible on their side, don't they? So I laid a trap in an empty room and left. But there's no way of knowing whether it was activated or not without going back to take a look."

"Your instincts, huh...? Was this 'trap' the pitfall you mentioned before?"

"Yes, that's why I filled up the entire first floor with concrete. This seemed like the perfect time to use it... At any rate, the worst-case scenario is that they may have escaped with vital information. In that case, we would have to shut down all the locations connected to that one. However...if they gained information but were then caught in our trap, that would be an excellent opportunity for us."

"...An 'opportunity'? How so?"

"There's not a Third Eye alive who could escape my pitfall. Whether black or red, all Third Eye users need to be able to breathe deeply in order to use their abilities. And sealed in three meters of concrete, they won't have enough air for a single breath. They'd die within moments... But unlike us, those Jet Eyes will invariably come to rescue their comrades even if they know it's futile."

"...You have a point." Finally realizing what Liquidizer was trying to say, Mikawa smiled. "If that's the case, I bet *he'll* show up, too..."

"Aren't you tired of playing with that samurai, boy? Just kill him already... Incidentally, have you seen the sky lately? The weather report said there was an eighty percent chance of snow today."

"Oh, is that so?" Forgetting that he'd been interrupted while meditating, Mikawa's smile broadened.

"But there's no guarantee he'll come alone, is there?"

"If there are any extras, I'll be happy to play with them. There's a perfect spot right near the Aoyama safe house, an abandoned factory. I'll send you a map, so make sure you take a look."

"Understood. I'll head out now."

Ending the call, Mikawa stood up lightly. A thin shell of ice fluttered down from his body, collapsing quietly on the floor. Looking over his shoulder into the dim light much farther down the passageway, he whispered to the other part of him that slept there.

"...I'll come back soon. Until then, sleep well..."

       * * *

As he sank down into the murky liquid and darkness obscured his vision, Minoru instinctively tried to spread his arms and swim to the surface.

But it was impossible. Once Minoru and Suu had been swallowed up into it, the liquid remained a liquid for only a matter of seconds. As he tried to stretch out his arms, they suddenly came up against an overwhelmingly hard surface that stopped them from moving any farther. In fact, his head, feet, and entire body were completely fixed in place, unable to budge in the slightest.

The only thing that stopped Minoru from flying into a complete panic was the body heat on his back. Focusing on breathing for a moment, he was able to calm down enough to speak up hoarsely.

"...S-Suu, are you all right?"

Her response was immediate. "Yes, about as much as you are."

"...Y-yeah, I guess that's true..." Since she was inside his protective shell, Suu would be fine as long as Minoru was. His stiff limbs somehow felt tired as he spoke again.

"So this...is our enemy's ability, huh?"

"Without a doubt. The concrete in the floor liquefied, submerging us inside. Which can only mean that that woman was Liquidizer herself... an executive from the Syndicate. If I had realized that before, we could have attacked her preemptively..."

Despite their trapped situation, Minoru couldn't help but smile drily at Suu's bitter words. "If I'd known that...I probably wouldn't have been able to move a centimeter. But if this is her ability, that means she was able to activate it from so far away that she couldn't even see the target..."

"I'd imagine she either set up a delayed activation of her ability or some sort of trigger that activated it."

"...Her abilities are that advanced?" Minoru found himself feeling a bit glad that they hadn't had to fight her directly, until he remembered that their current situation wasn't exactly anything to be happy about.

Minoru very carefully grasped the small LED light, which was fortunately strapped to his left pinkie finger. If he was to drop it, there was no way he would be able to pick it up again when he could move only his fingers and mouth. Pushing the switch with his fingertip, he shone the pure white light above them, keeping the darkness at bay.

Separated by just the three centimeters of the barrier was what could only be described as a concrete gray wall. But though concrete was theoretically a combination of gravel and cement, the surface was so smooth that Minoru couldn't see a single grain of sand.

"...Despite supposedly being concrete, this smoothness is more like plaster...," Minoru murmured a bit absently.

"I think rather than turning dried concrete back into its raw state, she may have broken apart the bonds on a molecular level. That's the only explanation I can think of for why we sank in so quickly."

"Then...does that mean she has the same ability as Oli-V?"

"Theoretically, yes. But..." Suu trailed off, uncharacteristically hesitant.

"But...?" Minoru prompted quickly.

"...They're on totally different levels. Divider can use his power only with a blade as an extension and can affect matter in only two dimensions, along the surface of his cuts... But Liquidizer can manipulate intermolecular forces in a three-dimensional space..."

"...!"

Minoru gasped sharply. Up until now, he had always thought that Olivier Saitou's ability to cut through anything at will was virtually unbeatable in battle. Of all the Jet Eyes in the SFD, his power probably had the highest attack power. The Accelerator, Yumiko, and the Refractor, Suu, would also be high in these ranks, since their abilities could be applied to weapons like a knife or a Taser.

But if Suu was saying that Liquidizer's powers were above and beyond

Olivier's, then the SFD as it was now wouldn't stand a chance against that woman.

"Minoru," Suu murmured, her voice increasingly strained. "We have to escape quickly. The Professor is probably going to send other members to rescue us. And Liquidizer will probably be expecting that. If a battle breaks out, she'll be difficult to beat even three against one."

"...Right," Minoru responded, his voice a low whisper. "But...it's going to be pretty difficult to escape this situation... I'm kind of, um, unsure about how long we're going to survive like this, actually..." The sense of imminent danger still hadn't really sunk it, but looking at the situation objectively, this seemed to be the only conclusion. "Um... there should be enough oxygen for us in the shell, at least. But it's not as though we can get food or water... And as far as breaking the concrete, I can't even move a centimeter..."

He trailed off, but Suu remained silent for a while. Hoping she was thinking up some kind of plan, Minoru waited quietly for the younger girl's response. Finally, she spoke in an odd tone of voice.

"...Wow, you're right."

＊ ＊ ＊

Mikawa reached out his gloved hands, catching the specks of snow that had begun gently falling from the sky. The hexagon-shaped crystals that landed on the fake black leather quickly melted into microscopic drops of water.

As he looked up silently at the sky, countless shadows began to fall from the heavy lead-colored clouds hanging overhead. It looked as though the first snowfall of the year would be as intense as the forecast had predicted. Last winter, there hadn't been a single heavy snowstorm; buzzwords like CO_2 and *global warming* had been tossed around quite a bit. But apparently, some scientists were saying that the current activity of the sun could bring on another ice age. If that were the case, perhaps people would start using even more CO_2 in order to warm the Earth.

Mikawa chuckled as he walked quickly along the twilit road.

An ice age would be wonderful. If humans were going to try to prevent that, then the Syndicate's goal of eradicating humanity was a perfect fit for him.

Truth be told, he hadn't really been eager to fight any Jet Eyes when his wound from the other day had only just healed; with this weather, it was another story. Every one of these water molecules was both weapon and shield to Mikawa. And unlike rain, which disappeared into drains shortly after reaching the ground, snow would industriously stick to the ground and serve as his reinforcements.

And on top of that, it seemed that Liquidizer was fairly serious about this battle as well. She had already been gone by the time he'd arrived at the Gotanda safe house, where he had just come from, but she'd left behind a present for him. The automatic nine-millimeter pistol, which was now tucked within his jacket's inside pocket, was undoubtedly a signal that her jocular "Just kill him already" remark had, in fact, been quite serious.

Unlike the black hunters, who often brought out handguns or sniper rifles at will, the Syndicate did not arm its lesser members so carelessly. This was the Syndicate executives' way of showing that they didn't have unconditional trust in even their most favored Ruby Eyes.

In other words, Liquidizer's orders this time around were essentially a test to determine whether Mikawa was worthy of the upper ranks.

Truthfully, Mikawa didn't have any particular desire to get ahead in the Syndicate. But there were some things he wanted to know. The thickly veiled top executives, who never revealed their faces or names, what were they really thinking? Was there serious intent behind their lofty goal of wiping out humanity, despite the fact that the Syndicate in its current state would hardly stand a chance against the Japan Self-Defense Forces? He didn't even really need to know what means they intended to use—just whether it was a real possibility. He wanted to know, whatever the answer might be.

Lightly checking that the hardness of the steel weapon was still there through his jacket, Mikawa continued to walk lightly toward South Aoyama through the falling snow.

* * *

"...Come to think of it..."

Having recognized the severity of their predicament, Suu paused a few seconds before speaking again in the same emotionless tone as ever. It was both very startling and very typical of her.

"...Where are we?"

"Where...? Um, we're inside some concrete, aren't we?" Minoru responded, looking at the smooth gray wall illuminated by the LED light.

"Well, yes. But this concrete is at least nine meters deep. Since we fell through the floor on the second story of the building, I'd imagine we're now on the first floor."

"Ah...I see, that makes sense..." Minoru shone the light around, but the only thing he could see was the same gray all around them. If they were in some sort of pillar, he imagined they would be able to see reinforcing steel bars, so the fact that there were none could only mean that they were indeed inside a giant block of pure concrete.

But a structure like that wouldn't exist in an ordinary building. Someone must have gone out of their way to build it—or rather fill it in—for a specific purpose. Someone had poured wet concrete into the entire first floor, or at least a significant portion of it.

"So that means..." Suu gave a small gasp, apparently coming to the same conclusion. "This is a large-scale trap designed to capture intruders. And it's based on Liquidizer's ability..."

"B-but..." Unable to accept that conclusion so easily, Minoru shook his head as much as he could within the small confines of the barrier. "That would make sense if the building were made like this from the beginning, but how would you fill a completed room or floor with wet concrete? It would be impossible to pour it in directly with a concrete mixer truck, and how would you dry it...?"

"It wouldn't need to be wet. They could've just carried concrete blocks to the second floor and then used Liquidizer's ability to pour it into the room below."

"Ah...r-right..." Minoru breathed out slowly. "...That woman should give up being a murderer and become an artist or an architect instead. She could make as many stone statues as she wants without needing any money or tools," he grumbled, then assumed a more serious tone. "At any rate, that means we're surrounded by at least a meter of concrete in all directions. In order to escape, we'll have to break through some of it somehow..."

Suu spoke quietly from close to his ear. "Yes. And to do that...we'll probably have to deactivate your shell."

Minoru nodded slowly. The shell would protect them from any threats, but since they couldn't move, it was also preventing them from interacting with the outside world. In order to feel the concrete and determine its strength, he would have to deactivate it.

But there was a problem. There was only about an inch between them and the concrete, which meant there could be very little oxygen. With both of them breathing, they would use it up in a matter of moments. Worse yet, they would probably then breathe in high concentrations of carbon dioxide. If they were to faint, it was highly unlikely they would ever wake up.

"...Umm, it might be dangerous to breathe outside the barrier too much. We should take a deep breath and hold it before I deactivate the barrier. Then we can try and figure out as much information as possible in that time."

"Understood. On three, then."

Minoru nodded and breathed out all the air remaining in his lungs. With the last shred of breath, he whispered, "One, two, three, go," then sucked in as much air as he could. Both of their chests expanded at the same time, but since they couldn't move outward, they were pressed against each other, Suu pushing into his back in a way that almost made Minoru blow the air right back out of his lungs.

Pulling himself together, Minoru deactivated the protective shell.

The deep pulsing sound audible inside the shell ceased, replaced with a silence so dense that it almost hurt his ears. None of the noise from outside the building could reach them. Minoru quickly moved his right hand to touch the concrete experimentally. It was icy cold to the touch, rough like sandpaper, and overwhelmingly solid. He tried tapping a fingernail against it, but it didn't leave a single scratch. Next, he made a fist and tried rapping on the surface, but there was no echo to indicate that the concrete was anything but solid.

After about half a minute, when they had more or less gathered all the information they were going to get in this situation, Minoru began to feel suffocated. He turned his head toward Suu. "Ready? I'm going to bring back the shell," he whispered.

Suu's response was immediate and just as quiet. "Ah— Change your posture a bit before you do it?"

"Um...sure." Minoru wasn't sure what the purpose of this strange command was, but he did as he was told, shifting his hands down toward the front of his stomach before he reactivated the protective shell.

Whump. He felt his hands being pushed into his abdomen, though not enough to hurt. Then he saw something unexpected. The re-formed barrier had pushed aside the concrete in the space where Minoru's hands had shifted. The concrete, which was about as hard as natural rock, had a new hole in it as if it had been scooped out with a spoon.

"Wh…what the…?!" Minoru cried, breathing in the air provided by the shell. Suu responded slowly, as if lost in deep thought.

"You should understand the nature of your protective shell better than I do, Minoru. When you activate it, foreign objects that exist within its boundary line are pushed aside… When you changed your posture, the radius of the barrier changed, too, so it pushed away that area of the concrete."

"Ah…s-so that means…" Blinking repeatedly, Minoru stared at the wall in front of him. "We can expand this space if I move my body while deactivating and reactivating the shell…?!"

"…That's the only method I can think of. It's too solid for us to do anything about it with our own physical strength. But…" Suu's voice faded for a moment, and Minoru looked over his shoulder at her, but she quickly continued, "…No, it's nothing. Give it a try, Minoru."

"O-okay." Minoru nodded, counted to three again, and deactivated the protective shell. Then he pushed up against the concrete with both hands and formed the barrier again.

This time, he felt sure he heard the sound of the concrete creaking. This was probably just a figment of his imagination, but in reality, he could indeed see small fissures spreading from where the concrete had been pushed in by his hands. The pressure he felt when he reproduced the shell this time was much stronger, too, but still not enough to cause any pain.

This is going to work! Minoru thought, clenching his fists, but then Suu spoke with some sort of anxiety still lingering in her voice.

"…I wonder why there's recoil…"

"Huh? Recoil…?"

"Yes. When you produce the shell, it pushes the concrete back, but it feels as though we're being pushed, too. Not enough to cause any damage, but…"

Suu sank back into silence, and Minoru frowned. Try as he might, he couldn't quite figure out what Suu was so worried about. The feeling of pressure was certainly unpleasant, but it was still well within the range of being physically bearable. He figured it was best to ignore it and focus on escaping as quickly as possible.

"Um, is it okay if I keep going?"

"…Go ahead."

Once again, Minoru deactivated the shell, shifted his body, and activated it again.

Crack! The hole in the concrete expanded again, now almost twice as large as it had been before. Without pausing for conversation, Minoru continued working. Before long, instead of his hands alone, he began to move his feet and the rest of his body as much as he could in his efforts to drill forward.

After repeating this process about ten times, though, Minoru finally understood the reason for Suu's concern. "Huh…? I'm being pushed back…"

The size of the gap in the concrete had expanded from a three-centimeter radius around their bodies to a long, narrow ellipsis, shaped like a cocoon. The wall was so full of cracks that it was beginning to look like old pottery. And the surface, perhaps because of all the pressure, was beginning to look a bit glossy.

However, when Minoru tried to expand the hole farther by pushing his hands forward and activating the shell again, he was repelled back toward the inside. Panicking, he pushed against the wall with all his strength this time as he activated the barrier. But the results were the same. As soon as he produced the shell, his hands were pushed back instantly, without denting the wall at all.

"…I knew it…," Suu murmured.

"What do you mean, 'I knew it'?!" Minoru asked, disconcerted. "Why did it stop working all of a sudden?"

"I think the space may have gotten too large. Think about it… Normally, when you've produced your shell at headquarters and such, it hasn't made a hole in the floor or anything, right?"

"Right... My body was always sort of lifted upward."

"The same thing is happening now. If there's enough space, and the mass of the object in question is large enough, the repellent force will be applied to you instead of the object. Which means...we won't be able to use that method to expand the hole any farther."

"But...that can't be!" Unwilling to give up, Minoru threw himself against the wall with both hands and feet as he activated the shell again, but the results were the same—he was simply pushed back with equal force.

As he took quick, shallow breaths to stave off the panic that threatened to creep up on him again, Suu spoke quietly. "This is bad... It's already been twenty-five minutes since we got sealed up in here. If the Professor was quick to send people after us, they're going to get here soon."

"What? It's been that long already...?" Flicking the LED light in his left hand around the wall, Minoru impatiently located the biggest crack and aimed a strike at it with his right hand. Though his ability was a defensive one, his punch while his protective shell was activated was fairly powerful. Since he didn't have to be afraid of hurting his hand, he could use all his strength, so he could easily put a dent in an iron plate, for instance.

However, since he didn't have enough room for a proper windup in this small space, his punch hit the wall with a thud and failed to cause any damage. The concrete wall that blocked them in remained the same, without so much as a single fragment falling to the floor.

"Damn it...!" Minoru cursed. Suu gently put a hand on his arm.

"We can't break it. The compression is actually making the concrete even harder."

"...Yeah, it seems that way..." Minoru sighed deeply and leaned his forehead against the wall with a thud. "I guess this is as far as we're getting... All we can do now is wait for help. I'm sure Oli-V will be able to cut through this wall..." With his ability, Divider Olivier Saitou's sword would slice up the block of concrete like butter and free them in no time.

We'll just have to wait. Minoru resigned himself to a long period of standby. But at that moment, Suu spoke from his back with a decisiveness he had never heard in her voice before.

"...No. We can't let any of them come near this place."

"Huh...?"

"If Liquidizer is lying in wait, they'll all be killed. The only way that Ruby Eye could ever be defeated is a surprise attack. There's a reason we can't beat her."

Taken aback by Suu's uncharacteristically clear, intense tone, Minoru widened his eyes. "I don't believe it... No matter how strong she might be, I'm sure Oli-V, DD, and Yumiko together could—"

"They would lose. I think you might be the only person who could take on Liquidizer, Minoru. That's why the Professor assigned you to this mission. We have to get you out before it turns into a battle even... if it's just you alone..."

Alone? Minoru shook his head. It didn't make sense. As long as they were bound together by the harness and his protective shell, they were in the same boat. There was no way one of them was getting out without the other. "Just me? There's no way—"

But Suu interrupted him by lightly putting her arms around his shoulders. "No, there is one way. A single method that can get you out of this place, right now."

"What...? Of course there isn't. It's not like we have a drill or explosives or anything..."

Suu's next statement caught him completely by surprise. "You've seen it before, too. The Third Eyes...disengaging."

"Dis...engaging?" Minoru repeated, dumbfounded. Before he could fully understand the meaning of the phrase, a memory came back to him all at once.

Late at night. A large figure rampaging wildly in an underground parking lot engulfed in flames. Most of the body had been hideously burned to the point of carbonization, and what's more, most of the head had been blown off.

Suddenly, there was a burst of red light from the remains of the body's neck. It shot straight up with ferocious speed, opening a huge hole in the ceiling of the parking lot, then streaking high into the night sky before dissolving among the stars.

The Third Eye "disengaging."

When a Third Eye host's vital functions ceased, or the Third Eye was removed from the host via surgery, the Third Eye parasite would shoot up toward the sky, returning to the same place it had come from.

Suu continued to speak as Minoru listened numbly. "When the

SFD performs Third Eye removal surgery, it's often done in an oper-
ating room in the back of a large vehicle with a roof that can open and
shut. But a while ago, when a different government-based research
team attempted to remove a red Third Eye from a dying host, it broke
through a triple-alloy barrier and the fifteen floors above them, leaving
huge holes in the ceiling of each. Nothing can stop a Third Eye disengaging to the sky. Not even nine meters of concrete—"

"What...are you saying?" Minoru interrupted in a pained voice,
unable to listen any longer. "Are you trying to suggest that we should
attempt to perform Third Eye removal surgery right here so that the
exodus phenomenon will blow a hole in the concrete? Don't be ridiculous! We don't have an anesthetic or anything to stop the bleeding...
And if it failed, you wouldn't be able to fight anymore!"

Minoru couldn't believe he had to explain his objections to such an
out-of-the-question idea. But Refractor responded in an even tone.
"Minoru. Even under ideal circumstances, my Third Eye can't be sur-
gically removed."

"Huh...?"

"My Third Eye parasite is inside my brain... It's fused with my thala-
mus. No surgery can possibly detach it. So..."

"What do you mean, 'so'?! What are you saying?!" Suu's arms were
still entwined around Minoru's neck, and he grabbed her right hand
instinctively. "That just makes your plan even more ridiculous! Even if
we were able to trigger Third Eye exodus and break through the concrete, it's pointless if we wouldn't get out alive!"

"But *you* would."

"I'm telling you that doesn't mean anything!" Minoru shouted,
squeezing her hand more tightly. "I... All I can do is shut myself away
in an invisible barrier! You're a hundred times more important to the
SFD—to the battle against Ruby Eyes! Getting me out of here isn't even
remotely worth you losing your life!"

His voice cracked as he choked out the words desperately, but Suu's
voice in response was still thoroughly calm.

"No, that's not true. Your ability has so much more potential than
you think it does. You could protect everyone from Liquidizer's attacks.
And on top of that, the data we copied before must contain information
about the Syndicate's headquarters. If we find out where that is, the 3E

Committee would definitely take action. You'd be able to protect every-one and bring down our enemies... Besides, if I can set you free from this prison, that's already worth more than enough to me."

"Th...that's not nearly a good enough reason to just sacrifice your life!"

Minoru shook his head furiously, continuing in a loud, shaky voice. "That's it...we can use mine. My Third Eye is just in my sternum. If we gouge it out, the wound wouldn't be fatal. We can escape without any-body having to die! Doesn't that make much more sense?!"

Minoru unzipped his jacket with his left hand and started to pull up his undershirt. But this time, Suu's left hand covered his to hold him back. Her slim white fingers stopped his impulsive action with a quiet strength, and she spoke in a voice that held equally strong conviction.

"I wouldn't be able to protect Yumiko and Olivier and the others."

Her words startled Minoru. Until now, Suu had always referred to the other SFD members by their last names or code names. The reason she was saying their names freely now was not lost on Minoru, but he pushed that thought aside.

"I-I can't protect them, either! I can't even break us out of this stupid floor! I...I don't have any of the power you're saying I do! All I have is a shell that I can use to run away and hide...!"

Click.

His desperate cries were interrupted by a snapping sound, then another. At the same time, the weight on his back started to become lighter. Suu was undoing the buckles of the harness that held them together. Even the straps around her waist that she had claimed she couldn't reach were unfastened, and her body heat on Minoru's back faded away.

"What are you...? No, stop! There has to be another way. I'm sure we can come up with something else if we think harder!"

"That may be true. But we don't have time to keep thinking anymore." Abruptly, Suu put her hands on his shoulders and turned him around. As he faced her, his protective shell shifted around them.

From point-blank range, Suu's deep violet eyes stared directly into Minoru's. There was no fear or impatience in her eyes. They simply shone with intense determination, and her voice, too, was full of resolve. "Minoru...I care about them. I love all the members of the SFD. I was always too cowardly to show myself around them, but still…they were my family. Please, Minoru…protect them."

"But…" Minoru still shook his head and replied pleadingly, "But I…I can't. If I sacrifice you to save Yumiko and the others, I…I can't just go on fighting after that as if nothing happened…"

"Don't worry. You'll forget." Suu smiled a little. "We've barely known each other for three days. I'm sure in another three, you'll be able to forget all about me."

"O…of course I won't!" Minoru cried, reaching out to take hold of her slim shoulders.

But before he could reach her, her violet eyes fluttered shut, there was a soft whooshing noise, and Suu vanished alone. No matter how hard he looked, he couldn't even find the black dots of her pupils. In the faint illumination of the LED light, Minoru stared at the spot where Suu's eyes should be.

"Suu…," he whispered desperately, his voice breaking. "You said my sight line was light gray…the color of apathy mixed with a trace of fear, right? It's true that I am afraid of other people. I don't want to get involved with them or get close to them… But that's only because I'm afraid of making more memories! Suu, you…you're already burned deep into my memory. I could never forget you!"

For a moment, silence filled the small gray room. Finally, Suu replied in a voice that trembled slightly:

"…Thank you."

"Wh…"

"Ah…even with the light blocked out like this, I can still see your sight line. It's beautiful…a warm color…I haven't seen it for so long…"

Suddenly, Minoru felt her soft hands on his own. Then, something indescribably soft and a little warm lightly touched his lips. Once it left, a quiet voice reached his ears.

"If you see my brother, just tell him…I'm going on ahead. Good-bye, Minoru."

Immediately, he felt a powerful impact on his chest. Suu had pushed him away with one hand as hard as she could, he realized instinctively. The instant his subconscious recognized the strong rejection implied by that action, whatever force had been connecting them and allowing them to share their abilities was severed.

And the Refractor, Suu Komura, was forced out of the protective shell toward the concrete wall at a terrible speed.

* * *

The snow was falling in earnest now. Soaking the asphalt black, it now began to pile up and cover the ground in white. It was still only about 3:00 p.m., but the light was already fading from the sky, and the temperature began to dive precipitously. Even if Mikawa didn't use his abilities tonight, the frozen streets were sure to cause plenty of accidents.

Mikawa blew lightly into his hands and peered at the Syndicate's Aoyama safe house through the resulting white steam. Then he posed a question to the person at his side. "…So, is there really a black spy pickling in concrete in there?"

"Well, my timed trap certainly was activated. Whether it caught a Jet Eye or a mouse or what, your guess is as good as mine."

"You don't want to dig it out to check?"

"Of course not! I'm not rescuing someone from my own trap," she huffed. Mikawa looked at her and shrugged slightly.

The two of them were encamped on the roof of an abandoned factory just southwest of the five-story building that served as the safe house. Of course, this meant they had no walls or ceiling to protect them from the biting cold, which Mikawa's flimsy jacket did little to abate. And yet next to him, Liquidizer, who was even more lightly dressed than he was, gave no indication that she was bothered by the cold. Stranger still, instead of her usual brand-name business suit, she was wearing a high school girl's sailor uniform.

He cleared his throat to prepare himself. "…So, I'm not sure I can hold this question in much longer. Is that a disguise? Or is it your true identity?"

Liquidizer responded with the same mysterious smile as always. "Which answer would you prefer?"

"…It doesn't really matter to me, since you're older than me either way."

"What a boring answer."

Perhaps to avoid her intense gaze, Mikawa looked over their surroundings again. The site of the abandoned factory stretched around the safe house building to the south and west—or perhaps it was more accurate to say that the hideout was nestled into the northeast corner of the factory. It seemed as if it had once been a metalworking factory, with milling machines covered in rust tossed aside underneath an overhang. The building itself was half-rotted, too, its roof dotted with holes.

Why was a ruin like this in the Aoyama area, even on the outskirts? According to Liquidizer's explanation, the real estate company that had owned this land had gone bankrupt, so the unused building had been abandoned. Thanks to this, there were no homes in use in the area, and in this weather, especially on New Year's Eve, there was nobody around to interfere, no matter how violent things might get. There was only one problem left…

"…Are they coming or what?" he muttered. The black ones were always prancing about like self-proclaimed knights in shining armor, but it was still hard to imagine they would casually show up knowing that the enemy must be lying in wait. If they had decided to cut their losses and abandon the spy caught in the trap, Mikawa and Liquidizer would be waiting in vain in the cold. Besides, the spy was almost certainly dead by now, anyway.

However, Liquidizer's response was simple. "They'll come."

"They'd come in the face of danger and go through all the trouble of breaking through the concrete just to recover a dead body?"

"Oh no, they're still alive in there. Otherwise the Third Eye would've disengaged by now."

"…"

Mikawa frowned and took another look at the building. Its roof was higher than the factory's, so he couldn't see for sure, but it was true that there were no broken windows or anything. The Third Eye exodus phenomenon tended to leave destruction in its wake, since it would break through any obstacles in its way, so it was doubtful that the fifth floor would be completely intact if it had occurred.

"…Alive? But it's been at least thirty minutes, hasn't it?"

"Indeed. Either they were carrying an air cylinder as a precaution, or maybe…" Liquidizer narrowed her eyes under her thick black glasses, and the rest of her sentence faded into a thin smile. Having long since learned that this expression meant she wasn't going to elaborate, Mikawa thought for a few moments before figuring it out on his own.

"Ah, I see. Or maybe it was that hunter from the spirit photography video who…" Before he could finish, Liquidizer suddenly placed a white fingertip over his lips.

"They're here."

"What? Really?" Following his former master's pointing finger, Mikawa saw a black van approaching rapidly from the south in the falling snow.

"Right there. Stop them."

"Understood." Right away, Mikawa inhaled deeply and blew the air out sharply toward the van that was still at least forty-six meters away. The snow that was piled up unevenly on the street froze at once, icing over the road. The van began to swerve left and right, its tires losing their grip on the road. But it didn't slow down, stubbornly careening toward the safe house.

"I don't think so," Mikawa muttered, this time aiming an airy breath toward the trees that lined the right side of the street. Instead of vaporizing the ice that had piled up on the dried leaves, he gently urged on just a bit of molecular movement, turning it into liquid. Once the water poured down onto the street, Mikawa quickly froze it back into ice.

The car's tires hit the freshly made ice slope on the road, and it quickly began to spin out. The driver recovered quickly, but the van was still off its original course, sliding left and right.

CRASH! The van smashed through a pair of locked gates, sliding not into the safe house but on the site of the abandoned factory.

"…Oh dear, they're in here now," Mikawa remarked. The van was scattering snow as it hit the brakes, and it screeched to a stop, its front bumper crashing into the wall of the factory. As he watched, the side doors of the black van opened, and three of the black hunters jumped out into the snow.

"Here we go. You take care of the one on the right, boy. Feel free to kill him, but try not to damage the brain. I'll have Empathizer get some information out of it."

Liquidizer's voice revealed no excitement as she gave orders. When Mikawa took one last glance at his former master, there was a cool smile on her lips.

"All right." Mikawa jammed into his jacket the object he'd made out of snow while waiting on the roof and leaped off, after Liquidizer.

Landing for a moment on the rusted emergency staircase, he jumped down again to the ground five meters below. Immediately, he spotted a fast-moving shadow charging at him from the right out of the corner of his eye.

Mikawa dove to the left. Milliseconds later, a sharp silver light flashed through the spot where his body had been moments before, and the snow on the ground flew into the air in two straight lines.

Mikawa gave a thin smile, watching the double-edged blade warily. It was glittering intensely, as if it were wet. "What's this? No time to chat with me today, Divider?"

The gangly, handsome Jet Eye shifted his blade back into position. "I'm not letting you steal anything else away from me," he spat in a low voice. "If you want to freeze stuff so badly, try freezing yourself in hell for eternity!"

Divider's blue eyes glinted, but Mikawa held his smile as he responded. "Goodness, how rude. I'm just following orders here, like always. Unlike you, still knee-deep in your own grudges…"

A fragment of a memory projected itself onto the screen of the thickly falling snow. Two months ago, shortly after joining the Syndicate, Mikawa and two of his colleagues had attacked a car that Divider had been in. Their target, however, was not him but the passenger in the backseat. Mikawa's job was to freeze the target in ice and capture them unharmed.

"…You know, Divider, I didn't even know anything about that girl when we 'stole' her…although I don't know if you could really call it that. After all, unlike you, she—"

"Not another word," Divider interrupted sharply, cutting through Mikawa's remark. Then, suddenly, he launched himself forward with a roar. Mikawa aimed a thin stream of air at the blade, just as he had a few days before.

He froze the water molecules inside the snowflakes as they touched the sword, expecting to see the blade turn into a dull stick of ice. But instead, he saw a small spark appear on the handle of the sword.

Whoosh! Suddenly, the blade was engulfed in orange flames.

So it looked so shiny before because it's coated in some kind of combustion agent, huh? But he couldn't come up with a countermeasure for it right away. The snow that would hit the sword as it swung through the air wouldn't be nearly enough to counteract the intense quantity of heat produced by the blade.

Quickly, he opened his mouth wide and blew. Instead of freezing, the water in front of him transitioned into steam. The pure white mist took over his field of vision immediately, but his lungs ran out of air after that. He couldn't produce steam hot enough to damage his opponent.

Passing through the steam, the fiery blade swooped toward him at a terrifying speed.

Mikawa bent his body backward as far as he could, trying to dodge the strike. A spasm from the wound he'd received from the same sword just a few days ago, still scarcely healed, slowed his movements a little. Luckily, the steam he'd created served as a smoke screen, obstructing Divider's aim. The tip of the flaming sword only nicked his left shoulder lightly, and Mikawa was finally able to catch his breath and release another cloud of steam, retreating as he did so. Divider, likewise, jumped aside, creating distance between them.

"…Well, that was a shock. As if that giant sword wasn't tacky enough on its own, now it catches on fire! What's the coating? Sesame oil?"

"Trioxane," Divider replied flatly. Mikawa had never heard of it. It was probably a chemosynthetically created high-efficiency combustion agent. This was just further proof of how advanced the black group's product development was.

"…Hmm. Well, it's too bad you weren't able to take me out with that strike. Looks like your party trick doesn't last very long." The flame that had engulfed the blade was already going out. No matter how effective the combustion agent, the small amount that could be coated onto a blade's edge was unlikely to last much longer than ten seconds.

Now it's my turn.

Mikawa reached his right hand into his jacket. However, before he could grab the object inside, Divider made an unexpected move: He quickly slid the now-flameless sword back into its sheath.

Shiiing! When he unsheathed it again with a sharp, metallic noise, the sword's blade was once more shining with fluid.

"…I see," Mikawa said darkly, the smile finally vanishing from his lips. Keeping a careful eye on his opponent, he glanced around to assess the other battle unfolding nearby.

On the other side of the car that had crashed into the factory wall, the sailor suit–clad Liquidizer fought against two black combatants. One was a young woman with long hair and a blazer-style black uniform—most likely the one whose code name was Accelerator. The other was a short male in a camouflage jacket, whom he'd never seen before. Both held suppressed automatic pistols in their right hands. A few empty shells lay scattered in the snow, suggesting that shots had already been fired.

Neither one was much farther than nine meters away from Liquidizer, so it was hard to imagine that all those shots could have missed, but somehow she was completely unharmed as she stood calmly between them. Just as Mikawa was wondering whether she had somehow dodged all the bullets, the two Jet Eyes fired again.

Pff, pff, pff! They fired at least ten times, the muted shots sounding like those of an air gun. In the face of such a merciless onslaught, Liquidizer casually raised her right hand and simply stretched it out in front of her, palm facing front.

Then Mikawa's eyes widened in shock, and he imagined that Divider's did, too.

Every one of the bullets that had been fired at Liquidizer's body with murderous intent, whether they made impact with her hand or not, melted in midair into lead-colored drops of liquid and fell to the ground.

Mikawa was all too aware of how terrifying Liquidizer's powers were. But he'd had no idea that she could use them on an object without directly touching it with her hand. It looked like the effect had a radius of only a half meter around the palm of her hand, but that was more than enough to protect herself from shooting.

As he thought it through that far, Mikawa hit upon a small problem. Even if she could liquefy a bullet, it should still have kinetic energy. Shouldn't the liquid stay clumped together and carry on forward to hit Liquidizer and deal some degree of damage before scattering into the air?

But this question, too, was answered once he saw the dissolved bullets forming a whirlpool in midair. Inside the barrel of a gun, there are spiral-shaped grooves called rifling. This causes the bullet to spin as it's fired from the gun, improving its accuracy. However, this spinning turned in Liquidizer's favor when she liquidized the bullets, the centrifugal force overwhelming the liquid and scattering it in all directions.

In other words, in order to shoot Liquidizer, a gun with a smooth, unrifled barrel—which Mikawa wasn't sure even existed—would be far more effective. The Jet Eyes were sure to have realized this by now. Unfortunately for them, they would never have the chance to act on this information. Because now that they had seen her trump card, she was certainly not going to let them escape with their lives.

All ten bullets were turned into little silvery droplets, the heat from the transformation diffusing into the cold air and creating little white clouds of steam.

At that moment, the girl, Accelerator, dropped her gun and pulled a knife from inside her skirt—perhaps thinking she had nothing to lose.

Fwoosh! She launched herself at Liquidizer with an explosive sound, snow whirling up around her. She was using her acceleration ability. All that Mikawa could see of her was an inky black shadow as she dashed forward at inhuman speed.

However, far from the metallic sound of steel piercing flesh, the sound that rang out was a simple splash of water. Liquidizer had pushed the fast-approaching knife away with the back of her right hand. The blade was liquefied immediately, drops of liquid steel scattering in the air.

This time, Liquidizer's left hand shot out toward her opponent, her white palm pushing against the right side of Accelerator's abdomen.

She's a goner, Mikawa thought with grim confidence. Her whole torso would be turned into liquid, collapsing into a puddle of protein soup.

However, the liquid that sprayed into the air from Liquidizer's left hand was pure black. All that she had liquefied was her opponent's blazer.

At the same instant, there was another explosive sound, and Accelerator retreated across an enormous distance. Once she stopped again, he could see that all that was covering her upper body now was a tight gray bodysuit.

"…You didn't really think you could beat me just by firing a bunch of bullets and hoping for the best, did you?" Liquidizer addressed the two Jet Eyes calmly. The faintest hint of a smile danced across her lightly colored lips and her eyes underneath the black-rimmed glasses. Somehow, that smile was even chillier than when her face was layered in makeup.

"You'll have to do better than that."

Watching his former master step forward smoothly, Mikawa concluded that her victory was only a matter of time and turned his attention back toward Divider. His bitter enemy's handsome features showed more killing intent than he had seen in any of their previous encounters as he lit another spark on his long sword.

Watching as the sword burst into flames again, Mikawa reached into his jacket with his right hand and pulled out a secret weapon of his own.

* * *

If Minoru had deactivated his shell even a split second later, Suu Komura probably would have died instantly. Pushed into the tiny three-centimeter space between the barrier and the concrete wall, every bone in her body would have instantly broken and her internal organs ruptured.

But as soon as Minoru felt her being ejected from the shell, he deactivated it almost unconsciously. As a result, he had prevented the instant destruction of Suu's body and the resultant exodus of her Third Eye, but this may have just been delaying the inevitable.

The sound of Suu's back crashing into the concrete at a violent speed was still reverberating as she collapsed forward into Minoru's arms. Her body crumpled, and Minoru saw a frightening amount of blood gushing from the back of her small head.

"Ah... Ahh...!" Minoru cried hoarsely. Desperately pressing his right hand against the area of the wound, he reactivated his protective shell. He could feel a weak heartbeat from her chest, but the bleeding showed no signs of slowing, and the color was draining quickly from her face, her eyes closed.

The injury wasn't only to the back of her head. A trickle of blood bubbling from her lips showed that it was much more extensive. Her lungs or alimentary canal must have been damaged.

"Suu...Suu!" he called desperately, but of course, there was no response. At this rate, it probably wouldn't be long until her heartbeat stopped, and the Third Eye would sense the death of its host's body and burst out through her head when it disengaged.

If he couldn't prevent that...then there was only one thing for Minoru to do. He would have to end Suu's life himself, right now, to force the Third Eye to disengage.

Because right now, the worst possible situation he could imagine was this: Suu's Third Eye would burst through the concrete and allow him to escape, only to find that Yumiko and the others had already been killed. If that were the case, Suu would have sacrificed herself for nothing. She had laid down her own life, entrusting Minoru with the task of rescuing Yumiko, DD, and Olivier—her family.

But...

But he couldn't do it.

There was just no way. Suu had said that since they'd met only three days ago, it should be easy for him to forget her—but by that logic, he had still met Yumiko and the others at Akigase Park only three weeks ago. He couldn't choose which of them to save and which to let die. Never.

"...I'll find a way. I'll save them. Yumiko and the others...and you, too." Minoru gritted his teeth, forcing out words in a wavering voice. "And if I can't...I'll die here, too. I don't care about fighting to save the world. I just...I just want to protect what's within my reach, what's close to me. And you're close to me too now, so...so..."

Unable to put the rest into words, Minoru instead held the unconscious Suu's head close to his chest with his left hand. If her Third Eye were to leave her body right now, it would put a hole in Minoru's body, too.

But he wasn't afraid. The feeling that resounded strongly in his chest was one he wasn't accustomed to. Unlike the burning heat he'd felt in his heart when he protected Yumiko from Igniter's explosion, this was more like a calm blue silence. Pressed on by this feeling, Minoru raised his right hand and pushed it firmly against the concrete in front of him.

He was already well aware that if he were to deactivate his shell now and then activate it again, all that would happen was that he would be pushed back. So in order to put more pressure on the concrete wall, he would have to expand the barrier itself. Currently, the invisible, unbreakable shield was projected three centimeters around his body; he would have to find a way to increase that radius to eight centimeters—no, even more.

It was something he'd never attempted to do before. But he felt certain it was the only way he could break out of here.

"Nn...nnngh..." With a low groan, Minoru pressed his right hand against the concrete wall with all his strength. The palm of his hand wasn't actually touching anything, but he could feel the joints in his wrist and elbow creaking.

Minoru's protective shell. For a long time, he'd thought that this ability, which he had gained from a jet-black sphere that came down from the sky three months ago, was the physical manifestation of his rejection of the world around him.

But that didn't seem to be true. After all, he had been able to bring Yumiko inside the barrier, then Suu. If the source of his power was the emotional wound that made him reject other people, that should have been impossible.

So the emotion inside the shell wasn't rejection or fear. It was the opposite.

It was love.

The one place on this earth that he could believe in and a place where he could feel at ease. This quiet world was a gift to him from the one person he had truly loved and trusted, his older sister Wakaba Utsugi.

"S...sis..." His face twisted in pain that ran from his right arm through the rest of his body, Minoru whispered intently, "Please...lend me your strength. I want to save her...to save everyone. I...I don't want to lose them...!"

Of course, there was no reply. But Minoru continued to cry out to his sister deep in his heart.

Eight years ago, a home invader had slaughtered his sister and their parents. Wakaba had hidden Minoru in a storage space under the floor of the pantry and gone to call for help.

But she hadn't made it. As she'd passed through the living room, she was spotted by the murderer and killed with a dagger. The last time Minoru ever heard her voice was in a whisper as she was closing the hatch above him. Her voice had been tense, but he could still hear that she was smiling.

"Don't worry. I'll protect you, Mii. Trust me and just count silently to yourself in there, okay?"

She had kept her word. The perpetrator had searched the kitchen for Minoru, overturning all the cupboards and cabinets, but he hadn't opened the hatch to the storage space beneath the floor where Minoru was hidden.

Minoru's protective shell was an imitation of that cramped hiding place. A place where he was completely protected, just as his older sister had wished. A world that couldn't be invaded by any threats or malice.

"Sis...I-I let you die without doing anything to save you. I...I don't ever want to do that again. So please...give me strength...to save Suu and Yumiko and the others...!"

As he spoke, Minoru heard a sharp cracking sound from inside his right hand—most likely, he'd broken a bone. Intense pain pierced from his right shoulder to his brain, sending sparks across his vision.

But at that same moment, a crack like a single thread from a spider-web formed in the concrete wall before his eyes.

"Hngh...aaargh!" Holding Suu's body tightly against his own, Minoru mustered all his strength and pushed his right hand even farther forward. The tip of a broken bone pierced through the back of his hand, scattering fresh blood.

Crack! Snap! More breaking sounds came from his right arm. He could feel his finger joints disconnecting, a crack forming in one of his thicker bones. At this rate, it felt like his right arm was going to explode before he could break through the concrete. But Minoru didn't slow down, focusing desperately on a single mental image. The space in his shell that he'd always thought was limited to three centimeters was expanding wider, farther.

One by one, more cracks radiated out from his hand in the concrete wall. But at the same time, he heard more crushing noises from his own arm, his tendons snapping apart.

"AAH! AAAAHH!!"

Brought on by sheer pain, tears began to stream from both his eyes, warping his vision. Cracks were forming in the body of the LED light in his left hand, too, and he could dimly see the white light flickering.

Finally, just as the light was completely destroyed and the space was plunged into darkness, Minoru saw it.

Someone's arm, illuminated with a faint golden glow, reaching over his right shoulder and gently placing a hand on his bloodied one.

* * *

Reaching into his jacket, Mikawa pulled out a simple sphere of ice, less than eleven centimeters in diameter.

There wasn't anything hidden inside it. He had simply shaped some snow into a ball and frozen it solid. Anyone could make the same exact thing with a freezer at home, given enough time.

Brandishing his combustion-coated flaming sword, Divider moved to attack. Mikawa tossed the ice ball at him with his right hand. At the same time, he breathed on it strongly with his mouth wide.

Narrowing his eyes slightly, Divider attempted to strike the ball as it approached in midair. Most likely, he had guessed that his sword could divide a ball of ice this small simply by touching it. And he was right.

However, the moment the flaming blade made contact with the ice and began to cut through it— *BANG!* The ball violently exploded.

Mikawa had instantly turned the water molecules in the center of the ball into vapor—in other words, transitioning it into steam. The resultant internal pressure turned the ordinary ball of ice into a tiny hand grenade, scattering countless tiny shards of ice toward Divider at point-blank range.

"Nngh!" Divider gave a low grunt as his upper body reeled back. Thin streams of blood began to leak from the cuts on his face and shoulder. Still, he stood firm, bracing himself without falling.

Mikawa reached into his left pocket and produced another ball of ice, hurling it at Divider's abdomen. At the same time, he fired off a short, broad breath.

This time the sound of the explosion was much lower, mostly absorbed by his opponent's body. Divider was blown back violently, falling toward the ground, when Mikawa huffed out a third large breath of air. This time, however, his target was not the enemy himself but the snow on the ground where he was about to land.

The white snow in that spot disappeared in a two-meter radius, turned not into vapor but water, so that Divider splashed down into a tiny pond when he landed. Immediately, Mikawa shot out a sharper breath.

There was a loud creaking sound, like a live tree being split apart.

The pond had frozen back into pure white ice, capturing Divider in the middle. Mikawa gave another long breath, but this time it was just a sigh, not another attack.

"…Well, it looks like that went pretty well," he muttered. "It's not easy to go back and forth between freezing and melting, you know. I have to keep jumping back and forth between imagining one or the other. Not that I expect you to understand that, since all you do is cut everything up."

He stepped toward Divider, who seemed to be ignoring the pain and struggling with all his might to force his way out of the ice. Coming upon the sword, which was still slightly aflame, Mikawa kicked it as hard as he could into a far-off snowdrift.

Kshh! A small sound turned his attention back toward the ice that held Divider. Small cracks had appeared in the ice's surface. "Oh, wow. Trying to break through my ice with brute strength alone, huh? But unfortunately..."

He grinned and blew another thin stream of air, and the snow that had already piled up on top of his frozen opponent and melted from his body heat promptly turned into more ice. *Kshh. Kshh.* Mikawa continued to spray breath around him, gradually entrapping his enemy in a thick shell of ice.

"Well, it was always going to end up this way, Divider. I'm sure even you must have known from the start that you wouldn't stand a chance against me on a snowy day like today. Was your colleague we caught in our trap there that important to you? Or maybe you just can't abandon a comrade no matter who it might be. That's the problem with you Jet Eyes..."

At this point, Mikawa wasn't sure whether Divider could even hear his rambling anymore. After all, his opponent's entire face, except for his mouth, was now completely covered with ice.

If I keep freezing more snow over him like this, will he eventually stop being able to breathe and die quietly? I don't know where his Third Eye is, but as long as it doesn't leave through his head, his brain should be perfectly preserved like this. I didn't even wind up having to use the gun, Mikawa thought to himself while looking back over toward the other battle.

It appeared that the two black hunters were utilizing Accelerator's speed to attempt some kind of disturbance strategy. The one in the camouflage hat would shoot at Liquidizer, and while she was dealing with that bullet, Accelerator would change positions at ultrahigh speed and fire from there.

It seemed like a decent strategy, but Ruby Eyes like·Liquidizer who were qualified to be leaders in the Syndicate far exceeded ordinary humans even in basic physical ability alone. As if she had eyes in the back of her head, Liquidizer easily followed Accelerator's position and liquefied both black hunters' bullets with both her hands. It seemed as though this back-and-forth had been going on for a while.

The man in the camouflage took a large jump back and reached into his jacket. Presumably out of ammo, he shook the magazine out of the pistol in his right hand and attempted to replace it with the new one he had just produced.

At that moment, Liquidizer dashed forward with a speed that seemed to rival Accelerator's, closing in on the male Jet Eye. Leaning forward and stretching her hand to its limits, she managed to brush a fingertip against the suppressed muzzle of his gun.

That was all it took. The metal of the gun from the tip of the muzzle to halfway down the slide melted into steely blue liquid and splashed onto the snowy ground. As her opponent's eyes widened in surprise, Liquidizer turned in midair and started to bring her hand down toward the nape of his neck.

However, just as her lethal fingertips were about to make contact, a black shadow slid up by her left. Accelerator was trying another close-quarters attack. This time, her left hand held not a knife but a black baton-shaped device.

Watching from a distance, Mikawa's mouth dropped open in surprise. It was an extremely high–voltage stun baton. Even Liquidizer couldn't do anything to electricity. She would get hit by the shock before she could touch the weapon itself.

Giving up her attack on the camouflaged opponent, Liquidizer ducked her body downward and nimbly leaped back. But however impressive her physical abilities might be, her movement was no match for Accelerator's. The Jet Eye caught up in a single step and doused her in an electric shock.

Or so it seemed, but moments before the strike landed, Accelerator's body suddenly wobbled and pitched forward.

On closer inspection, the sole of the speedster's right shoe had suddenly sunk three centimeters into the asphalt that had been exposed by the raging battle. As she retreated, Liquidizer had touched the ground's surface for just an instant, liquefying just a bit of the asphalt. As soon as Accelerator stepped onto that asphalt, the pavement had most likely rehardened, fastening her shoe to the ground.

The Jet Eye's face froze. She bent over quickly, trying to unfasten the buckles of her waterproof boot. However, presumably to support her ultrahigh-speed movement and braking, Accelerator was unluckily wearing tight ankle-length boots instead of ordinary shoes.

Before Accelerator could get out of her shoe, Liquidizer's right hand pushed down on the asphalt.

Gloop.

Accelerator's leg sank into the pavement up to the knee, and the ground immediately hardened again. The technique was similar to how Mikawa himself had trapped Divider, but undoubtedly even tougher to escape.

"Damn...!" Tossing aside his melted pistol, the camouflage-wearing young man pulled out a small revolver.

"Don't move!" Liquidizer ordered sharply, freezing him in his tracks. Her right hand was still level on the asphalt as she continued, "Drop your weapon. Unless you want me to bury this girl up to her head."

"..." He stayed frozen for a second but obeyed before long, tossing aside his revolver.

"There's a good boy." Liquidizer gave a thin smile. "Now, as long as you're here, tell me something. That friend of yours caught in my trap over there...the boy who makes the invisible barrier. How does that ability work? It's been more than thirty minutes, so why on earth hasn't he died of suffocation by now?"

She really is terrifying, Mikawa thought. *I'm sure she plans to kill these two—no, probably all three of them, counting Divider—but she's still trying to get information out of them while they're alive.*

Standing stock-still, the camouflaged young man visibly set his jaw.

"Don't say anything! Get out of here now!!" the trapped Accelerator cried out despairingly.

Her other leg sank into the ground. Presumably, Liquidizer had used her ability again for just a moment. The other Jet Eye grimaced and started to open his mouth.

Then, suddenly, Mikawa heard a mysterious noise.

Rrrrg... Something creaked heavily. Coming up from the ground, it was almost more like a tremor than a sound. Alarmed, Mikawa looked around for the source of the noise. Then he gasped when his eyes fell on an unexpected scene.

The Syndicate's five-story safe house building about eighteen meters away. Snow was tumbling over the sides of the roof. The cause wasn't wind or an earthquake. The building itself was trembling, shaken by some enormous unknown force.

In his shock, Mikawa was momentarily distracted from the frozen Divider behind him. As a result, it took him a moment to notice what was happening. Divider had managed to work free a single finger, and dangling from it was a sharp object, an icicle less than eight centimeters long, with which he was slowly cutting up the ice around his hand.

Crack! The sound made Mikawa whirl around, and his eyes widened. Divider had already broken his arm free of the icy pond. His hand now gripped a much larger weapon—a pointed shard of ice more than a half meter long. Before Mikawa could freeze his arm again, Divider slashed it horizontally with a flash.

Don't tell me his ability even works on a blade of ice? I thought it had to be metal!

As panic flashed across Mikawa's mind, Divider broke free and leaped toward him, cutting from his chest to his left shoulder with the icy blade.

"Uuugh..." Mikawa groaned and jumped back, but Divider didn't follow him. With fresh blood gushing from the wounds that covered his body, he held the icy sword aloft and bellowed, then threw it toward the outside wall of the trembling building.

Sparkling brilliantly, the white shard of ice rotated in the air as it flew toward its target. When it struck the concrete of the building, instead of breaking, it silently cut right through the surface. Then, as Mikawa collapsed to the ground, he saw some kind of energy burst forth from the deeply cracked cement.

BOOOOM!

An overwhelming sound reverberated from the building as a large portion of the front wall was blown to tiny pieces. It seemed like it could have been caused only by some kind of explosives, but then the person inside would have presumably been blown away along with the wall.

However...as he clutched his fresh wound, Mikawa heard something.

Out of the darkness of the hole that was almost two meters in diameter, the faint but unmistakable sound of footsteps approached.

Mikawa wasn't the only one who'd heard it. Divider, who had returned to a crouching position; the trapped Accelerator; the camouflage-wearing Jet Eye; and even Liquidizer all stared transfixed at the hole in the building.

After a few moments, a figure appeared beneath the falling snow. It was, indeed, the young man who'd appeared in the spirit photography video.

There was no way that the building should have exploded just from the shard of ice Divider had thrown at it. It was hard to imagine how he could have broken free from the middle of the concrete, but it looked as though it had cost him, as his right arm was clearly wounded and bleeding. And in his left arm, he was carrying a young woman Mikawa had never seen before, who was in far worse condition than even he himself was. Half her face was covered in blood, and she looked to be near death.

In other words, these two posed no threat in the current battle, he thought. It would be easy to take them out with a preliminary attack from a distance. But there was one problem...

His eyes. At first glance, the boy's eyes looked weak, but there was something in that look that made Mikawa hesitate. Liquidizer, too, backed about three meters away from the trapped Accelerator and surveyed the situation intently.

The first person to move was the one closest to the building, the camouflage-wearing Jet Eye. As if a switch had been flipped, he suddenly rushed over to the boy, took the unconscious girl into his arms, and laid her gently on the ground. Producing something like a first aid kit from his jacket, he began to treat her wounds. The other boy watched this for a moment and then continued to walk forward.

Finally, Liquidizer spoke in a low voice. "So, you actually managed to break out of my trap... How very interesting. What's your name, boy?"

The young man wore a black jacket, and his hair was tinged with gray.

"Isolator," he replied shortly, not slowing his approach.

"Hmm. As in separating yourself or as in being alone, I wonder..." Her split low ponytail bobbing behind her head, the powerful woman

of ambiguous age smiled slightly. "A pitiable name. But perhaps a fitting one, since you can't protect anyone but yourself with your power."

The boy stopped in his tracks. Perhaps Liquidizer's words had hit a nerve. But a faint smile appeared on his face, albeit one tinted with transparent sadness. "I'm sure you've realized this by now, Ms. Liquidizer, but all of us Third Eye users—Jet and Ruby Eyes alike—all our powers, without exception, originate from a fear of the world beyond ourselves."

For once, Liquidizer didn't have an immediate comeback. The boy spoke to her again, his voice as quiet as the falling snow.

"The power to enact violence on the world. The power to run from the world. And the power to learn about the world. Their forms may be different, but they all come from the same source... We're all afraid of the world that has hurt us so badly. In that sense, every Third Eye user is an 'isolator.'

"But...despite all that, I still have people I want to protect. A world I want to protect. What about you, Ms. Liquidizer? Is there anyone you want to protect with that incredible power of yours? If nobody comes to mind, then..." Pausing for a moment, he gazed at the Syndicate executive with even more sadness...no, perhaps even *pity* in his eyes.

"You're much more isolated than I am."

Forgetting for a moment that Divider was still crouching nearby, Mikawa stood stock-still.

How could he say something so stupid to Liquidizer without fearing for his life? He ridiculed the boy silently, but then his thoughts shifted. Despite himself, annoyance bubbled up in his mind.

...Fear? Fear of the outside world?

Don't be stupid. I love all the water that fills this world. And I hate the humans who pollute that water without realizing its worth. What part of that sounds like fear to you? I don't believe it for a second. I'm not afraid of anything...

Then someone's voice rang in his ears, unbidden.

Then why won't you wake me up?

"Huh...?"

Why are you still keeping me asleep? Why do you leave me alone in such a cold, dark place...?

"...B-because...if it melted...if the ice melted..."

Are you afraid? Are you afraid of what might happen to me if the ice melts...?

Mikawa was shaken out of his trance by Liquidizer's voice, low and tense, as she addressed Isolator.

"...I see. Well, let's see you protect them, then, boy. The people you love...and yourself."

Blinking his eyes back into focus, Mikawa saw that the snow falling in Liquidizer's immediate vicinity was being turned into large drops of water. Her intense power was seeping out, liquefying the snowflakes without even touching them. Just moments ago, Mikawa had been telling himself that he knew no fear, but at this moment he felt it deep in his heart. Liquidizer, the incredibly powerful and usually calm and collected Ruby Eye, had dropped her languid smile. She was angry.

Mikawa's instincts told him he should get away now to avoid being involved in this, but he couldn't move. He needed to know.

How was the ashen-haired boy planning to protect his friends?

Trapped in the ground, Accelerator obviously couldn't move, and neither could the seriously wounded Divider or the camouflaged boy treating the dying young girl. If he wanted to protect them, he would have to fight without running away. But fighting Liquidizer empty-handed was an impossible task. The gray-haired boy must know this all too well.

Liquidizer took a step forward.

At almost the same moment, the black hunter known as Isolator broke into a run.

Watching him, Mikawa noticed that Isolator's feet were floating slightly above the ground. This must be his ability, the "invisible barrier." Leaving strange footprints in the snow, the young man dashed in a straight line, simply charging forward with no apparent plan.

As he ran, he pulled his left hand back, forming a fist and winding up with an exaggerated motion. He clearly had no knowledge of martial arts or how to throw a proper punch. It should be easy for the nimble Liquidizer to dodge his attack. But perhaps planning to take the hit and liquefy his arm, she simply stood with her right hand outstretched.

No matter what substance the barrier was made out of, Mikawa knew that once it touched Liquidizer's hand, it would melt in an instant, followed immediately by the liquefaction of the fist itself.

However…

An unpleasant cracking sound echoed, and Liquidizer's hand snapped backward. Two of her fingers were bent at unnatural angles.

It's not solid matter!

Unconsciously, Mikawa's face warped into a smile.

If Liquidizer couldn't melt it, that meant it wasn't ice, glass, diamond, or anything like that. So was it some kind of energy, a powerful repulsive force, which warded off all chemical elements around it? If so, the code name Isolator was truly a fitting one.

He guessed that Liquidizer must have been surprised, too, but the sailor suit–clad woman hadn't stopped moving. As if she didn't feel any pain from her two broken fingers, she smoothly twisted her body and moved closer to the ground.

The young man moved to throw another punch with his left hand, but before he could do that, Liquidizer's hand touched the ground beneath his feet.

Gloop. The boy's body sank downward. Liquidizer quickly retreated, her hand still touching the ground. Even if the boy's barrier was an immaterial field, his damaged right arm was proof that escaping from concrete was still no easy task. And this time, he was trapped in the ground that stretched out endlessly in all directions. Being buried in that, even if he could escape somehow within a few hours, his friends would all be long dead.

"…Oh." Mikawa heard a strange noise escape his own throat.

The boy who had been sinking into the ground just moments ago pulled himself out with a single step. Concentric circles formed in the asphalt-colored pond that Liquidizer had created. But he didn't sink. The liquid, its molecular forces manipulated by Liquidizer, had a specific gravity of close to zero, yet the boy was standing calmly in the middle.

Did he have a floating ability? No, it was something else.

The ability that created his isolation power was isolating him even from the Earth's gravity.

* * *

The protective shell Minoru produced held many secrets that even he didn't understand.

Why did there seem to be an unlimited amount of oxygen inside? Why was visible light the only thing that could penetrate it? And what was the low rhythmic noise that he always heard inside?

Compared to these questions, the problem of why he could walk without slipping despite the shell's zero coefficient of friction seemed trivial. So Minoru hadn't even stopped to consider it strange, never mind trying to figure out why.

But now, standing upright above the swamp that Liquidizer's ability had created, he felt as if he understood. When he was walking while in the protective shell, he wasn't moving forward by using friction to push off the ground. He was fixing himself to the area he stepped on—in other words, the point of contact with material outside the shell—by force of will. That was how he had walked down the slippery stairs without falling and how he could run at full speed even on a sandy beach.

Since he was still affected by gravity, he would, of course, sink if he was to suddenly find himself in the middle of liquid. But if he prepared in advance, it would be possible to deal with. All he had to do was fix himself on the point of contact with the liquid's surface.

Standing on the surface of the asphalt lake, Minoru turned his gaze toward Liquidizer, who had her hand on the ground nearby.

Her eyes showed no hint of emotion from behind the thick black-rimmed glasses. But she was giving off a level of pressure that seemed strong enough to blow Minoru away if he let down his guard for even a second. Clearly, he had found a way around her "liquefied ground" attack, though that was only one small aspect of her abilities.

However, he couldn't show any fear. It was doubtful Minoru could beat her with nothing in his arsenal but an amateurish punch—or whether she would even let him land another hit—but he had to drive her away somehow. And he had to do it quickly. Suu needed serious medical care, more than DD's emergency treatment could provide.

Which meant there was only one power he could rely on in this situation: Yumiko's acceleration. They would have to attack her with the same combination strike that had beaten Igniter.

Minoru took a big leap back, landing near Yumiko, whose legs were still trapped in asphalt. He deactivated his shell and felt, along with the biting cold, the chilling murderous intent of the Ruby Eye pressing down on him. Though it was coming from Liquidizer, her face was still completely expressionless as she stood up. The asphalt hardened again, forming a smooth surface that looked like black glass.

"...Don't worry about me," Yumiko murmured, her voice strained. "Just focus on fighting." It looked as though she had exerted all her strength trying to get out. Her tights were ripped where they touched the asphalt, and the exposed skin was bleeding.

Turning his eyes back toward his opponent, Minoru answered quietly, "No...I need your power to do that."

"But...you can't bring me inside the shell..."

True, his attempts to accept her into his protective shell hadn't succeeded in a single one of their experiments. But Minoru suspected that he had some idea of the reason why.

In the past few days, why had he been able to bring Suu Komura into his shell countless times while continuing to reject Yumiko? Most likely, it was because by bringing her into his protective shell, he would be contradicting the very purpose of its existence by transforming it from a protective ability into a strong offensive power. Unconsciously, Minoru was afraid of that contradiction. He was afraid of using this ability, created from Wakaba's final wish of a safe and sacred place for him, to hurt someone.

But right now...

Right now, unlike any other time, he needed that power. In order to protect the people he cared about. And so...

"Don't worry," he whispered. Then he put his left arm around Yumiko, drawing her toward him, and activated his ability.

He couldn't hear the sound of the hardened asphalt breaking. But cracks radiated out in the ground around Yumiko's body, and both of her legs were set free.

For just a moment, he felt Yumiko's body tremble as she was pressed up against him in the shell. Her voice, too, was shaking as she wrapped her arms around his back and pressed her forehead into his shoulders. "...H-honestly...if it was that easy, you should've done it sooner."

"I'm sorry." Once Minoru had apologized, they both turned at once to look at Liquidizer, who was standing about nine meters away. Despite the fact that Accelerator had been freed from her trap, the Ruby Eye's expression was unchanged. If anything, she looked more focused than ever.

Just as he was thinking that, Minoru saw a flash of red in her eyes underneath her glasses, but it was no illusion. She put out her right hand with the palm facing upward, raising it high in the air.

"Run!!" Yumiko cried, and Minoru took a single step sideways. Yumiko accelerated the movement, instantly sliding them more than three meters across the pavement. At the same time, the spot they'd been standing in just a moment ago burst into a geyser of liquid.

"?!"

Minoru gasped sharply, staring in shock as the liquid quickly solidified again, forming a rocky stalagmite more than nine meters tall. No, it was more like a spear. But they had no time to be surprised, as Liquidizer moved again, using both hands this time.

Right as they jumped out of the way, a second spear of rock shot up from the ground, grazing the shell. Then a dark brown torrent of liquid rose up from directly underfoot, clouding Minoru's vision. But of course, the liquefied gravel couldn't scratch the protective shell.

Then Minoru suddenly felt his whole body suddenly trapped in place. The spurt of liquefied asphalt and soil had covered the entire shell and then solidified around it, obstructing his movements.

"Rrgh...!" Minoru put all his strength into moving his limbs, breaking through the wall of rock. With Yumiko's ability, they used a slide dash to put distance between themselves and Liquidizer.

It seemed that the range of her ability to remotely liquefy and solidify the ground was about nine meters. Liquidizer stopped her movements and smiled again, and Yumiko glared at her.

"We can't get anywhere near her!"

"...No, we can. With your acceleration, we can smash through rock like that without a problem. There's no time to lose. Let's end this with our next charge!"

Minoru braced his legs firmly, lightly lifted Yumiko into his arms, and got into position for an all-out dash. All they needed to do was crash into Liquidizer one time, and she should be out of commission. Minoru and Yumiko together weighed at least one hundred kilograms. There was no way she could take a hit from that at ultrahigh speed without being hurt.

"Here goes!" he shouted, and launched himself forward with all his might.

✳ ✳ ✳

Watching his former master, Liquidizer, bring out even more new abilities—liquefying ground from a distance, jetting it upward, and hardening it again—Mikawa sharply sucked in his breath.

Just the ability to liquefy the ground from almost nine meters away was terrifying enough, but he could accept that level of power from her. She had scarcely moved from the same spot in the past three minutes. Given that she was in the midst of a battle, perhaps she had synchronized with the ground around her, controlling it for a ridiculously long time.

But did the ability to create a spire of ground far taller than a person fit into that theory? The Syndicate's research had long since proven that all Third Eye users' abilities, whether red or black, were fundamentally based around the manipulation of atoms and molecules. Igniter, for instance, had simply been able to manipulate oxygen molecules, and Biter had altered and reconfigured his body by manipulating protein molecules.

Within this infinite variety of possible abilities, Mikawa's phase transition abilities and Liquidizer's closely resembled each other. That was why she had taken him on as a pupil. No emotional reasons were involved.

When Mikawa changed water into vapor or ice, he was controlling the vibration of the water molecules. If he stopped the vibration, the molecules would join together and form ice, and if he made them vibrate intensely, they would fly about and form water vapor. That was the full extent of his power. He couldn't, for example, form water out of hydrogen and oxygen or manipulate the form or movement of the water.

Liquidizer, on the other hand, could manipulate any solid material within her reach, weakening the van der Waals forces that made it solid. She wasn't changing the vibration of the molecules like Mikawa, so her ability didn't produce heat. And she couldn't manipulate something that was already a liquid. In theory, the full extent of her ability should just be liquefaction. Any other manipulation, like causing her target to shoot up into the air regardless of gravity, should be impossible. If she could do that, then the Syndicate, or at least its executives, must be hiding some logical knowledge that Mikawa wasn't aware of...

All these thoughts flashed through Mikawa's mind in only a moment. During that time, the gray-haired boy brought Accelerator into his protective field and used the help of her ability to dodge two, then three attacks from rocky spears. More accurately, the third one caught them as it covered their shield and then solidified again, but it was too weak to hold them for long before they smashed through it.

His resolve perhaps strengthened by that success, the boy called Isolator turned to face Liquidizer, who was standing near the wall of the abandoned factory, and took an assertive stance. A powerful light filled the eyes of Accelerator, who was pressed close beside him, glaring at their target.

After a moment, the boy gave a soundless cry and launched himself forward. The two charged at a frightening speed, but to Mikawa, who was so focused on the battle that he forgot the pain of the wound in his left shoulder, the actions that followed seemed to play out in slow motion.

First, Liquidizer raised both hands above her head, creating multiple earthen spears from the ground at the same time. Immediately, the spikes hardened directly in the Jet Eyes' path, but they were quickly pulverized by the pair's charge. The spears were formed from the earth and sand below, so they should have been about equal in hardness to natural rock once resolidified, but the process of gushing into the air before hardening probably created too many air bubbles in the center, weakening the structures. They would certainly be hard enough to stop an ordinary human body, but against the boy's defensive shield, they were utterly useless.

Then, with her rocky spears destroyed, Liquidizer raised her right hand up again, as if in a last-ditch effort to defend herself.

* * *

Just as Minoru had predicted, the rock spires that Liquidizer produced weren't strong enough to stop the combination attack of his protective shell and Yumiko's acceleration.

Smashing through the first two spears slowed their speed a little, but they still had plenty of force behind them as they approached the enemy.

As Minoru lowered his head and braced himself for direct impact, suddenly, Liquidizer raised her right hand a third time.

This time, instead of opening her palm, she extended only her long index finger. Then she aimed it directly at Minoru.

A terrifying scene unfolded before his eyes.

The steel frames that held up the abandoned factory behind her suddenly melted into bent half circles, twisted together in midair, and formed three enormous metal spears that launched directly toward Minoru and Yumiko.

There was no time to dodge them. Just a meter away from Liquidizer, the metal spears crashed into Minoru's protective shell.

Inside the shell, they didn't hear any roar or crash, and the shock of the impact itself felt strangely gentle, as if they were bumping into a polyurethane foam wall back in the experiment room. The biggest effect was just dull, heavy resistance against their movement. The spears were bent and crushed before Minoru's eyes, but the speed of their charge was greatly reduced as well.

Minoru's face was only ten centimeters away from Liquidizer's when their momentum from inside the protective shell stopped. For just a second, he locked eyes with the powerful Syndicate Ruby Eye.

The eyes behind her thick glasses were at once like bottomless pools of darkness and perfectly polished mirrors. Her gaze seemed to suck in Minoru's soul without revealing a single hint of herself or the inner pain that she surely carried as a Third Eye host.

In her eyes was nothing but rejection. Not a single trace of desire for anything. Just abject enmity toward everything around her.

A smile spread across Liquidizer's beautiful face, as if she sensed Minoru's fear.

Immediately, the three metal spears pressed against Minoru's protective shell dissolved into liquid again, spreading over the surface of the shell in an instant. He heard Yumiko let out a sharp gasp as the metal blocked their vision. "Oh no…!"

We have to get away!

Minoru put all his strength into his right leg. But just as he was about to launch them away, all his movement was stopped in an instant. The thick layer of metal covering the protective shell had hardened again, trapping them inside. He tried to break through it as they had when they were suspended in rock before, but this time there was no sign of success, no matter how hard he pushed.

"No…DD and Komura…!" Yumiko's voice rang out desperately near his ear. With the two of them cut off from the world like this and Olivier occupied with fighting Trancer, there was no one to protect DD and Suu from Liquidizer's attacks.

Minoru squeezed his eyes shut to think and made an immediate decision. "Yumiko. I'm going to destroy this metal shell. But once I do that, I won't be able to make my barrier again for another three minutes or so. We have to end it in one attack as soon as we break out, or else…"

We'll be killed. Minoru tried to say it, but he was interrupted by Yumiko nodding.

"I understand. I can do it." Her voice rang with determination in the total darkness. Minoru nodded, too, and inhaled deeply, filling his lungs with as much air as he could. He felt his chest creak under the pressure, but he ignored that pain and focused intently.

Ba-bump. The sphere embedded in his chest pulsed heavily, and energy poured forth from it, filling the protective shell. The energy increased in density, flooding the inside of the shell with little points of faint golden light. The light gathered together, glowing brighter, and turned into a steady surge.

Minoru shouted a wordless battle cry.

The protective shell itself spread—no, exploded—in all directions. Minoru heard the thick metal shell being smashed into tiny particles.

Through the fading golden light and the scattering pieces of metal, he saw Liquidizer's back as she started to walk toward DD and Suu. As the woman in the sailor uniform whipped her head around in surprise, Yumiko took one long step toward her, aiming at her back.

The air vibrated sharply as Accelerator charged without hesitation. Sparks flew from the Taser in her left hand, leaving thin blue traces in the air. Liquidizer's face darkened as she turned her right palm toward the Taser.

The black baton-shaped weapon dissolved, dark droplets flying in all directions. At the same instant, a high-ampere electric shock zapped out of the reinforced battery inside, bursting over Liquidizer's entire body.

Minoru watched as Liquidizer was blown away as if she'd been struck by the hand of an invisible giant, tumbling over and over before finally collapsing in a heap. Even as he watched this unfold, he still couldn't move.

The Ruby Eye lay motionless on her side, not stirring a centimeter. She appeared to have passed out, but Minoru was unable to shake off the fear that this might be another trap. He stared at her warily. With her eyes closed and lips slightly parted, Liquidizer looked strangely defenseless. As he stared at her face through the falling snow, an unbearably strong feeling boiled up inside his chest.

Although they were all Third Eye hosts, the Jet Eyes and Ruby Eyes continued to fight solely on the basis that the spheres they possessed were different colors. In fact, if Minoru had received a red sphere instead of a black one three months ago, he might have become one of Liquidizer's subordinates. And if Liquidizer's sphere had been black, she might have been a dependable asset for the SFD.

The only factor that divided them was pure chance. In all likelihood, up until that day three months ago, Liquidizer had been a lonely, isolated person who feared the outside world, just like Minoru...

As this thought washed over him, Minoru heard Yumiko releasing the magazine of the pistol she had pulled from its holster on her right side.

Yumiko checked the amount of remaining bullets and loaded the magazine back into the gun. Then, gripping it with both hands, she pointed the pistol directly at Liquidizer.

"...Yumiko?" he said quietly.

"...This is our only choice." Her voice was strangled as she gave a short reply.

She was right. None of the usual restraints they used on Ruby Eyes would work with Liquidizer. Whether they used belts made of aramid fiber or chains of titanium alloy, she would liquidize them the instant she regained consciousness. Attempting to remove her Third Eye was far too dangerous.

Minoru turned away, holding his breath as he waited for the sound of the gunshot.

* * *

Leaning against the partly destroyed wall of the abandoned factory, Mikawa watched as his former master was flooded with blue-white electricity and collapsed.

His first reaction was surprise. He had always thought the only way to kill Liquidizer would be with a flamethrower or poison gas or something along those lines, so he couldn't believe she had ultimately been brought down with a single electric stun baton.

Still, he supposed, electricity was another form of attack that she couldn't liquidize. It was ironic that after the black hunters had come prepared to kill them with guns and knives, in the end they had brought her down with a weapon meant only to paralyze enemies.

It was just a simple twist of fate. No matter how strong their abilities, nobody is invincible.

Reflecting on what would probably be his former master's final lesson to him, Mikawa breathed in quietly. He planned to turn the surrounding snow into steam and slip away in the mist. There was no way he could help Liquidizer out of this situation. The wound in his left shoulder from Divider's sword was deep, and though he had stopped the bleeding by freezing it over, it would surely open again if he moved too much.

And yet.

When he saw the pistol being pointed at Liquidizer on the other side of the van, he suddenly blew a thin stream of air toward the weapon.

The little sigh was far too weak and too far away to freeze the entire gun. However, it was just enough to obstruct the hammer, stopping it with a little click. Immediately, Accelerator and Isolator turned toward him, and he started to walk forward, mindful of his wound.

"You…" Suddenly, he heard a low, hoarse voice from his right. "Why aren't you…running away…?"

Turning, he saw Divider, who he thought had fainted from the injuries the explosive ice grenades had caused, glaring at him with fiery eyes from a bloodstained face.

"Why indeed?" Mikawa shook his head vaguely. Up until now, he had always feared the woman called Liquidizer, leaving no room for feelings of loyalty or trust, much less affection. In the end, he had followed her only because it suited his goals of refining his abilities and growing stronger, in the hopes of one day realizing his dream of covering the world in frozen silence. So there was no motivation for him to try to save his former master now, knowing full well that he would probably die here along with her.

And so Mikawa smiled wryly. "…I don't know why, either. Oh, that's right…your princess is still safe. They're taking extremely good care of her. Not that I have any idea what the top brass is thinking."

"…"

Divider glared at him silently, and Mikawa looked away, walking onward. He went around the back of the crashed van and headed straight toward the gray-haired boy. As he pressed his right hand against his wound, he felt warmth growing there as he began to bleed again.

Having cleared the ice from her pistol, Accelerator quickly pointed it straight at him. But Mikawa paid her no mind, stopping about three meters away from the boy and opening his mouth to speak.

＊ ＊ ＊

"Hello, I'm Trancer. Nice to meet you, Isolator."

Minoru stared wordlessly at the Ruby Eye man—no, just a boy—who had suddenly introduced himself. He was still recovering from the protective shell's burst attack and thus unable to use his Third Eye abilities, but the other boy looked even more drained of power than he was. Blood from his wound, which looked like a cut from Divider, had soaked as far down as his jeans, and his face was pale; he seemed as though he could be defeated with a simple push.

But however much he appeared to be a boy of about the same age as Suu, he was still the perpetrator behind the catastrophe at Akasaka three days ago. Minoru watched him carefully as he replied, "…Isn't it a little late to be doing this?"

"It really is, isn't it? …But there's a question I wanted to ask you. You said earlier that all of us Third Eye hosts are afraid of the world around us, right? If that's the case, why do you people want to protect that world so badly? Even after it's rejected, hurt, and opposed us all?"

"…"

Minoru didn't have an immediate response. Yumiko, too, inhaled deeply without anything to say. The response that finally came was a woman's voice, low and husky but with some strength yet behind it.

"That's because the hearts of the black ones…are being manipulated. Just like…just like us reds…"

Minoru turned his head in surprise to see that Liquidizer had somehow regained consciousness, her eyes weakly half opened. But it seemed that she still couldn't move freely, as her limbs were convulsing sporadically.

Unsteadily, Trancer hobbled over to her. He slumped to his knees, a few flecks of his blood hitting her cheek.

"That...that's not true!!" Yumiko cried sharply. "We set out to stop you Ruby Eyes from murdering people of our own free will!! No...out of basic human compassion! Nobody's manipulating our hearts at all!!"

"Sooner or later...you'll understand. You'll run into an enemy...who doesn't fit into your simple sense of right and wrong...so easily..."

"Our only enemy is you!" Yumiko shouted, and she pumped the trigger of her gun.

But the moment the shots rang out, Liquidizer and Trancer disappeared.

More accurately, they sank abruptly into the liquefied ground. The bullets sank into the black liquid, sending ripples through it. Then, with the pattern of the ripples still intact, there was a grating sound as the ground solidified again.

Since, after some time, no red light appeared from below to signify the disengaging of their Third Eyes, it was obvious this had been a risky escape maneuver, not a double suicide. Most likely, there was a sewer system or an underground utility tunnel directly beneath the ground the Ruby Eyes had sunk into. This was certainly no coincidence. Liquidizer must have known about the underground structures when she chose the safe house.

"How dare she...!" Yumiko snarled, apparently still angry about Liquidizer's parting words. She stomped on the ripples in the ground with her bloodied right leg.

Putting a hand on her arm, Minoru spoke softly. "Take care of Olivier's injuries. I'm going to contact the Professor and get her to send help."

"...All right."

Yumiko sighed and put her pistol back in its holster. Minoru watched her back as she accelerated herself away, then turned and started to run toward the northwest corner of the abandoned factory. His fractured right arm wouldn't do anything he told it to, so he reached into his jacket with his left hand and pulled out the small mobile communicator, awkwardly pressing the speed-dial button.

As the phone rang in his left ear, Minoru breathlessly addressed DD, who was looking up at him. "Is Suu all right?! How are her injuries?!"

Under the brim of his hat, DD looked unusually grave, and he lowered his eyes again as he replied, "…The bleeding's stopped. But her breathing and her heartbeat are very weak. It looks like her skull and her ribs are fractured in several places. To be honest…her heart could stop beating at any moment."

True to his words, Suu Komura's face was whiter than the snow on the ground around her as she lay wrapped in DD's camouflage jacket. Minoru dropped to his knees beside her, placing his injured right hand softly over her heart. Quietly, DD spoke again.

"Stay with her. I'll go get the AED from the van."

As Minoru heard DD's footsteps heading toward the van that was lodged in the factory wall, the Professor's voice finally came from the PDA's speakers. "Sorry I'm late. What's the situation?"

"L…Liquidizer and Trancer both escaped. But Suu is seriously injured. We need an ambulance…"

His mouth was stiff and his voice desperate, but the Professor sounded perfectly calm. "DD already called. A medevac helicopter is on its way. Mikkun, I need you to send me the data you retrieved from the enemy safe house right away."

"Wh…? This isn't the time for that! Suu is on the brink of death. I… There has to be something I can do…a blood transfusion or something—"

"Send me the data!" The Professor cut in with a pragmatic command. "I need to analyze the data quickly so that we can raid the enemy base as soon as possible. The Self-Defense Forces' STS is on standby with a helicopter. But the weather is getting worse. We're running out of time!"

"On standby…?" Minoru repeated. Suddenly, his face darkened, and he slowly shook his head. "If you had a helicopter of soldiers on standby, why didn't you send them here? We would have been able to fight off the enemy so much faster. Suu is fighting against time for her life. Why wouldn't you just postpone finding the base and—"

"We knew the risks of this mission. There's a reason it has to be this way! Listen, send the data right now. That's an order!"

"You knew the risks?!" Minoru was shouting now. "Are you saying this is all according to plan?! If Suu…if Suu doesn't make it, will you still be able to say that?!"

Suddenly, he was silenced by a voice even quieter than the sounds of the falling snowflakes.

"M...Minoru."

Minoru gasped, his eyes widening. Suu's long eyelashes had fluttered open ever so slightly, and her violet-blue irises peered out through half-closed eyes as if she lacked the strength to open them any farther.

"S...Suu...," Minoru choked out.

Suu smiled faintly. "...Don't blame...the Professor... I knew this... mission...could put my life in danger. Besides, I...volunteered for this. Right then...I made up my mind. That if I...could give my life...to save you...I would do it...without hesitation. Because..."

Suu coughed violently, and a vivid red stream of blood trickled from her lips.

"Because you...you are the best hope...for everyone...with a Third Eye......and because...for the first time in my life, I..."

The rest of her words were drowned out by the sound of helicopter rotors whirring overhead.

A red-and-white medevac helicopter landed in the battle-torn front yard of the abandoned factory, letting out two men in matching jumpers. Apparently briefed on the situation by the SFD, they approached quickly and skillfully lifted the once-again-unconscious Suu onto a stretcher.

While one of the men examined Suu's injuries, the other looked at Minoru's arm. "We have room to bring one more person to the hospital with us. Will you be coming on board?"

Yes, Minoru wanted to reply, but instead he shook his head. "No... bring the man over there with you, please." He pointed over to Olivier, who was leaning heavily on Yumiko's shoulder for support. The man who seemed to be a flight nurse nodded and gestured to the other man to bring Olivier onto the helicopter, then turned to head back. As he walked away, Minoru called after him wretchedly.

"Sir...p-please save Suu. Please."

The flight nurse glanced over his shoulder. "We'll do everything we can."

And with those brief words, he disappeared into the helicopter along with the stretcher. The rotors started up again, scattering snowflakes as the helicopter quickly took off into the dark gray sky. Watching it until it vanished, Minoru put the PDA back up to his ear.

"...Professor, please answer me one thing. Why didn't you tell me how dangerous this mission might be?"

"Because if I did, I thought you might refuse to do it. Not for your own safety, but for Komura's."

"...I see." She was absolutely right. He knew he would have almost certainly refused, but the fact that Suu Komura had been told the risks and had still agreed weighed on his mind. Minoru's voice trembled.

"...I'm sorry. I'll send the data to you now."

He pulled out the small USB flash drive from his pocket and plugged it into the connector on the small communicator. With a few button presses, the data transfer was set into motion. As he watched the progress bar, his eyes blurred with tears.

As he chewed on his lip and lowered his head, a hand gently patted his right shoulder. Her snow-soaked gray skirt fluttering, Yumiko spoke quietly. "Utsugi, the public security department of the police will be here soon to block off this area and clean up. You should get yourself to the hospital, too... DD says he'll drive you."

As if to back up her words, the sound of sirens blared in the distance, drawing closer. But Minoru still couldn't move, aside from his left hand trembling.

"Yumiko..." His voice quavered. "How are you still able to fight? Even knowing that Sanae...that your beloved partner might never wake up...? I...I don't know if I can take it. We get hurt, we hurt others, and in the end...the people we started to care about...they just get taken away...? I can't..."

"I fight *because* Sanae was taken away," Yumiko replied immediately. Her voice was full of barely suppressed emotion, but she kept it quiet and even. "Maybe that's just your average thirst for revenge, I don't know. But I know that's not all it is. I'm fighting for the things Sanae wanted to protect. And besides...I think I mentioned this before, but if I give up, she'll be furious with me if I ever see her again."

Minoru stood in silence, unable to reply. Yumiko put an arm around him and brought her lips close to his ear as she continued even more quietly:

"Don't worry. Komura's not going away just like that. I told you—she's the strongest Jet Eye in the SFD. Both in terms of her ability...and the strength of her spirit. I'm sure she'll be back before you know it."

"......Yeah. You're right..." Minoru managed to murmur a few words. Seeing that the data transfer on the PDA had finished, he put it away. The pain in his right arm was belatedly making itself known again, but Yumiko supported him with her left shoulder.

As they walked together toward the van, which DD had extracted from the wall, Minoru tilted his head back and gazed up into the snowy sky. The helicopter that had taken Suu and Olivier to the hospital had long since disappeared, lost in the light of the skyscrapers in the distance. But Minoru gazed intently in that direction, making a silent vow in his heart.

I want to hear the rest of what you started to say before.
So I promise we'll meet again.

The End

AFTERWORD

Minoru is finally starting to seem like a real light-novel protagonist...!

Hello, this is Reki Kawahara, and I'm guessing that's what all of you, my dear readers, are thinking. Thank you very much for reading the third volume of *The Isolator*!

It's been a whole year since the previous volume came out! In this volume, it appears our protagonist, Minoru, has started getting used to his work as a member of the SFD, so there aren't as many scenes of him shutting himself away in a metaphorical protective shell (not a literal one). But I don't want it to seem like he's lost his original intention (?), so I think he'll probably still end up hiding in the corner, clutching his knees and such, from time to time. So I hope you'll continue to support Minoru and his friends—including the new member, Suu!

So.

I know I'm changing the subject, but ever since March 11, 2011, I think many novelists and manga artists have been hesitating over a common issue: When writing a story set in modern times, should we include the Tohoku earthquake and the resulting nuclear accidents in the timeline? Of course, I'm no exception to this, and I still haven't come up with a clear answer. Within a year or two after the Tohoku earthquake, aside from works that focused on it as their subject matter, I don't remember any books that touched upon earthquakes or nuclear accidents as plot devices. But now that it's been almost five years, it seems like books without such an incident in their timeline are currently in the minority.

The Isolator has thus far taken place in December 2019, so it's set in the very near future. If the earthquake occurred in 2011, then it's likely the nuclear accidents would still be a major problem. If people with abilities like Minoru's were to appear, and important members of the government were to know about them, don't you think the government might try to use them...? I thought about this question for quite a while. The details of these nuclear incidents are constantly changing, and furthermore, I was concerned they might be a sensitive topic for fiction.

I spoke to my editor, and in the end, we decided to set *The Isolator* in a "parallel" timeline where a major nuclear accident had occurred in the fictional institution of Tokyo Bay. There's even an observation base on the moon in this 2019 setting, so even without the "Third Eye" incident, it'd probably still be a parallel universe, but... At any rate, the "Retriever" interlude is a realization of my thoughts on the matter. It features a suspicious new organization and a nonhuman new character (?), so I hope that even readers of the web version of this story will enjoy it. I did my best to write accurate depictions of nuclear power plants, radioactive material, and so on, but I'm sure there are still mistakes here and there...which I hope you can forgive me for. Also, if there are any descriptions that bring back memories of actual nuclear accidents or make someone uncomfortable, I would like to use this space to apologize.

If possible, next time I'd like to write an interlude where Minoru gets sent out to another unexpected new location. If any of you have requests as to where that place might be, please let me know online through Twitter or something! I was thinking maybe the inside of a volcano, but I'm not sure how he would get out of there...

Finally, I'd like to thank my illustrator, Shimeji, for drawing an extremely cute and cool cover image of Suu and her Copen to follow up the first two covers with Yumiko and her Agusta! By the way, Shimeji's main job is as an animator, and he did the character design and animation direction for a commercial for a mobile game that's currently on the air. You can see the video on the website of Studio Colorido, the company that created the game, so please check it out!

I would also like to thank my editor, Miki, who manages to help me create books every year without fail, despite the fact that each year is busier than the last. And to all of you who have read this far, I hope we'll have a great year together in 2016!

A certain day in January 2016
Reki Kawahara